A DRUID HEXED

A DRUID HEXED

CHRONICLES OF AN URBAN DRUID BOOK 6

AUBURN TEMPEST

MICHAEL ANDERLE

DISRUPTIVE IMAGINATION

Copyright © 2021 LMBPN Publishing
Cover by Fantasy Book Design
Cover copyright © LMBPN Publishing
A Michael Anderle Production

LMBPN Publishing
PMB 196, 2540 South Maryland Pkwy
Las Vegas, NV 89109

First US edition, March 2021
eBook ISBN: 978-1-64971-604-0
Print ISBN: 978-1-64971-605-7

THE A DRUID HEXED TEAM

Thanks to our JIT Team:

Dave Hicks
Deb Mader
James Caplan
Diane L. Smith
Thomas Ogden
Dorothy Lloyd
Paul Westman
John Ashmore
Rachel Beckford
Kelly O'Donnell
Micky Cocker
Larry Omans

Editor
SkyHunter Editing Team

CHAPTER ONE

"You're in trouble now." I take possession of the torn envelope and grin. "Drum roll, please."

It's twenty to twelve and time for the annual Cumhaill New Year's Eve resolution assessment. Technically, now that we're druids, the New Year should be November first after the celebrations of Samhain, but old habits and all that.

Emmet and Dillan start the rhythmic hammering of our dining room table as I prop open the envelope sealed on December thirty-first of last year. I pull out my neatly folded sheet of paper, shake it in the air with a flourish, and read what I wrote.

"I, Fiona Kacee Cumhaill solemnly swear that in the year to come, I will drink less, exercise more, find a decent guy who looks great in a pair of jeans and plays the guitar. I will also convince Da to let us have a cat and figure out what I want to do with my life."

"Remarkably sensible this year," Calum says.

Kevin nods in agreement. "I'm sure those are the same things more than half the twenty-three-year-old girls in Toronto aimed to do. Very sensible."

"Sensible is boring," Emmet counters. "I liked the year she vowed to become an artisan glass-blower and travel the Renaissance circuit."

Dillan snorts. "I got out of a blind date to take her to the hospital to get stitches."

"Stitches?" Sloan repeats. "Did ye get cut?"

"No. She keeled over in class."

I lift my chin so Sloan can see the scar. "Fainting isn't uncommon with glass-blowing. I won't be shamed."

"How'd you score?" Dillan points at my page.

"Well, I don't think I get a point for drinking less."

Emmet laughs. "No. You don't."

"Your cat turned out to be an ancient warrior bear," Kevin says.

"Half-point?"

Emmet snorts. "No."

Tough crowd. "Okay, but I think I get full points for exercise, guy, and life goals. I train every day, if not every other, Sloan is a decent guy, and I have the druid thing rolling out in front of me for the foreseeable future. Bam. Drop the mic!"

"Do you play the guitar, Irish?" Dillan asks.

Sloan looks sideways at me and smiles. "No. Piano and a little fiddle, sorry."

"Hey, close enough," I shout. "Have you seen his ass in a pair of jeans? I should get a bonus point for that alone."

"Sloan's ass has my vote for a bonus point." Kevin grins and holds up his beer.

Dillan makes a face and waves that away. "The man's ass doesn't do a damned thing for me, but I'll count it. He doesn't play guitar, so you only get two-thirds of a point for finding the man of your dreams."

"Total?" Emmet asks, pen poised to add my response to the tally sheet.

I flip Dillan a middle-finger salute and flop back in my chair. "Two and two-thirds."

"*Ohhh*, so close," Dillan says. "But close only counts in horse-shoes and straight-razor shaving. Suck it, losers. I rule."

Sloan rolls his eyes and finishes his drink. "Are we done now? Can we get ready to ring in the new year?"

I point at the pad and pen each of us has before us. "No. Now we have five minutes to write down our things for next year and seal them up."

Sloan grabs his paper and leaves the room.

Emmet busts out laughing. "Oh, he's going the secrecy route. Remember when we used to do that?"

"Yeah. When we were nine," Dillan shouts.

I lean back in my chair and call after him. "It won't help you, Mackenzie. I'm going to get full points next year."

I pick up my pad and tap the end of my pen on the paper. I, Fiona Kacee mac Cumhaill—yes, I added the mac in honor of Fionn—solemnly swear that this year, I will… I check the clock and squeak. "Three minutes, people."

Wow, it's much more difficult this year with so many more things open to me as possibilities.

I check the clock again and wince.

Okay, four or five things.

I start with the one I start with every year—I will drink less. Who knows, maybe this year that will be true.

With the tip of my pen madly scribbling over the surface, I jot down the next four things that come to mind. Reading them over, I snort. "Okay, one of mine is cray-cray."

Emmet grins. "Good. That makes it more fun."

I finish before the egg timer *dings* and fold my answers away. Kev and Calum hand theirs in, then Emmet and Dillan, and Aiden and Kinu. At the sound of the bell, Sloan jogs into the room, folds his, and adds it to the pile.

Da collects them all and seals them in the envelope Jackson

and Meg colored for us. Crayon images of balloons and rainbows and Manx, Bruin, Doc, and Daisy cover it.

"Done." Da passes his hand over the envelope and seals it. The air tingles with the unique fae signature of his magic, and that finishes the game. "Until next year."

"Until next year," we repeat, raising our glasses.

I look at the one folded piece of paper left in the envelope on the table, and my heart hurts. "Da? Can we keep Brenny's predictions for another night? I'm not ready."

Da reaches forward and picks up Brendan's predictions, leaving the paper closed. "Another time then. I'll tuck it into yer Mam's photo album in the cabinet by yer chair. Everyone can read it in their own time and in private."

I nod and take another drink. "Thanks, Da."

"Red, the man on the telly says it's time," Bruin hollers from in front of the TV. Scrambling up from the table, we grab our drinks and race to watch the ball drop.

"Countdown time!" Kinu shouts.

We crowd close in the open concept kitchen/family room of the Victorian home I now share with Sloan. I take in my family's smiles, Bruin and Manx standing by at their respective bowls of midnight booze, and Daisy and Doc curled up with the kids asleep on the couch.

Life is good.

When Nikon snaps in at the last minute, it's perfect.

"Five, four, three, two, one...Happy New Year!"

Turning in the arms of my decent guy, I grin as he claims my lips. Sloan Mackenzie is the first and only man who can simultaneously steal my breath and make my head spin.

I was never that girl...until him.

"Happy New Year, *a ghra*," he whispers against my lips.

"Happy New Year, broody. I heart you."

"I'm glad because I heart ye right back."

"My turn." Before Sloan can muster an argument, Nikon spins

me by my shoulders, plants one on me, and dips me back like something in an old movie. Despite the show, he doesn't give me anything more than a friendly peck.

When I'm back on my feet, I smack his arm. "You only did that to get a rise out of Sloan."

Nikon busts out laughing. "Hells yeah, I did. It's the icing sugar on my *bougatsa* to see smoke curling out his ears. Look at his face. Hilarious."

I laugh and push him off. "Go kiss someone else."

"If you insist." He turns from me, grabs Calum by the scruff of his shirt, and plants one on him.

Kevin busts up laughing. I roll my eyes.

My phone beeps in my pocket and I return the holiday well wishes to Suede, Dora, and Myra.

I text HNY to Liam and send him hearts and fireworks and red kissy lips. He's working the bar, but he'll get it later when he checks.

"Are ye as happy with yer life as ye seem?" Sloan hugs me from behind and rests his chin on my head.

"Even more so."

"Good. Then I guess I'm doin' my job."

I can't get over how much one year changed things. Brendan is gone, and we will forever mourn him. On the other hand, we've added so many amazing people to our lives.

Kinu and Aiden separate from kissing, and he runs a loving hand over her rounded belly.

Twins—two more amazing people coming this May.

Doesn't get any better.

I wake the next morning with the wisdom of my resolution to drink less pounding in my head. This year fo shizzle. I lay there a few more minutes and gather strength. One of my favorite things about King Henry is that I never have to face the world before I'm ready.

The massive wooden frame of Sloan's antique bed boasts a carved ceiling and heavy, brocade drapes. They make it easy to lie in bed and pretend it's still the middle of the night and I have nowhere to be.

That is until I raise my wrist and check the time on my Fitbit. 10:32 a.m. The spell is broken.

It's not unheard of for me to waste the day away lounging in the luxury of Sloan's bed. It is, however, beyond weird that I'm not alone. Sloan's an early riser—always.

Rolling onto my side, I check that he's still breathing.

Yep. His bare chest is rising and falling, the motion in sync with the whisper of breath escaping his lips.

All righty then, I shall let sleeping druids lie.

Reaching along the curtain, I find the seam and roll out of bed. The cool air gives me a shiver at the same time the scent of Gran's hangover remedy hits like a violent punch to my senses.

Gran's cure is kinda like taking Buckley's cough syrup when you have a cold. It tastes awful, but it works great.

The first time I made Gran's hangover recipe, Kevin likened the aroma to festering maggots. It was as accurate then as it is this morning. With a hand on my sloshing belly, I slide into my slippers, wrap myself into my ugly but comfy-cozy cardi and head downstairs.

"There she is." Emmet beams up at me from the kitchen table with a million-dollar smile. He's showered and dressed in the new sage green collared shirt Sloan bought him for Yulemas. "Rough ride this morning, Fi?"

"A little." I pour myself three-quarters of a cup of coffee and top it up with Gran's concoction. After stirring things together, I take a wary sniff and start sipping. "What time are you heading to Ireland?"

"Nikon's snapping in at eleven and dropping me off at Sarah's on his way to Greece."

It blows my mind that we even get to say things so beyond the realm of normal life. "What have you crazy kids got going on this weekend?"

"Sarah and her two roommates are having a New Year's day afterparty game day. I think it's food and board games."

"That sounds fun."

Emmet nods but doesn't look convinced. "I don't think they do game night up like us. Still, I'm sure it will be fun."

It sounds like he's trying to convince himself more than me, so I leave that alone.

"Is Dillan alive?"

He shrugs. "Not sure. I haven't been over this morning. I saw Da and Aiden leave for work before you came down."

"And Calum and Kevin?"

"Left for Kev's parents' house a couple of hours ago."

I can't even imagine needing to be somewhere a couple of hours ago. "This year, less drinking."

Emmet snorts. "I think those are the exact four words you said to me last year on New Year's morning."

"This year I *mean* it. I'm settling down and growing up. I'm going to be mature and responsible for twenty-four."

Emmet clears his dishes off the table and puts away the carton of almond milk. "Speaking of mature and responsible, where's Sloan? When do you expect him back?"

"Back from where?"

"From wherever he got off to this morning."

Oh, that explains it. He's been up and gone back to bed. "Did he go out?"

"Didn't he? He's usually first up and milling around. I haven't seen him all morning."

I shake my head. "He's out cold upstairs in bed."

Footsteps outside the kitchen window bring my attention to

someone crossing the boards we laid down to join our deck to next door temporarily.

Dillan passes the window and shuffles inside. His ebony hair sticks up off the side of his head like he recently resurrected from the dead. He has a blanket over his shoulders, and a mug of coffee clutched in his hands. "I knew you guys would have the hangover cure rolling. Bless you."

I laugh at how much he looks like a homeless man begging as he holds out his mug.

Emmet tops up Dillan's coffee with an infusion of Gran's recovery octane and hands him a spoon to stir things together.

Dillan accepts the offerings and scowls. "Why the fuck are you so chipper?"

"I'm going to Sarah's, remember?"

Dillan makes a face. "What's on the agenda for this weekend? Is she teaching you to crochet? Does she have a rousing puzzle waiting for you?"

Emmet scowls. "I'll have you know, that puzzle was very difficult. It took a lot of teamwork to get it done."

Dillan arches a dark brow. "I don't give a flying fuck if it was genius-level. Your girlfriend made you sit around all weekend and jigsaw puppies and kitties playing with mittens."

"It was—"

"—lame. There's no other word to end that sentence, Em. It was lame. You're twenty-four and have been snapping to Ireland for two months, and you're doing puzzles. Wherever your balls have crawled up inside you, it's time to coax the poor boys back down."

Emmet points a finger and scowls. "Rude. You don't know as much as you think you do about our relationship."

"Oh, yeah? What's on the excitement meter for tonight?"

I bite my lip and focus on popping down a bagel to keep from laughing.

"It's board game night," Emmet says.

"Oh, for the love of all that's holy," Dillan snaps.

"It's fine." I cut Dillan off before he hurts Em's feelings. "If Emmet's happy, we're happy for him. Change of subject."

Dillan grunts and takes another sip of his coffee. "Where's your other half? I want to talk to him about ideas for creating an ultimate man cave."

I chuckle. "By man cave, you mean adding a bar beside the pool table in the basement?"

"For now...but I have ideas for how to build onto the theme. That's a good space. We could do a lot down there."

I butter the cinnamon bagel and offer him half. "I'm sure you have lots of ideas. Who do you envision paying for all of your great ideas?"

Dillan bites off a chunk of bagel and ignores my question. "So where is he?"

"In bed sleeping."

He gives me a double-take. "Irish wasn't up and buzzing around at the ass-crack of dawn?"

"Nope. He's still sawing logs."

Dillan raises his mug. "Maybe his New Year resolution is to pull the stick out of his ass and unwind. Maybe sleeping in is a small step toward learning how to chillax."

I swallow a long gulp of my remedy coffee and chuckle. "I don't think chillax is in his vocabulary."

"I didn't either, but the guy's still in bed."

"Is he coming down with something?" Emmet asks.

"He hasn't mentioned anything."

Movement on the floor above has me straining to hear if he's coming down. When no sounds build toward the stairs, I figure I'll go up. Pouring another mug of coffee remedy for him, I head back upstairs.

I meet him at the bay window of the master bedroom. He's looking out over the snow-covered street blinking against the glare of white.

"You slept in. You feeling okay?"

He runs a hand across his belly and makes a face. "A bit queasy. I didn't think I drank enough to be off this morning, but apparently, I did."

"Welcome to my world." I step in beside him, and he wraps his free hand around to rest on my hip. The two of us have made this a bit of a ritual. Standing together, studying our end of the street and the wild space beyond.

"What have I missed by being so lazy?"

"Liam is expecting me at Shenanigans in an hour for our annual New Year's lunch, Emmet is leaving soon for Sarah's for a board game night he doesn't seem jazzed about, and Dillan is wondering about expanding the basement into a full-on man cave. He says he has big ideas."

Sloan chuckles. "I'm sure he does. Give me fifteen minutes to shave and dress, and the bathroom is yours." He takes another long drink of his coffee and makes a face. "That's not sitting well either. I'm finished with it."

"You sure you're okay?"

"Fine. I'm sure it's nothing."

I accept his unwanted mug and head back downstairs.

CHAPTER TWO

At noon, I turn into the side alley of Shenanigans and pull up tight to the bumper of Liam's black Honda. There isn't much available parking on this block and with the wind gusting and swirling up snow like it is, I don't relish the thought of parking down the block in the pay lot and having to walk.

It'll be fine. I'm blocking the dumpster, but I doubt there are garbage runs on New Year's Day.

I turtle into my coat as I dash between my SUV and the back door. It's brutally cold today, and I hate it. As quickly as I can, I punch in the code and let myself in.

A warm rush of air hits as I stomp my boots and unzip my coat. The scent of pub fare and ale sets the stage for a few hours in one of my favorite places, and I start to thaw.

Liam is in his usual spot—working behind the bar—and I climb up on a stool. Pushing up on my boots, I lean forward on my elbows to kiss his cheek. "Happy New Year."

"And to you, Fi. Did you have a good night?"

We catch up on our evenings, and when he finishes restocking the beer fridge, we head into the kitchen to make ourselves lunch. Liam doesn't spend time working the grills anymore, but there was a time when he was the best line cook this pub ever saw.

"You think you still have the golden touch?" I hand him two Angus burger patties and smile.

"I'm sure I can handle a couple of burgers. How do you want yours done?"

"Medium rare with caramelized onions."

"Sweet potato fries?"

"You know it."

He chuckles and gets us set up. "If you were a potato, you'd be a sweet potato."

I laugh. "Because I'm sweet or because I eat so many?"

"Your pick."

I leave it at that and swing open the stainless steel door to the ice machine. After scooping a bucket full of cubes, I fill the reservoir beneath the drink station and tend to our drinks. "Coke Zero?"

"That's good."

Before long the two of us are carrying our lunch out to the front and sliding into a booth. Being a holiday, the rest of the staff won't arrive until three, so we have the place to ourselves for the next couple of hours.

Which is the way we like it.

As I lay my napkin in my lap, he jogs over to the bar and grabs the remote for the sound system.

"All set?" he checks the table.

"Yep. Everything's perfect."

The two of us dig in and before long, are laughing like always and getting caught up on the nuances of every day that get missed when people lead busy lives.

"I can't believe he bought you a house for Christmas."

I dip a fry and point it at him. "No. He bought me this beautiful Irish sweater from the Blarney Mill that I wanted. He bought the house for himself."

"Uh-huh. If you say so."

"I do." I fill my mouth with another bite of my burger and turn the tables. "What did Kady get you?"

He grins and pulls up the sleeve of his shirt. "She wanted to keep it small for our first holiday together so we had to make something for one another. I made her dinner and a little photo album of the shots and selfies we've taken on my phone, and she made me this."

He holds his wrist forward and I put my burger onto my plate so I can check out his bracelet. It's woven strands of leather holding a nickel plate engraved with his initials on it.

"That's super cute. I approve."

His grin is so genuine it's easy to gauge how it's going between them—and I'm glad. He means too much to me as my closest friend to muck it up.

He has Kady, and I have Sloan, and it's all good.

"How's the new arrangement going with the RCMP guy?" Liam finishes his lunch and wipes his fingers. "What was his name again?"

I push my almost empty plate toward him and lean back while he picks at my leftover fries. "Deputy Commissioner John Maxwell. So far so good. It's only been a couple of weeks, and nothing has happened in the fae disaster category yet, so nothing to bite me in the ass."

He laughs. "That's your glowing endorsement? Nothing's blown up in my face yet, so we're good."

"With me, that's as much of a win as I can hope for."

He holds his knuckles out and laughs. "True enough."

I meet his bump and poke my straw around in my ice. "Garnet said he wants to meet with Maxwell, Da, and me in the new year and hammer out how things will work."

"The new year is upon us, Fi."

I make a face. "Don't remind me. I'm not sure I'm ready to face the angry lion on this one. Every time the Lion King ringtone goes off on my phone, I think it's him calling me to my doom."

"Meh." Liam waves that away. "I'm sure that's alpha bravado. He likely loves you the same way everyone else does. Didn't you set him up with an orphaned bear child he claimed as his daughter?"

"Imari, yeah. The three of them are so freaking cute together it makes me ache."

"Ache? For babies of your own?"

I choke on my drink and pound my chest. "Oh, hells no. I told you, Sloan and I are working on ourselves. That's our priority. I'm learning and growing as a druid, and he's learning and growing as an independent man."

He finishes chewing and stacks the plates to the side. "You realize him growing as an independent man because he's moved in and is falling for you is an oxymoron, right?"

I roll my eyes. "Don't make more of things than there are. We are who we are, but we're miles away from aching for babies. I'm twenty-three, and we've only been dating a few months. Talk to me again when I'm thirty."

He nods. "All right. Thirty it is. Until then, you intend to kick ass and rule the fae world."

"Exactly. Now, what kind of establishment is this? I finished my lunch five minutes ago. What does a girl gotta do around here for a little dessert?"

Liam laughs and shifts the stack of dirty dishes onto a tray. "Get off your lazy ass and go back to the fridge."

I giggle and hop out of the booth. "That's it. You screwed yourself. No tip for you."

By the time I get home, it's nearly three in the afternoon, and I'm looking forward to changing out of civilized clothing to spend a quiet afternoon in my jammies. I park in my old spot behind my family home and laugh at myself as I pull my keys. It's not the first time I've done this.

It seems anytime I'm driving home distracted, I end up parking at my old house next door instead of the skinny lane that came with the new house.

Makes sense I guess. Twenty-three years in one house and two weeks in the other.

I reach to the passenger seat, grab the bag of groceries I picked up on the way home, and let myself through the gate. When the weather cooperates, we'll remove the fence between the two properties, but for now, only two eight-foot sections between the back decks are gone.

Before I head inside, I step into our sacred grove to say hello to my fae friends. They don't understand what New Year's day means to us here, but I don't want to leave them out of the celebration.

"Hello. Anybody around?"

In truth, they're always around. They live in this forest, and though I don't completely understand how the magic works, the grove is much larger within than it appears from the outside.

When the world thaws in April and May, it'll be even bigger. We intend to expand into our property next door.

I sit in one of the two hanging basket swings and dig a few things out of the grocery bags to leave out here. Over the past months, I've found that the Ostara rabbits love pretzels, the deer like anything salty, the faeries like nothing and won't deviate from whatever it is they eat, and Pip and Nilm love sour cream and bacon potato chips.

Sloan thinks I'm tainting their natural lifestyle, but I say, "When in Toronto, do what Torontonians do."

Flopsy and Mopsy flutter down from the canopy, and I get my fluffy rabbits set up. I open the box of pretzels and the plastic bag inside and feed them a few. They nibble away happily, and I set out another handful on a flat rock on the ground for when they've finished.

The deer plod out from behind the screen of greenery, and I set out a pile of sweet and salty popcorn.

I'm not sure if Pip and Nilm are busy or sleeping or enjoying private time as a couple, so I open the bag of chips and leave them to be found later.

"Enjoy, guys. Love you." I pick up the rest of the groceries, wave over my shoulder, and tromp through the snow in the back yard to get to my back door.

"Honey, I'm home."

There is an uproarious call from the basement, followed by a round of panicked cursing. I unzip my coat, afraid to go down and see what that's about.

When Sloan first told me about the house, and we discussed inviting Calum and Kevin to move in, I added Emmet thinking it would be perfect if my brothers could share in the new adventure with me.

I knew Aiden and Kinu needed the space for the kids and Dillan wouldn't care about the shuffling of rooms if he got to have his own space.

What I failed to realize was that Sloan has never had brothers or besties and having the boys live here with us would mean as much or more to him.

While I try to support him making relationships and expanding his support system, sometimes it's a little like living in a college frat house.

"Hey, you're back." Sloan jogs up the stairs, two at a time, and blocks me from going down. His cheeks are flushed, and he looks guilty as hell. "How was your lunch with Liam?"

"It was great." I hang my coat in the closet and my purse on the rack of pegs on the wall. "Why do I get the feeling I don't want to know what's going on down there?"

Sloan grins. "Likely because you're an incredibly intuitive woman with strong instincts."

"Should I go with my instincts on this?"

"Yes!" Dillan shouts from downstairs. "It won't do any good for you to involve yourself in this, Fi. We got this."

I peg Sloan with a look and frown. "Which means you absolutely don't have it, right?"

Sloan runs a hand over his face and sighs. "I don't suppose I could convince you to go upstairs and treat yourself to a bubble bath or something, could I?"

Hilarious. Still, I get sucked into those pleading dark eyes and give in. "Can you fix whatever is happening?"

He hesitates but then slowly drops his chin. "I'm ninety-five percent sure."

"No one is bleeding or in need of emergency care?"

"No."

I think about it and shrug. "Okay, fine. Have at it, boys. I had a great lunch, and I'll go up to treat myself to a comfy, cozy afternoon instead of harshing my mellow. Consider me tapping out of your mayhem. If you need me, I'll be lounging with King Henry and my laptop watching a movie."

"Thanks, luv." He looks relieved.

"Can I watch too?" Manx trots into the hall from the living room.

I extend my hand and scrub my fingers through the long, gray coat of Sloan's lynx companion. "Sure, puss. I'd love the company."

"Will there be snacks?"

I snort. "Would you like there to be snacks?"

He lets out a long, throaty purr and smiles up at me. "Did ye happen to bring home any of those meat sticks I like?"

I pick up the grocery bag from the table by the door and nod. "I have ye covered, buddy. Give me five minutes to put things away and pour a glass of water. Bruin? Are you coming out to watch the movie or resting?"

When my companion bear flutters in my chest, I release him. He takes form by the stairs and yawns a wide, roaring yawn. "I think a nap in my room if yer good."

"I'm good, Bear. Go ahead. Nap away."

When he dematerializes, I meet Sloan's gaze and smile. "I'm tossing these in the kitchen, grabbing our snacks, and removing myself from the playing field. Good luck with fixing whatever it is."

Manx and I watch *The Spy Who Dumped Me* and are laughing about the gymnast assassin when my phone chimes the melodic tones of the Lion King theme song. I fish around in the duvet and answer. "Hey, Garnet. Happy New Year. How're things at the compound?"

"Happy New Year, Lady Druid. Are you busy?"

I assess my current state of loungewear, snacks, and activity. "Nope. You caught me during a lull in actively trying to change the world. What can I do for you?"

"I spoke to your father a moment ago. He's off duty in twenty minutes. Is there any chance you could contact your Mr. Maxwell and invite him for a meet and greet?"

"I can call him, but twenty minutes isn't a lot of time. I have no idea about his schedule."

"That shouldn't be a problem. He took the day off and is working on home improvements. I am certain repainting his living room walls can wait a few hours."

I scoot out of bed and set my laptop onto the bedside table where the plug is. "Are you having him watched?"

The deep bass chuckle at the other end of the line doesn't sound the slightest bit remorseful. "Of course, I am. He's human and an unknown entity in a world I'm bound to secure. I've had a team on him and looking into him since the evening of Yule when you first handed me his file."

I guess that makes sense. "How's he looking?"

"It's early in the game, but nothing has flagged my concern yet —other than the obvious."

"That he's human and an unknown entity in a world you're bound to secure?"

"Exactly."

I finish plugging in my laptop, call Bruin to me through our bond, and close the bedroom door to get changed. "Okay, twenty minutes. Is Anyx coming to escort me?"

"He is."

"He knows I now live in the house next door?"

"He does."

"Then I guess we're set. I'll be ready."

Anyx knocks on the front door promptly twenty minutes later.

"Hey, Lion, come in." I step back from the door and wince as a gust of ice-pellet-laced wind whips me in the face. When the burly lion shifter steps inside onto the mat, I close the door behind him. "How were your holidays? Did you get a chance to unwind a little? Is there a Mrs. Anyx?"

Over the past months, the two of us have worked on him being a little less strong and silent bodyguard and a little more good guy to have at your side when the world goes to hell.

It's a slow transition, but we're getting there.

He dips his chin, his blond hair hanging noticeably longer these days. "My mate is Zuzanna. I believe you met her at the compound once or twice."

I brighten. "Absolutely. Congrats, dude. I didn't know you

were together. She's stunning and has always been lovely to me. You're a lucky man."

He nods. "That I am. Thank you."

"Anyx." Sloan rounds the railing of the basement steps. His sleeves are rolled up, his feet bare, and the pantlegs of his jeans soaking wet. "I thought I heard the doorbell. What brings you by?"

"Garnet called," I say. "It's time for the John Maxwell meet and greet session."

"Oh, and you're headed out?"

I nod. "I called down, but you didn't hear me over the noise of the Shop-Vac, so I texted you the update."

He makes a face and smiles at Anyx. "There's a bit of a work zone issue in the basement at the moment."

I chuckle. "How's the 'handling it' coming along?"

"Slow but steady."

I shake my head. How can I be so curious about what happened and totally not want to know what's going on down there at the same time?

"Well, we don't want to keep the big man waiting, so we'll leave you boys to it."

Dillan jogs upstairs and rushes into the kitchen. A moment later he runs back downstairs with the entire box of large Ziploc bags.

I shake my head and grab my purse from the hook. "Okay, then. Laters."

"Safe home, *a ghra*. Have ye got Bruin with ye?"

I pat my chest. "Snug as a bug. So, we're off. Good luck with your work zone."

With my spirit bear in place and everything taken care of, I move next to Anyx and grip his forearm. The magic of his transportation tingles over my skin, and we're off.

CHAPTER THREE

A moment after Anyx flashes me from my front hall, I find myself outside a snazzy office suite. The décor is high-end metropolitan with glossy black granite floors, glass walls, and chrome fixtures.

"Nice digs." I look through the glass wall.

Anyx places his hand on a scanner, and the mechanical *click* of the door signals our approved entry. When I head in, he doesn't follow. "I have another party to pick up. Are you comfortable waiting here alone?"

"Perfectly. You do you, Lion."

Anyx flashes out, and I wander around. There are four enclosed offices along the inside wall and an open area with a conference table and a long corkboard and whiteboard wall taking up the rest of the suite.

Judging by the atmosphere, I wonder if this is maybe our new clubhouse.

Garnet flashes into the foyer with Da only moments before Thaos flashes in with John Maxwell, Deputy Commissioner of the Royal Canadian Mounted Police.

They all enter the office together and Garnet gestures for them to come deeper into the space.

Garnet stands tall and lifts his chin. He's in full, scary intimidation mode and I assume it's for Maxwell's benefit and not ours. I think we're past that. "We'll begin in a moment. We're expecting one more. When she arrives—"

Andromeda Tsambikos flashes in with Anyx. She looks as elegant and confident as ever, wearing a long cashmere jacket and carrying a black Gucci workbag. She has the same Mediterranean skin tone and flaxen blonde hair as her brother, Nikon, and I'm immediately thrilled to have another woman involved in setting up Team Trouble.

Once she sets her bag on the boardroom table, she unbuttons her jacket, removes her gloves, and extends a hand to the man of the hour. "Deputy Commissioner Maxwell. It's a pleasure to see you again."

Since the first time I met John Maxwell, I've been blown over by how much he reminds me of Anderson Cooper. The premature silver, the slim face and build, the intelligence and insight that seems to glitter in his eyes. "Miss Tsambikos. I, uh...it's a lovely surprise to see you here."

Andy waggles her manicured brows as she tucks her gloves and scarf into the sleeves of her jacket. "Now you're wondering how I fit into this new world you're learning about, aren't you?"

His cheeks flush an adorable shade of pink. "I honestly know very little about this new world. So far, witch, wizard, druid, and immortal trickster are the only things that we've discussed."

Andy points at herself. "I am immortal but not a trickster. I'm also a damned good lawyer and have a few questions about the SIU position opening and how things would look if I were to step in and join this merry band of rule-breakers."

"I'm calling us Team Trouble," I say. "Because the only time we'll need to be activated is when there's trouble."

Garnet gestures at the table. "You're getting ahead of us, Lady

Druid. How about the five of us sit and discuss the workings of this plan before we get team jerseys made and pick our positions for the softball team?"

I shrug off my jacket and take the seat next to my father. "I'd be more of an asset with hockey, but I'm game. If softball is the game, I'll be third base. Hey Da. Good day?"

My father sits back in his seat. He's in plain clothes so he either changed at the station or had court duty today. "Weel, it wasn't a bad day, so I suppose that's a yes in itself."

True enough.

"Everyone, take your seats," Garnet says.

The guest of honor sits down opposite me, and Andy sits beside him. When Garnet takes the seat at the head of the table, and Anyx and Thaos sit at the opposite end, it seems we're ready to begin.

"What do ye like to be called, Mr. Maxwell?" Da asks. "Deputy Commissioner, John, Mr. Maxwell?"

"Just Maxwell is fine." He folds his hands together in front of himself. "I'm used to it from my years in the ranks of policing, and it eliminates the stuffiness of titles."

Da nods. "All right. Maxwell it is."

Garnet nods. "All right, introductions first. I'm Garnet Grant, and despite who and what you likely believed me to be, I'm not Toronto's most wanted."

Maxwell's blank and relaxed expression doesn't weigh in on that either way.

"I am, however, the Grand Governor of the Lakeshore Guild of Empowered Ones, as well as the Alpha of the Toronto Moon Called community."

He gestures at the opposite end of the table. "Anyx and Thaos are my men. They are loyal and can be trusted. If they come to you as an extension of me or my wishes, you can trust them without question."

Maxwell nods. "Good to meet you."

I wait for his curiosity to rise to the surface and for him to ask about what Moon Called means...he doesn't.

Garnet seems to appreciate that. "I know Fiona told you very little about the empowered world, and that was wise for both our security and your safety. We'll move slowly on this and make no mistake, we will be watching. If you betray our tenet of secrecy, we will end you."

Rude. Note to self. Buy Garnet a copy of *How to Win Friends and Influence People.* I scowl at Garnet, but he's paying no attention to me. He's locked in a serious staring contest with our RCMP officer.

Garnet is an alpha predator, so locking stares with him is tantamount to a challenge of authority.

It's a bad idea any way you look at it.

Thankfully, Maxwell makes his point and drops his gaze. "I'm taking that as more of a warning of what to expect than a threat because I don't respond well to threats, and I don't want to get off on the wrong foot. As I told Fiona, I have every intention of abiding by your wishes and making this work."

"Why?" Garnet asks. "I'd like to hear your reasons for getting involved."

Maxwell sits back in his chair and reflects on that. "For one, I think it's important to keep a lid on something like this. If it's as big as I've been led to believe, I think both communities are better off with a team like this overseeing events. I'll sign any kind of NDA you put in front of me with no issue."

"That won't be necessary, Mr. Maxwell. A non-disclosure agreement would only benefit us if we were the kind of community that dealt with infractions through a penal paperwork system. You'll find the empowered community have a much more final deliberation when we're betrayed."

Maxwell gestures at me across the table. "Fiona mentioned there are members of the community who will kill me simply for knowing they exist."

Garnet nods. "That is true."

"I can't be effective in my position if I don't know what I'm dealing with."

"Also true."

Maxwell frowns. "It's a Catch-22."

"So which side of the conflict do you wish to fall on, not knowing and being unprepared or knowing and putting yourself in the hot seat?"

"I'd rather know what's coming at me."

"You realize it puts you in mortal peril."

Maxwell nods. "I accept that."

Garnet nods in return. "Very well. I'll lift the secrecy ban so you know what you're getting into. In return, Thaos will be your shadow until further notice. He'll work as a bodyguard for you as well as eyes for me. If he sees any sign you've either been compromised or are compromising us, he'll intervene. Otherwise, you won't know he's there."

Maxwell doesn't look pleased about having a shadow, but he doesn't argue the point. "In my capacity as the Deputy Commissioner, I deal with other top security and privacy issues. While I appreciate your position, I won't betray my oath to my office either."

"Agreed," Garnet says. "When you're working your human position, Thaos will remain outside the room, and you'll have a panic button in case you need him. If anyone asks, you've received unsettling calls and have a sense you're being followed. You hired personal security until you establish if there is or is not a credible threat."

"If I agree with this, I'm all in?"

Garnet smiles. "You will be made aware of everything within our community that is public knowledge and can help you help us. I won't open up the vaults of little-known facts or give you free access, but yes, you'll know as much or more than everyone else in the community."

"If I choose to walk away, you'll scrub my memories, and I'll simply go back to life as I knew it?"

"Those are the two choices, yes."

Maxwell considers that and looks at me.

I read the question in his eyes. "That's it in a nutshell."

Maxwell stands and reaches down the table in front of Andromeda. "Very well, Mr. Grant. We have an accord." Garnet meets his palm, and the agreement is struck. "Now, if it's not considered too much to ask, may I know what type of empowered member you and your men are? What does Moon Called mean and how will that make Thaos an asset if I'm attacked?"

Garnet's amethyst gaze glimmers with amusement. "By all means, Thaos. Show the man what it means to be Moon Called."

I know it's not nice to laugh at someone's expense but the look on Maxwell's face when Thaos vanishes from his seat and reappears a split-second later standing on the boardroom table as a roaring lion is too hilarious.

Garnet's glimmer of amusement builds to full-on delight as he waves Thaos off the table. "Moon Called is what today's fiction stories call shifters, Mr. Maxwell. Thaos, Anyx, and I are lions, but within our kind, we also have wolves, bears, hawks, coyotes, foxes, eagles, and a dozen more."

"But that's different from what you are, Fiona." He turns his attention to me. "You have a bear, but you aren't a bear, right?"

"That's right, but what I don't think I mentioned to you earlier is that the bear you saw in my home that day lives within me as a mythical spirit until I call for him."

"Will you show me?"

Come on out, buddy. Do me a favor though, don't scare the nice man too badly.

Bruin bursts free from me, swirls around us, brings up our hair in a gust of wind, and assumes his grizzly form in the open space behind me. "This is Bruinior the Brave. You can call him Bruin or Bear."

Maxwell reclaims his composure quickly and accepts the glass of water Andy pours for him. He looks at her and his gaze narrows. "You don't turn into anything, do you?"

She shakes her head. "No. I'm as human as you are. I simply happen to be immortal—and I may have a few little magic tricks up my sleeve."

"Are you a witch?"

"Not unless you consider that a commentary on my lawyering skills, no."

"But you're part of the empowered community."

"I am."

"You're allowed to know about all this without the threat of death?"

She giggles. "Threat of death isn't very effective against an immortal. Besides, once you've been around a few thousand years, you kind of become part of the landscape. My family is well-known in preternatural circles."

His jaw falls slack. "A few *thousand* years?"

"I'm killing it, don't you think?" She winks and looks over at me.

"Yeah, you are." I reach across the table to meet her palm in a high-five. "At least you don't have to go through life looking like you're not old enough to go into a bar. Your poor brother."

She laughs. "Why do you think we live here instead of the United States? He'd never pass for twenty-one even when, in reality, he's twenty-one hundred."

I sober and meet Garnet's gaze. "Okay, back to Team Trouble. Are we a go? Can we assume we're doing this?"

Garnet nods at Andy, and she starts pulling things out of her bag. She straightens with a green folder and slides it in front of Maxwell. "Yule is over, but there is always time for presents. Mr. Maxwell, here is my CV. I think you'll find that I meet all the criteria to become an agent of the Special Investigations Unit and will be able to fulfill the duties of that appointment while serving this team."

He flips it open and scans a few pages before setting it on the table. "I look forward to going through it."

"My contact information and address are in there. You should call me so we can begin your immersion into the world of the empowered."

He opens the folder, pulls out his phone, and enters the info. "Thank you for taking this on. I look forward to hearing all about things."

Next, Andy pulls out a small cardboard box and a bunch of business cardholders. "Everyone take a bunch of cards. The idea is when you come across someone at the scene of a fae event, if there's a risk of exposure, you provide the contact information to put them in touch with our group. I will man the phones and, in turn, assess if the caller needs physical, legal, or magical intervention. Then, I will put them in touch with one of you."

I take one of the brushed nickel cardholders and a wad of cards. The cards themselves are pretty cool. They're a sexy matte black with embossed gold lettering that says *The Guild* across the center and a Toronto extension and phone number below.

"May I take some for Sloan and my brothers?"

She nods. "That's the idea. When things go wrong on the streets, and there's no way to make it go away, we want people of the community to know how to get the right kind of help."

I fill the cardholder in my hand and slide it to Da, then fill another for myself. "Are these our offices?"

Garnet nods. "They are. Now, if you need to have a tactical meeting, you have the place and the resources needed to respond appropriately."

"Do we get to know where we are or is this like Guild Headquarters, and we'll get flashed here?"

Garnet chuckles. "This is your Batcave, Lady Druid. You can know where you are."

"To that end," Andromeda pulls a manila envelope from her briefcase next. Opening things up, she slides out a whack of expensive platinum pendants on substantial chains.

"You may have noticed the doors to get in here work on a hand scan security system. What you likely don't know is that scan works in conjunction with a personal beacon found in these pendants."

"So you need both for the door to open?" I ask.

"Correct. This way you don't have to worry about pulling out your wallet to tap an ID card or forgetting the card at home. Once you arrive, the scanner will detect your pendant, and when you set your hand on the reader, it will grant you access."

I lift the pendant to examine it and recognize the design from Garnet's insignia ring he wears to Guild meetings. "This is the insignia of the Lakeshore Guild."

"That's right," Garnet says.

I lean forward and point out the meaning of the components to Da and Maxwell. "The pentacle represents the unending connections of the elements, earth, wind, fire, water, and spirit. The centurion's helmet in the center represents the honor of battling for our people. This sigil dates back to Babylonian times as the symbol for truth and justice. Isn't that right, Garnet?"

"Exactly right, Lady Druid. One of the most important features of the pendant is that if you press the sigil and speak the word, 'backup,' everyone else who is wearing their pendant will be alerted you require help."

I undo the clasp and put one on. Then I pass one to Da and Maxwell. Garnet, Anyx, and Thaos already have one hanging around their necks, so I finish with Andy. "Have you got one, Andromeda?"

She tilts her head to the side and taps on the silver chain. "Yes, thanks. Those are for your brothers and Sloan, and I suppose my brother if he's interested in getting involved."

I tuck the extra chains into the envelope and smile. "Oh, I

think I can convince him. Now, should we talk about what we'll be doing?"

Andy pulls out a stack of ring-bound notebooks and hands them around the table. "You took the words out of my mouth. Everyone take one, and we'll get started. These will be our procedures and protocols. I expect, knowing the group, they'll be adhered to very liberally, but it's good to set our expectations from the start."

———

By the time Anyx flashes Da and me home, it's close to eight o'clock, and I'm tired. I say goodnight to my father, release my bear, and rid myself of my coat and boots. All I want to do is heat something to eat, change into my jammies, and tell the boys about my afternoon.

The house is pretty quiet, so I hope they resolved the Shop-Vac issue. I don't hear anyone moving around up or down, so I lean over the basement railing and call, "Hello, basement people. I'm home."

Calum jogs up the stairs with Kevin close on his heels. Neither of them looks wet or harried, so I take it as a good sign. "How'd it go with Garnet and Team Trouble?"

"Good, actually." I fish around in the envelope and hand him one of the pendants and chains. "Wear this from now on. It has a security chip to allow you entrance into our new Team Trouble Batcave."

"Cool." Calum fastens it around his neck.

"Here, Kev, you might need one too. You help us with computer stuff and art stuff. Odds are you'll end up there too at some point." I hand one to him as well.

"Thanks, Fi." He puts his on and lifts it to admire it.

"Where's Sloan?"

Calum frowns. "He's up lying down. Apparently, it was a rough day, and he needed a nap."

"Do I want to know what happened?"

Kevin shrugs. "Sorry, we've been sworn to secrecy. I think it's safe to say there was a gross miscalculation, but a life lesson was learned, and things seem to be well in hand now."

"And the dash for my Ziploc bags?"

Calum twists his fingers against his lips and throws away the key. "They'd taken care of the crisis by the time we got home from visiting Kev's parental unit. I'm sure things will be sorted out completely at some point soon."

I sigh. "I don't even want to get into it. I'm too tired to deal with one of Dillan's half-assed disasters."

"Likely a wise choice." Kevin points toward the kitchen. "Are you hungry? My mom sent home a couple of food prep containers. We had lasagna earlier if you want to nuke up some leftovers."

"Amazing. Thanks. Then, I'm snuggling into King Henry and calling it a night. I'm beat."

CHAPTER FOUR

"Look what the cat dragged in."

I laugh at my boss's sense of humor as Garnet and I arrive at Myra's Mystical Emporium. "I'm late for my shift, sorry. In my defense, it was your mate who made me late."

She waves that away and smiles. "I suppose you're forgiven. Garnet says you've done a great job getting your Mr. Maxwell caught up on what it means to be part of the empowered community in the city."

I hug Garnet's arm and bat my eyes up at him. "Why do you only say nice things about me when I'm not there to hear them? A girl needs to hear them. Go ahead. I'm listening."

Garnet rolls his eyes and tugs his arm out of my clutches. "You need positive reinforcement about as much as I need more drama in my life. I'm not concerned about your fragile feminine ego."

I laugh and shuck off my jacket. "Fine. I'm pretty secure in who I am, but Myra's right. I have been rockin' it with Maxwell the past three weeks. He's a fast learner, and he's gelling with Andromeda and my father well too."

Garnet frowns. "I admit—as far as humans go—John Maxwell is a decent, capable male. Although I've never had much of a taste for the race, he surprises me now and then."

That's high praise coming from him.

"Have you told him about vampires and hobgoblins yet?"

I shake my head. "No. We decided not to introduce the most violent races until something happens and we can't get around it. He knows about some of the darker and more dangerous members though."

"It's still a case of need to know versus keeping him alive," Garnet adds. "It would be a shame to go to all this trouble of educating and vetting him for weeks and weeks, then have him killed because we shared too much too soon."

I snort. "It would also be a shame if he got killed simply for the fact that he's dead."

Garnet shrugs. "I suppose that's true as well."

Myra chuckles and waves her fingers at him to leave. "I love you like crazy, but you need to go. You've hogged her long enough. I need to get my Fiona fix before she flutters off to Ireland this weekend."

Garnet holds his hands up in surrender. "Who am I to stand in the way of willful women?"

***

I work the rest of the week, splitting my time between tutoring John Maxwell with Andromeda and working in the bookstore with Myra. By the time the weekend rolls around, I'm more than ready for a few days away. Unfortunately, Sloan's stomach is acting up on him again, and I'm worried we might have to cancel.

"We're not canceling." He rinses his hair in the shower. "It's the annual Imbolc feast, and we're not missing the festivities. It's part of our heritage, and we promised your grandparents."

"Maybe the urge to hurl has more to do with the thought of facing your parents than anything else. Maybe it's nerves."

He runs his hands over his face and pushes the water off his forehead. "While I don't relish the idea of a confrontation with my parents, I'm certainly not going to make myself sick over it. No. The problem is definitely related to what's happening in my stomach. Maybe I'm developing a food sensitivity. Emmet says my malaise sounds much like his when he eats dairy."

I accept his explanation for now and finish corralling the toiletries I want to pack from the counter. "When Emmet was getting queasy, we tracked what he ate and when his discomfort got the worst. Once we narrowed it down to dairy and eliminated it, he felt better."

He shuts off the water and reaches out for a towel. "Then I'll start jotting down my meals and how I feel afterward. That's easy enough."

The steam from Sloan's shower means the bathroom is warm for my turn. Unlike in the house next door where the four bedrooms all share one bathroom, in this house—our home—there's a master bathroom with a big two-sink counter and a Jacuzzi tub, a glass walk-in shower, and a little room for the toilet with a separate door for privacy.

To have a bathroom to ourselves is a luxury I never knew I'd cherish, but I do. It's one of my favorite things.

As he slips out of the shower, I step in. He'd just turned the water off, so it's warm almost instantly. "Can you pull out the clothes you want to bring? I brought up the basket with the clean undies and socks. I only need your clothes."

"I can do that." He finishes toweling his hair and wraps the mile of plush terry around his hips.

"Then check on the boys and see if they're almost ready to roll."

"I can do that too."

After I'm finished in the shower and done blow-drying my

hair, I hustle back to the bedroom wrapped in a towel. Sloan looks up at me from where he's piling his packing and whistles. "I think ye should go like that."

I giggle as I head to my dresser. Unwrapping myself, I open my drawers and pull on a pair of underwear. "Ha! Hard pass. What kind of sex talks do you think that will spark from my grandparents?"

He groans in the corner. "May we never suffer through that humiliation again."

"Amen."

I shuffle over to the closet and frown. "Hey...did you see...I thought I hung the dress I was going to wear here. Did I move it?"

"Yer dress? Ye can't find anything to wear?"

"No. I had something." I pivot, scanning the room, and catch sight of three pink and gray checkered boxes stacked on King Henry's mattress.

There is a big black bow on the large one and a simple black ribbon on the two smaller ones. I shuffle over to take a closer look. "What's this?"

"Open it and find out."

I cast him a sideways look. "What did you do?"

"Read the card and see."

I find the card on the top package and tear open the envelope. The card is a picture of fireworks with Sloan's beautiful penmanship beneath it.

> I vow to cherish you every moment of forever,
> And even if your world crumbles, I will never.
> Each day we embark on a life fresh and new,
> "When did I first know?" I always knew.

I chuckle at that last line. "You borrowed that one from *Black and White*."

"You got the reference immediately."

The fact that he quoted one of my favorite Niall Horan songs is endearing in itself.

I pull the end of the bow and open the box.

Tossing the lid on the bed, I rummage through the layers of tissue and sparkles to find an emerald green silk dress. The sheen catches the light as I lift it free and my jaw falls slack.

"Do ye like it?" he whispers, stepping in behind me.

"It's beautiful. Elegant. Do you think I can pull it off?"

"In a heartbeat." His fingers grip my hips as he kisses the shell of my ear. "I know ye said ye'd wear something out of the back of yer closet, but I didn't want that. Ye deserve to have beautiful things tailored to yer colors and tastes. Come, let me help ye dress."

He turns me in his arms, and I press a firm hand against his chest. "I know that rasp in your voice and appreciate the ogling gaze, but if you help me, Cinderella will never get to the ball. You better let me take care of the dressing. You can be in charge of the undressing later."

He grins and steps back. "I accept your terms. How about I watch from over here?"

I watch him cross the floor. He looks good in a classic black tuxedo.

He catches me checking out his ass and laughs. "Now who's ogling? Get back to it. There should be an asymmetrical bra and stockings in one of the smaller boxes. The lady at the store assured me we had everything ye need."

I open a smaller box and smile at the strappy, silver shoes before opening the other one. Yep. The store lady thought of everything. I figure out the one-shouldered bra and unzip the side of the dress. Once I get it over my head and straightened out, he steps in to zip me up.

When that's done, I sit on the edge of the chair by the window and wrap the silver straps around my calves and back to the front again.

"Ye forgot yer stockings." He points at the unopened package.

"I didn't forget. I passed on them. I'm a bare leg girl." I stand when both shoes are in place and smooth a hand down the dress. It's a floor-length gown with a split-thigh-slit that rides high on my left leg and an asymmetrical neckline that swoops over my left shoulder.

I check myself in the mirror and arch my brows. "Wow, this is quite a transformation."

Sloan chuckles. "Yer always beautiful, Cumhaill, and I love that ye don't need to flaunt it, but now and then, ye need to let me show the rest of the world what I see."

I avoid the intensity of his gaze and grab my brush and toiletries kit off my dresser. It only takes a couple of minutes to pull back my hair and pin it in place. Then I paint my face.

I'm not big on makeup but can manage a bit of blush and smokey eyes when the occasion calls for it. When I finish, I straighten for inspection. "There. How do I look?"

He assesses me and shakes his head. "You need..."

Reaching into his jacket pocket, he closes the distance to step behind me. I watch in the reflection of the mirror as he hangs a delicate silver knotwork pendant against my throat.

"There's no need to wear Garnet's necklace tonight. Ye won't even be on the right continent for it to work. Tonight ye can wear one from me."

I lift it to see better. Bands of shiny silver weave to create a detailed triquetra pattern and at the center of the pendant sits a chunk of emerald gemstone.

"What's with all the presents, hotness? Yulemas is over."

"You don't want me showering you with gifts, so I have to pick my moments. The Order's Imbolc dinner seemed a perfect excuse to flex my shopping muscles. Ye needed a dress, and I provided one. Dresses need adornments, so I got you a few of those too."

"You're spoiling me."

"It is my greatest pleasure."

I run my finger over the uneven emerald nugget and smile when my connection to the stone warms my fingertip. "You flexed your shopping muscles well. This is stunning."

"Emerald is the stone of infinite patience and embodies unity, compassion, and unconditional love. It also promotes balance between partners and strengthens domestic bliss, contentment, and loyalty. I thought you'd appreciate it in its natural form more than milled and polished for perfection."

I grin as he finishes securing the clasp at the nape of my neck. "How is it possible you understand me better than anyone who came before you and almost better than I understand myself?"

That wins me a glorious smile. "I guess I'm plugged into your kind of crazy."

I check how we look in the mirror one last time and nod. "Nailed it. Okay, let's go round up the boys."

One of my favorite things about Sloan's abilities is that his wayfarer gift allows us to pop over to Ireland for the weekend or special events or emergencies. The distance drains his mojo pretty badly, so he needs a few days to power up again before a return trip, but if we intend to stay for a few days anyway, life is good.

"Happy holiday, Gran." I hug her and step back to admire her shimmering, silver sequined gown. Gran's a classic beauty, wearing dresses and heels every day. Tonight is extra special, though. She looks worthy of striding down the red carpet. "You're killing it in that dress, Gran. I love your hair like this."

Gran pats the updo and checks the curled tendrils beside her face. "It was a chore to get it just so, but it turned out well, I think."

"You're resplendent, Lara." Sloan leans in to kiss her cheek. "Blessed Imbolc."

I move along to hug Granda. "Looking good, oul man. You're pretty spiffy in your man-skirt." The men of the Ancient Order of Druids will all wear their traditional leather kilts tonight. I love Celtic traditions.

Granda tugs on the cuffs of his jacket sleeve and winks. "The Order's annual Imbolc dinner is a time to shine. Speakin' of shinin', yer gonna turn heads tonight, *mo chroi*. Yer utterly beautiful."

I look down at the form-fitting silk and how it flatters my figure and blush. "It's the dress Sloan bought more than me."

Granda steps over to pull Sloan in for some chest-to-chest backslap action. "Ye did well, son. She looks lovely. We're glad to have ye stayin' fer a few days."

"We're glad to be here, aren't we Manx?" Sloan reaches down his side to scratch Manx's head.

"It's too bad everyone couldn't come," Gran says.

I shrug. "The guys had to call in some big favors for the entire clan to come in September. Twice in six months was more than they could get away with."

"The only reason it worked in September was because Da insisted we needed to take care of family traditions after Brendan's death." Dillan hugs Gran and Granda, then hitches the strap of his bag higher onto his shoulder. "I'll drop the bags in the spare room so they're out of the way."

Gran nods. "Can ye tell Dax we're ready to leave? He's likely curled up on my bed."

Emmet takes his turn hugging Gran and smiles. "I might not be sleeping here, but you'll see lots of Sarah and me. She took the weekend off, so we're free to hang out."

"Ah, yes, we're lookin' forward to meetin' yer Blarney witch," Gran says.

Emmet's grin is so sappy I can't believe that he's my goofball brother. "I'm running late to pick her up, so we gotta *poof*. Irish, do you mind?"

The two of them disappear, and Gran smiles at me. "He's quite taken with the lass, is he?"

"Sarah? Yeah. He's crazy about her."

"It won't last," Dillan comes back into the fold. "She's too good...too sweet...too tame. Emmet's greatest charm stems from his lack of impulse control. It's a shame to see him always twisted up trying to behave."

I'm not sure if Dillan's objection is completely focused on Emmet and Sarah or if he's projecting...but he's not wrong. Emmet's a prankster and gets a kick out of getting into trouble. Being on his best behavior at all times is tough.

"Let him come to his own conclusions." I give Dillan a serious look. "He adores her. It's not up to us to put their relationship in a box and check yes or no."

Dillan lifts a shoulder and smiles. "I'm not worried. He'll figure it out like I did with Kady. It'll just suck for him when he does. He doesn't guard his heart well enough, the dummy."

"What about yer heart, luv?" Gran brushes the lapel of Dillan's jacket and rests her hand over his heart. "Any special lady makin' it beat faster these days?"

Dillan winks. "No one special enough to make me settle down yet, Gran. Why take all this off the market and away from the world of females?"

Even as his sister I can see his appeal. He's our heartthrob looker. Sparkling emerald eyes. Square jaw. Crooked smile. Dressed in slacks and jacket as he is tonight, the women will eye him up and down all night.

"Besides," he continues, "becoming a druid opened an entirely new playing field for me. I haven't even begun exploring the opportunities in this exciting new world: witches, vampires, shifters, nymphs, elves...so little time."

Granda chuckles. "Och, when the right woman comes along, ye'll be a goner like the rest of us."

"Truer words have never been spoken." Sloan winks at me as he strides over to kiss my temple. "One day ye'll be rollin' on the ground cuppin' yer knackers and cursing a blue streak, and the next ye'll be buyin' a house and beggin' her to build a life with ye."

I chuckle. "I don't recall any begging."

"Och, I was beggin' on the inside."

I laugh and turn the attention over to Emmet. The poor guy is bursting to introduce Sarah to our grandparents. While he's doing that, I slip off to the loo and get ready to leave. By the time I get back, Emmet is showing off Doc.

Emmet points at his shoulders where his chunky brown marten is lounging across the back of his neck like an old-fashioned lady's stole.

Gran smiles and reaches up to stroke his ears. "Well, hello, Doc. It's nice to meet ye. How do ye feel about meeting lots of new folks this weekend?"

Doc braces his paws against Emmet's shirt and lifts his head to greet her. "A journey shared with new friends is a journey well enjoyed."

I giggle. "Our Doc possesses quite a poetic soul."

"So he does." Gran scrubs her fingers on his head. "Well, far be it from me to keep us from our evening. Boys, if ye'll be so kind as to nip into the kitchen and grab the jugs of wine to bring with us, we'll be all set."

Emmet, Sloan, and Dillan strike off to the kitchen and return with large glass jugs filled with a rich burgundy liquid.

"That's a lot of wine," I say.

Granda chuckles. "Yer gran's famous blackberry pear wine is the highlight of every Imbolc dinner. It'll be gone before ye know it."

Sloan looks stricken. "There's more, isn't there?"

Gran chuckles. "Och, my boy. I'd never leave ye without yer own supply. I know how much ye love it. I saved a few jugs to take home with ye as a housewarming gift."

Sloan settles, and I laugh at him. He doesn't get excited about much. It must be amazing.

I hook my finger through the ring in one of the glass jugs that Sloan is holding, and Granda takes the other. With his hands free, Sloan reaches into the space between us and makes sure we're all touching before he *poofs* us out.

"Imbolc festival, here we come."

I admit, when it comes to parties, the druids kill it. Within a circle of ancient druid stones is an area set with thirty or forty tables of eight. The linens are pale champagne, the centerpieces and swags of garlands the rich green of healthy plants.

Twinkling fae winnots light things from above, fluttering and playing among the branches and leaves magically woven across the tops of the stones to create a canopy.

The effect creates a living ceiling and makes the setting feel secluded and intimate.

A vast open area with a wooden dance floor undulates with couples in crisp suits and elegant gowns. They flow as a coordinated sea, shifting and turning to the dulcet tones of Celtic flute music. It's mesmerizing...like something you'd see in a romantic movie.

I love magic.

And it *is* magic...because there's no way all those people know how to move like that. Clearly, they've cast a spell to make them light-footed and coordinated enough to float like Fred and Ginger.

"May I take your jackets, ladies?" Granda asks.

Sarah, Gran, and I shuck off our coats, and even though it's the first of February, we're as warm and dry as if we were in a grand ballroom in the middle of summer.

Magic.

Gran sets Dax down, and the crabby badger waddles off without so much as a goodbye. I'll never understand how a loving and fabulous woman like my gran got stuck with such a miserable animal.

"Go ahead and let Bruin out to look around," she says. "Companions are welcome and celebrated at these events."

Sloan chuckles. "Bruin's not an animal companion, Lara. He's a mythical battle bear."

Gran blows him a kiss. "He's Fiona's animal companion, and so, he's welcome to join the fun."

I release my spirit bear, smiling as he takes form beside me and the people around us startle and give us a wider berth. "Lookin' good, Red." He checks me out. "Ye clean up well."

"Thanks, buddy. Here, I made you this." I open my clutch and pull out a black bow tie. It's oversized to look normal when situated around his massive neck and took a lot more fabric than I expected to make the straps long enough to wrap around him, but when I snap the ends together, it's a perfect fit. "Now you look snazzy too, Bear."

He lifts his chin and grins. "Much appreciated, Red. I do like to look my best among my peers."

I scrub his ears and kiss the top of his head. "Have fun tonight."

"I don't suppose there will be any killin'?"

"Likely not, sorry."

Gran points to the area at the back of the dancefloor. "There's a companion's bar next to the druid bar. The three of ye can get yer fill there."

We follow her pointed finger toward the low trough running along the ground. It has a champagne fountain feeding it and a gathering of feathered and furred friends congregating.

"That doesn't look very bear-friendly," Bruin growls.

Gran pats his head and winks. "I let them know to bring a roasting pan for ye, luv. Ye should be able to get yer drink on without issue."

Bruin presses his head against Gran's hip and lets out a happy grunt. "Yer the best, Gran." Before he trots off, he looks back at Manx and Doc. "Are ye ready, lads?"

Emmet looks wary at first, so I step in. "Stick with Manx and Bruin, Doc. You'll be fine. You're the Toronto boys, so do us proud."

"Represent!" Dillan pumps a fist in solidarity.

The three of them toddle off toward a gathering of animals, and I laugh at myself. "Is this what it feels like when your kids first go off to school?"

Emmet frowns. "I don't like it."

Gran chuckles. "Och, ye must let them find their way, my boy. Now then, shall we claim our table?"

We find the Cumhaill table without a problem as it bears the ancient crest of our family. And what a surprise, Sloan's parents are lying in wait, loitering at their son's assigned seat.

Sloan squeezes my hand as we draw closer and I'm not sure if he's trying to keep me from bolting or taking strength from me being there. Could be either. "Hello, Mother. You look lovely this evening." He leans forward and kisses her cheek. "Da, it's good to see you looking well."

"It's good to see you too," Sloan's father says. Wallace is equally formal and cool when he looks over at me. "Fiona. Happy New Year and Blessed Imbolc. You look well."

I nod. "I am, thank you."

When the silence builds, Sloan's father lifts his chin and gestures to a table closer to the bar. "We had hoped ye would sit with us tonight, son. Yer a Mackenzie, after all. We haven't seen or spoken to you in months and thought it would be nice to catch up."

Sloan wraps his arm around my back and squeezes my hip. "And Fiona? Will ye welcome her to our family table?"

His mother stiffens at the mention of it. "Fiona's a Cumhaill. She has a family table of her own. This is her first year as a druid. I expect she wants to spend time with her grandparents and learn about our ways."

Sloan draws a deep breath and forces a smile. "I am proud to be a Mackenzie, truly. I have nothin' but the greatest respect fer our family heritage, but until the two of ye can respect I'm my own man and have ideas on things, it's best to leave the seating plan as it is."

Before they can say anything more, Evan Doyle *clink-clink-clinks* the side of his glass with a knife and the music dies down. All heads turn toward him standing at the head table. "If everyone would take their seats, we'll begin."

I watch Sloan's parents as they back away. Their chins are high, and their backs are iron-rod straight, but their disappointment is obvious. "That's sad. I feel sorry for them."

Sloan pulls out my chair and seats me like the gentleman he is. "Yer too kind. They wouldn't give yer emotions a second thought if the roles were reversed."

He unbuttons his jacket and takes the seat next to me. When he's settled and placing his napkin on his lap, he reaches over to squeeze my hand. "Let's not talk about them. This will be a wonderful night, and I don't want to ruin it."

Leaning closer, I give him a polite kiss. "Agreed. Let the good times roll."

The evening progresses as any event of its kind does. The food is delicious. The ambiance is magical. Spending an evening out with my brothers, my grandparents, and my guy is pretty much perfect.

"The only thing that would've made the night better would be if Da, Aiden, and Calum could've come."

Emmet wipes his mouth and sets his napkin back into his lap. "Maybe next year. Who knows what the year will bring?"

I chuckle. "I doubt Aiden will be doing much of anything this time next year. He'll be buried in babies."

Gran lights up at the mention of the twins. "Och, I can't wait. I was thinkin'...since yer friends with that nice blond boy who can travel distance without penalty, perhaps when the babes arrive, I can come to visit for a day. Do ye think he would mind poppin' me home?"

Gran's tie to her sacred grove and the nature of her animals and property is so strong that she rarely leaves home. Having Nikon snap her back and forth is likely the only way we're going to get her to Toronto.

"I'm sure he won't mind."

"He definitely won't," Sloan says. "Even if he did, he'd do it anyway. He has a soft spot fer Fi."

"He's a dear friend."

"Who lives to flirt with ye."

"And tease you."

Sloan arches a brow but doesn't look annoyed. He returns his attention to Gran and smiles. "I'd love fer ye to come and see our home, Lara. By the time the babies arrive in May, we'll have the fence down, the deck built across the two houses, and the grove expanded."

"It's a very exciting time fer all of ye," Granda says.

While Emmet tells Sarah and our grandparents about the house, I pat Sloan's leg and gesture at his plate. "You didn't eat much. Is your stomach still off?"

He flashes me one of his glowing smiles, and I know he's

fronting. "I'm fine, *a ghra*. Nothing to worry about. No better but no worse than it's been lately."

"Well, I wish you were feeling better."

While no one is looking, he slides his scalloped potatoes onto my plate. "No sense of them going to waste. I know ye love them."

I pick up my fork and help the guy out. "I do."

CHAPTER FIVE

By the time coffee and dessert rolls around, Evan calls for the heads of the Nine Families to stand at the podium. Together, they recap the past year's achievements and lay out the projected efforts for the year to come.

They speak about the conflict with the necromancers and the need to return to our prime directive of protecting nature and fae creatures.

They mention the dark witches, the destruction of the shrine, how they attempted to steal from the source, and how the Divine Mother tasked us to put an end to that.

Then, they marvel at the miracle of having a revived population of dragons and what it means to have them once again thriving on the Emerald Isle.

There's a great deal of excitement about that, and the overlapping voices make things very loud for a bit.

I finish swallowing the last of my pastry and pause between bites. "I'm still not sure the whole dragon thing will go as well as most people hope. How do we keep them hidden?"

Granda shrugs. "Dragons are magical creatures, Fi. Once they're mature, their magic will cloak them from sight."

"That won't explain the torched fields where the Westerns charbroil a flock of sheep or the giant holes where the wyrms come up to feed or the tidal waves as the wyverns fish along the coastline."

"Perhaps not, but we have time to plan and prepare."

Gran smiles and leans over the table. "Did we tell ye that the Perry twins asked to begin their Order dedication to focus on ancient dragon care?"

"No. Have the twins met them yet? Do they know what they're in for?"

"Not in the slightest," Gran says, chuckling. "I told them what I know, but they're very interested in speaking with you. Perhaps ye can put them in touch with the queen and yer friend Dora. As far as I know, she's the only druid alive who is classically trained and dedicated to the care of dragons."

"I have no idea what they'll think of the idea, but I can certainly ask."

"—never been in more capable hands. Despite the advancements over the past year, the folly of youth within our ranks has brought chaos and some truly violent days. The Order has a longstanding reputation for calming the waters. I ask each family head to reassert the importance of traditions and propriety going forward."

I sit straighter and shake my head. "Wait a minute. Am I drunk or did he give all the credit to the advancements and battles won this year to the old guard while simultaneously crapping on the heirs?"

Dillan is glaring daggers at the current speaker. "You might be drunk, but that's what he did."

"Who is that douche canoe, Gran?"

"Och, that's Riordan McNiff."

"Tad's father?"

"The same."

I assess the man twisting the truth of events and decide Tad's not as bad as I first thought. If this is the role model he grew up with, he's done pretty well not to be more of a dick than he is.

"—focus on curbing the instinct to cause trouble, to leave the other communities to their business and concern ourselves with what directly affects us."

I raise my hand and stand. I don't interrupt. I simply wait until it registers with him that I have something to say and he stops to give me the floor. "Apologies, everyone. I was wondering how you have an opinion on how the youth handled ourselves poorly and what we could've done better when you weren't there?"

Cue the sourpuss faces from most of the guests.

"I don't mean that with any disrespect, but the heirs of the Nine Families have rallied to do some amazing things both with the elders and not."

Riordan McNiff arches a haughty brow and scowls. "Miss Cumhaill, I presume."

I curtsy. "Correct."

"You think you have more valuable insights into our community than I?"

"I didn't say that, but you were speaking about the battle at Ross Castle, and you weren't there. You mentioned the heirs mixing it up with the dark witches on Samhain at the Ring of Rath. Again, you didn't come to help. If violence ensues and dangers need to be faced, you can't point at the folks who show up and save the day and blame them for being there. If the heirs *hadn't* been there, those battles would've been lost."

"In your very new, very untrained opinion."

I cast a glance across the sea of our fellow druids. Yep. Classic. Maybe I should buy *myself* a copy of *How to Win Friends and Influence People*.

I catch the venomous glare from Janet Mackenzie and shrug. The can of worms is open now.

"Yes, I'm new to the game, but it was me who revived the

dragon population. I faced Baba Yaga and won. I was the one chosen by Fionn to wear the Fianna crest and represent."

I scan the tables and meet the gazes of the heirs I've met over the past months: Sloan, Tad, Ciara, Jarrod, Eric, and the twins. I really must learn their names.

I look up at where Granda stands with the other elders. "The traditions of the Order are the foundation of who and what we are—I'll never argue that—but it's new blood and new insights we need to face what's coming."

"And what is that?" McNiff snaps. "Have ye got the power of divination now?"

"No, but don't you find it strange that after years of normal life and the other communities doing their thing, the aggressive empowered groups are seeking more power to gain a foothold in a world where they already dominate?"

"What do ye mean, Fiona?" Evan Doyle asks.

"The dark witches stole from the goddess herself to enlist the help of an Unseelie prince. Barghest, a group that considered themselves druids, desiccated groves, and siphoned power from the fae. The wizards of Toronto opened a rift in the plane of Hell to summon a Greater Demon. Why? What's going on that has everyone in such a stir for more power?"

"Do ye think it's connected, *mo chroí?*" Granda asks.

I hadn't given it much thought, but now that I'm saying it out loud like this, yeah, I do. "Even in the human world, people have noticed it. The rise in violence, the natural disasters, the division and hostility between races, genders, religions..."

"To what end?" Mr. Perry says. "What are ye sayin'?"

What *am* I saying?

I close my eyes as the shield on my back warms. It's not a warning, but it's trying to communicate something. "Fionn activated the Fianna mark on me and tasked me to be ready for what's to come. Since druids are the protectors of the natural world, we'd do well to stop pointing fingers. Instead of creating divisions among ourselves, we should celebrate the accomplishments of our members, of every generation, and band together for a new druid order."

"There's nothing wrong with the *old* druid order."

I read the expressions of the eight men and one woman standing at the front. As much as I regret thinking it, the heads of the Nine Families isn't a very inspiring group. I'm sure they have an amazing amount of amassed skill, but they became complacent.

"If life were continuing status quo, I'd agree, but it's not. The earth is suffering. Violence and greed are on the rise. Pollution, consumerism, deforestation, the scales are tipping."

"All it takes for evil to win is for druids to do nothing." Tad raises his glass.

I nod. "The heirs have responded to my call for help more than once, as have Mr. Doyle, Mr. Perry, and Granda. We accomplished great things on those occasions. Instead of you and us, we need to all be us—*we the druids.*"

"We the druids." Sloan chuckles on the dancefloor a short time later. "Ye have a flair for the dramatic when yer fired up. I'll give ye that, *a ghra.*"

"I wasn't trying to be dramatic."

He kisses my forehead as we spin as one and cover the dancefloor.

"I've already ordered t-shirts." Tad speaks over his shoulder as he whisks a starry-eyed brunette past us. "We the druids. Good one, Cumhaill."

Ciara and Jarrod dance past us and I giggle against Sloan's neck. "And you accuse *me* of being dramatic. Wow. That's some hat she's wearing."

He finds Ciara as she dissolves into the ebbing sea of dancers and starts laughing. "That's more than dramatic. That's madness."

The two of us dance for a few more minutes before Sloan starts looking a little green. "Is your tummy going to revolt?"

"It's a distinct possibility."

"Healing yourself isn't working?"

"No. Nothing's working."

When the song ends, the two of us head over to the bar to get him a glass of soda to settle his stomach.

"Fiona, come have a drink with me."

I follow the call of a man's voice and find Riordan waving me over to the McNiff family table. He has several of the elders sitting with him, and it looks like they're deep into Gran's wine. Once Sloan has his drink, we join them.

"Hello, gentlemen."

"Have a seat, young lady." Riordan gestures at one of the empty chairs.

Sloan sets his glass on the table and helps me into my seat before sitting next to me.

"Will ye have a drink, little miss? If ye think to challenge yer elders, ye ought to be able to hold yer own in a one-on-one conversation, don't ye think?"

I draw a breath and smile. Gonna be like that, is it? "Sure. Why not? For the record, I wasn't challenging the elders. I was simply pointing out times are changing, and division isn't in anyone's best interest."

"To unity, then." Riordan sets a line of shot glasses in a row before him and draws a steady pour across the tops. When the amber liquid fills them up, he sets the bottle down and gestures for everyone to take their pick. "*Slainte mhath.*"

"*Slainte mhath.*"

We all raise the shots and down them on a oner.

Riordan watches me expectantly, but whatever reaction he's hoping for, he's left disappointed. The whiskey is homebrew.

That's easy to tell. It's strong and oaky and burns going down, but it's nothing that's going to get the better of me.

After living with Patty for weeks and drinking the leprechaun version of homebrew, I'm now immune to anything. I likely don't have a stomach lining left to object to drinking anything shy of turpentine.

Tad's father frowns and gestures for everyone to bring them back in. After another pour across the tops, we go again.

"So, how do ye find the world of the Irish, Fiona?"

I sit back and shrug. "As opposed to what?"

"As opposed to bein' an American."

Why is it that wherever Canadians go, they get mistaken for Americans? Hello...different country. Or better yet, we get the "Oh, I knew a fellow in Vancouver named Jim Patterson. Do you know him?" Yeah, we love that.

Hello...thirty-seven million people.

"I'm Irish-*Canadian*," I say, emphasizing the last word so it might sink in. "I was raised Irish, worked in a pub my whole life, took Irish lessons and dancing classes on the weekends...what exactly did I miss out on, other than the druid side of things?"

"So, ye consider yerself full-blooded Irish then, do ye?"

What an asshat. "If it pleases ye more, oul man, I can lay on me best accent and speak the Irish to fit yer mold."

He tosses me a sly grin and raises his glass. I match the challenge and swallow it down. "And yer set to come to live here and take over after Lugh?"

We go again. Pour, raise, swallow.

I push my glass forward, and now it's only two of us in this pissing match of wills. "That's the long-term plan."

Sloan's father, Wallace, and Evan Doyle come to sit on the elder's side of the table as Tad and Ciara join our side.

"Ye think ye'll be ready? To take over after such a short time?"

I make eyes at my grandfather. "I think he's killing you off, Granda. Watch your back."

"Ye know what I mean."

I nod as he raises his glass and we down another.

"It would be no different than if he had passed this summer and I had to catch up. However, now that he's recovered, I expect he'll live a long and healthy life. *Slainte mhath.*"

I push my glass in and smile. Yes, my world is spinning, and I feel like my head weighs as much as a ten-pin bowling ball, but Riordan's pour is getting increasingly sloppy.

He feels it too.

I am stubborn when someone locks horns with me.

When my shot glass sits unattended, I sit back in my seat and give us both a moment to breathe. "You know, when I was researching Barghest and the druids in that sect, it didn't escape my notice that a barghest is a mythical black dog and your surname, McNiff, means...black dog. Crazy, right? Black dog druids and black dog druids. Quite a coincidence."

Riordan's gaze darkens, and I'm not sure if he's insulted or upset that I made the connection. Hey, anyone with the Internet could have Googled the same info.

He glares and points at the shot glasses. "Drink up, ye wee bitch."

I point back and chuckle. "You need to pour first."

Tad reaches for the bottle and does the honors. "I'm impressed, Cumhaill. My granda's Teeling Whiskey packs a walloping punch."

I accept the glass and hold it at the ready, waiting for Riordan to assume the position. "You can take the girl out of Ireland, but you can't take Ireland out of the girl."

Riordan picks up his glass and smiles. "*Slainte.*"

"*Slainte.*"

We tip back, and the standing stones start dancing around me. I pick a spot over Riordan's shoulder and focus until the world slows its roll.

With deliberate care, I push in my glass.

Riordan sets his on the table, and he still has half an ounce in the bottom. I'm about to call him on it when he makes like he's melting and slides off his chair.

"Whoa," a couple of the men roar, catching their fellow elder and trying to right him on his seat. There's no use. He's done. He flops forward and faceplants on the champagne tablecloth.

"Well, this was fun." I stand and press my palms flat on the table while I steady my footing. Once I'm sure my legs will hold me and I have control of my stance, I reach forward, grab the last of Riordan's shot and finish it for him.

Turning the glass over, I slam it down and end the game.

"Gentlemen."

I straighten and head to the opposite side of the stones to where they have a portable bathroom station set up. Sloan slides in on my left and Dillan takes my right. I grip my brother's bicep and focus on the path ahead.

"Can you tell I'm shitfaced?"

Dillan covers my fingers with his hand and squeezes. "No one who doesn't know you will know. What do you need? Are you gonna hurl?"

"Absolutely."

"Are we gonna make it?"

"Where there's life there's hope."

In the end, we do make it. The washrooms are built within a semi-truck trailer and have a little porch where you pick a door for lads or lasses.

"I have her," Ciara says when Dillan opens the door.

"We won't be long." I smile at my entourage, which, now that I'm looking back includes Emmet, Tad, and Eric too. "Back in a flash."

"Take my jacket fer yer knees, *a ghra*. I don't want ye on the dirty floor with bare legs."

"Oh, my beautiful black knight."

Sloan chuckles. "Away with ye."

I return soon after, empty of my self-poisoning and fit as a fiddle. Standing tall and walking steady, Ciara and I exit the lass side of the trailer and find my cheering section.

"Hello, good folks. Thank you for your support."

Dillan's eyes brighten, and he chuckles. "That was a quick turnaround."

I shrug and point my thumb at Ciara. "Girlfriend here has an insta-sober pill that works wonders."

"Noice," Dillan says. "That's coming to the occasion prepared, beautiful. Well done."

While the party banter starts up again, I notice Sloan has fallen eerily still.

"Hey, are you okay?" The chatter stops, and I feel his forehead. "You're warm. Are you still not feeling well—"

Sloan bolts left, almost plows over a guy coming out of the lads, and rushes to the sink. Gripping the counter on either side of the white basin, he heaves forward and throws up.

"What the hell?"

"Okay, so, really not feeling well." I head inside to stand with him and press a hand on his back.

A man at the urinal gives me a dirty look, but I don't care. I focus on Sloan as he retches a couple more times and try not to think about it as my recently triggered gag reflex starts to tighten again.

More focused on my situation, I miss the cue when things go south. Sloan pitches sideways, hits his face on the edge of the counter, and collapses to the floor.

"Emmet! Dillan!"

My brothers barrel inside the trailer, followed by Tad and Eric. Ciara looks in the open door.

"What's happened?" Emmet snaps, rushing over.

Dillan rolls him onto his back and looks up at me. "What's wrong with him?"

My throat flexes and the sterile white of the interior spins. I point into the sink. "I don't know for sure, but I'm guessing that's a big part of it."

Dillan straightens from checking on Sloan and curses when he looks in the sink. "Fucking. Hell."

"My thought exactly. Someone, get Wallace. Hurry!"

CHAPTER SIX

I'm kneeling on the floor at Sloan's hip when his eyes flutter open. Wallace is busy checking him over, and I have my *Ice Palm* pressed against his forehead, soothing the swelling from where he smacked his face on the counter. Even when his dark gaze settles on me, I can tell by the foggy confusion that he's still a little lost.

"Hey there, hotness. We've got you."

He lays statue-still while he struggles to get his hamster back in its wheel. "Did I vomit up a nest of festerbugs?"

I glance back at where Granda and Evan are working on cleaning the sink and disposing of a writhing mass of shiny, royal blue bugs. "Yep. It looks to be about a hundred or more. When you said you had a stomach bug, you weren't kidding. You've been royally mockered."

"Are you making light of his suffering?" Wallace snaps.

Sloan scowls. "No. She's coddin' me to make me smile. It's her way. It's one of the things I love most about her."

Wallace harumphs and goes back to assessing his son.

"It's the witches hex, then," Sloan says to me.

"The gift that keeps on giving."

"Any chance I can return it?"

"Likely not until after the holidays."

He closes his eyes and his throat bobs as if he's fighting to hold back another flood of bile or barf or something nasty.

I move my spelled palm from his forehead to his cheek. "I have you, Mackenzie. Whatever this is. Whatever we need to do to excise the little buggers. I'm on it. I called Patty, and he'll be here any minute."

He doesn't open his eyes.

There have been moments since Moira's coven kidnapped him when I catch him unaware and see the depth of how badly they hurt him. He won't talk about it, but I'm sure that forcing him to swallow an evil parasitical bug to nest in his belly isn't all of it—maybe not even the worst of it.

Normally, he's strong enough or proud enough to hold it at bay. Tonight, he's neither.

I collect the tear that escapes his pinched eyes and kiss his forehead. "I heart you hard, Sloan Mackenzie. We'll beat this, I swear."

We sit silently together for a few more minutes while Wallace does his thing and Sloan glues himself back together.

"Sorry about that."

I chuckle. "Don't be stupid. After all the times I've come apart at the seams, and you reassembled the pieces, I think you owe me a dozen more fall apart sessions. You don't want me to get a complex, do you?"

"I suppose not."

"My shoulders might not be as broad and beautiful as yours, but they're yours whenever you need them."

"I appreciate that."

Voices on the porch outside signal the arrival of our leprechaun first responder. "How about we sit you up so Patty can have a look at you?"

Wallace frowns. "I don't know why you thought it necessary to call him, Fiona. I'm a healer and Sloan's father."

I shrug. "Getting Sloan help has nothing to do with sharing blood or whether or not you know your way around a clinic. Patty was there when we got Sloan back from the witches, and he excised the mother bug. He knew what we were dealing with from the beginning, and I want everyone who knows anything to be involved in fixing this."

Wallace either sees my point or realizes there's no sense arguing because he straightens and steps out the door to chat with someone on the porch.

"Do you think you're good to sit up, babe? No second wave of wriggle, jiggle, and tickle inside you?"

His gaze narrows as if even the mention of it makes him nauseous. "Can we strike *The Old Lady Who Swallowed a Fly* off our song list for our children?"

"No problem. I'm more of a Disney girl. Or Passenger. Or Niall Horan. Have I mentioned I love Niall Horan?"

He chuckles. "Only every day since ye found out I know him. Yer givin' me a bit of a complex. Should I be worried? Am I yer gateway Irish lover?"

I palm his cheek. "Enjoy it while you can. I'm using you for sex and foot massages."

He offers me a genuine smile and my nerves ease a little. "It's good to know where I stand."

"Howeyah, kids." Patty steps inside the loo to join us. With Sloan sitting up against the sink cabinet and me on my knees, we're almost at eye level to greet my leprechaun friend.

"I heard yer night went into the shitter." He swings his green hat toward the stalls, and both Sloan and I get a chuckle out of that one.

"Yeah, he's feeling pretty crappy."

"And lookin' a little flushed."

Sloan groans and I regret adding to his misery. "We could use one of your fester bug fumigations if you're game."

Patty tosses his hat toward the wall, and it settles as if it's hung on a magical hook that just appeared there. He smiles and tugs his vest straight. "We'll start with fumigation, o' course. I'm sorry, son. I didn't realize the witch's bug had spawned inside ye."

Sloan winces at the mention of it, and I'm not sure which disturbs him more, talking about the witches or their torture. "Not yer fault, sham." Sloan holds out his hand and clasps wrists with him. "Yer not responsible for this in any way."

"What about gettin' ye home to yer da's clinic? He's likely better equipped to help ye there once we make sure we've got all the wee bastards out."

Sloan frowns. "We're estranged at the moment. I'd rather not go that route if we can help it."

As far as I know, Sloan hasn't spoken to his parents since he found out they confronted me about him changing his financial directives. They had a big fight about him ruining his life...but this isn't about that.

I squeeze his hand and smile. "I think going back to Stonecrest Castle and getting the care you need from your father is a good idea. I can weather the venom and disdain of your parents if it means you get better faster."

"That's big of ye, Fi." Patty winks at me. "Wallace Mackenzie may be short-sighted, but no one will ever dismiss his healing abilities."

"Patty's right." Granda finishes at the sink. "Whatever the ill will is between the lot of ye, Sloan's health is much more important."

Sloan frowns. "They rang up yer granddaughter and accused her of bein' a money-grubbin' whore. They insulted her character, her intentions, and her value to me as anythin' beyond a sexual conquest. Now, they have a team of solicitors challengin' my right to remove them as the beneficiaries of my trusts, citing her as an unfit influence."

I straighten as that sinks in. "They're discrediting me to sue you for the right to inherit your money?"

I didn't know that. Man, that sucks big.

Sloan grips my fist and brings it to his mouth. "It's gotten ugly but has nothin' to do with us. I'd rather not open any doors to let them into our lives right now."

"Unbelievable. So, their focus on your money keeps you from getting the help you need? Don't you think you being sick might smack some sense into them and give them a wake-up call about what's important?"

"No, *a ghra.* I think they'll use it to say I was altered at the time of the changes and my decisions should be nullified."

"How did you get there? Who thinks like that?"

"They do…and by extension, I do."

I run my fingers through my hair and sigh. "Well, that's a sad commentary in itself."

"It is." He leans his head back against the sink cabinet. "Have Tad come in. He can portal us home to Lugh's and Lara's. I'll accept any help Patty and Da can offer me there. Then we'll see where we are."

Five minutes later, Emmet and Dillan move the coffee table out of the way so I can kneel on the floor in front of where Sloan is settling on the couch. Patty is on the cushion sitting beside him, and Gran is sitting at Sloan's other hip. Tad has taken Wallace home to gather a few essentials he needs to deal with a festerbug hexing. Once he drops him off, he'll return to the party to pick up Granda and the animals.

"We gotta stop meeting like this, hotness." This is exactly how we ended up the first time we had a festerbug problem. I meet his worried gaze and waggle the puke bucket. "I have you covered, Mackenzie."

"Are ye ready to do this, boyo?" Patty asks.

"As ready as I'll ever be," Sloan says.

Patty stands on the couch. Then, like the night when we rescued Sloan from Moira's basement, he strokes his hand up Sloan's back and forces an eject of his stomach contents.

Sloan's discomfort breaks my heart.

Since the druid turmoil began in our lives, we've talked more than once about how it's easier to be the one suffering than the one on the sidelines watching.

Not that I want shiny blue beetle babies wriggling around inside me, but I hate the thought that they're inside him.

As Patty's hand nears the back of his neck, Sloan lets out a pitiful moan and doubles forward over the bucket. This isn't like me ejecting too much alcohol less than an hour ago. That came up like a tidal wave of fluid that didn't belong inside me anyway —this is intentionally inflicted pain.

If Moira Morrigan wasn't already trapped in some unknown fate at the hands of the Unseelie Prince Keldane, I would hunt her down and make her pay for this.

Sloan's whole body shakes until the retching stops.

I glance into the bucket and wince at another dozen shiny blue bodies crawling through his stomach contents. "How can we be sure we got them all out?"

Patty pushes his glasses up his nose and pegs me with a serious, crystal blue gaze. "Festerbugs are a witch weapon. I can make him throw up the bugs in his stomach, but ye'll need witches to undo the hex and take care of the ones that traveled deeper into his system. My apologies to ye both. I thought we got it out of ye fast enough to avoid all this."

Sloan shakes his head and touches Patty's arm. "Not yer fault. Ye've been a great help."

"All right." Gran pats Sloan's leg. "Let my boy lay down for a bit and rest. I'll make some healing broth, and Fi can speak to Sarah and find out if the Blarney witches might want to help us out to break the hex."

Gran might be small-statured and sweet, but she's a mighty warrior in her own right. When she sets people on task, things get done.

I thank Patty and send him off with a hug and a promise to come to the new dragon lair as soon as things settle down. Then, I head into Granda's study where Dillan, Emmet, and Sarah are hanging out—or maybe hiding out.

"How is Irish?" Emmet asks.

Tad *poofs* in with Granda, Manx, Bruin, and Doc at that same moment. I update them all at once. I tell them everything Patty says and ask Sarah if she thinks her coven might be able to help.

By the end of it, I'm done. I sink into one of Granda's desk chairs and wish this night were over.

Granda kisses my forehead, takes the bucket, and strides off to take care of bug disposal.

I pat my chest. "Bruin, do you mind, buddy?"

"Not at all, Red. I'm happy to help ye."

My bear takes his place within me, and his strength is an instant remedy for my weariness.

"So, when will you know about going to Blarney and whether or not Sarah's coven will be able to help?" Tad asks.

"I'm sure my sisters will gather to help," Sarah says. "The only problem will be that tonight is the druid festival Imbolc, but it's also the Wiccan Sabbat, Candlemas. I likely won't hear back from most of them until tomorrow morning."

I sit straighter in my chair. "That's fine. It's not terrible if he rests tonight and comes back at this fresh in the morning."

Sarah's ponytail bobs as she nods in agreement. "Then if that's all right, I'll take a portal home and start leaving messages for everyone to set it up."

Tad nods and *poofs* off with Sarah and Emmet.

I hold up my arm to Dillan. "Help. I've fallen, and I can't get up." Dillan gives me a heave-ho, and I'm on my feet and moving again.

Back in the family room, I find Sloan lying on the couch with his eyes closed. His father's glowing hands hover over him as Wallace's healing magic activates crystals set over his chakra points. While the healing grooves on, his mother glares at me. Always a pleasure, Janet.

"Are ye happy now?"

I frown at Sloan's mother and focus on what I said earlier about weathering his parents' dislike if it means he gets the care he needs.

Take the high road, Cumhaill.

This isn't the time to air family discord.

I cross my arms and rub the goosebumps on my bare arms. "No. I'm not happy at all. This is awful."

"Ye should've left him alone and let him be safe and happy with us."

I reach back and unclip my hair, letting it fall loose. It releases some of the pressure on my skull but not all. "Sloan was captured by the witches when he responded to an alarm on the druid shrine at Ardfert Cathedral. It was Order business and had nothing to do with me. And...I might add, I was the one who gathered a team and rescued him from the witches."

"Ye always paint yerself as the hero, don't ye?"

"Mam, stop," Sloan groans, his eyes flipping open. "If ye can't be civil fer my sake, go home. Tad will take ye."

"Yer mother's understandably upset," Wallace says. "To see you brought down like this is alarming."

"But Fi's right," he says. "The witches takin' me had nothing to do with her or us. They took me because I'm Lugh's apprentice and they wanted inside the shrine."

"They took ye because Lugh didn't respond to his alarm system and ye walked right into a trap," Janet snaps.

I scowl. "So now this is Granda's fault? If you stop pointing fingers long enough to think, you'll see the only ones responsible for this are the witches."

"The leader of the dark witches is Lugh's old flame. She wanted to get back at him fer passin' her over. No matter how ye look at it, Sloan got caught up in Cumhaill drama."

Gran is back from the kitchen and stiffens. "I think it best ye leave, Janet. Yer not helpin' anyone right now, includin' yerself. Sloan's been through enough without havin' to hear ye tear at people like ye always do."

"*I'm* his mam, Lara. I have every right to speak my—"

Gran turns her head and smiles at Tad. "Be a dear, and portal Mrs. Mackenzie back home."

Tad looks like a deer caught in the headlights with two trucks barreling at him from opposite sides. When he turns his panicked gaze on me, I know I'm getting dragged into this. "What do I do?"

I swallow. "Gran's right. Bickering helps no one and Sloan is exhausted. Janet, please allow Tad to take you home or back to the party. Wallace, if you've finished, he can take you too. I'll text you if anything changes and update you in the morning about how he feels."

Wallace straightens and gathers his crystals. "I've done what I can for tonight. He's by no means cured, but he should be able to sleep."

"Thank you, Wallace. We'll address the hex tomorrow. Sarah is gathering the Blarney white witches for a mocker meeting in the morning. I'll let you know how that goes."

I turn my attention from Wallace to Tad. "If you're around and feel like joining, that would be okay too. I'm not sure what they'll need or if they'll need me to *poof* anywhere while they work on him."

He nods. "Consider my gift at yer disposal. I'll take them back and text in the morning for details."

I sigh, relieved not to face this one alone.

When he *poofs* off, Dillan and I move Sloan into the spare room and get his suit off him. Closing us in for the night, I unpack my PJs, hang up my dress and his dress clothes, and take a moment to strengthen my resolve.

"You're going to be fine," I whisper at him from across the room. He's softly snoring and sleeping off his night. "There's no other option. I won't lose another person I love."

I think about that. Love? Is that where we are?

I study him lying there so still and rub the ache in my chest. Yep. There's no denying it. I'm a goner.

CHAPTER SEVEN

I wake groggy, having suffered a night of fitful sleep. I find Sloan up and helping Gran in the kitchen with his usual vitality and charm. I won't give him a clean bill of health yet, but it's nice to see him back on his feet.

Having his stomach free of parasitical poisonous bugs has given his system a chance to recover. Add to that an extended treatment from Wallace and being touched by the luck of a Man o' Green, and things are looking up.

After we've all had a chance to eat and down a cup of coffee, Dillan texts Tad that we're ready. A moment later the McNiff heir knocks on our front door.

"Thanks for coming." I lean in for a polite hug as he steps into the front hall.

"My pleasure. How is he today?"

I grin. "Much improved."

Sloan strides in from the kitchen and extends a hand to bump knuckles. "Well enough that they needn't have bothered ye to come. If ye have other things awaiting yer attention, yer free to pass on the day's events."

He shakes his head. "Nope. I've already had my fun takin' the piss out of Da about Fi drinkin' him under the table. Step-monster took her shots at me, sayin' I have no manners and should learn some respect, and the housekeeper found my dope and is likely turnin' it over to my da as we speak, so I'm pretty much set for the day."

He says it like it's a joke, but I hear the vein of truth in his words.

The more I learn about how other people my age interact with their families, the more I realize how lucky I am. "We should get you to Toronto sometime soon. That way, if we ever need to call in the cavalry or you need to run away for a bit, you've been there and can *poof* over."

His grin is cocky, but I see he's affected by the invitation. "Smart. If the world goes to hell like yer predictin', it can't hurt to have a 'break the glass' scenario in place and ready to activate."

"True story."

Sloan chuckles at the two of us and reaches to the hook on the wall to grab my coat. "Shall we?"

I slide my arms into my sleeves as he holds them open for me. Once he and Dillan are ready, Bruin takes his place within me, and we're good to go. "Manx, are you coming?"

"Comin'." Sloan's lynx drags his furry tufted paws over from behind the living room tree.

"Rough night, dude?"

"The worst." He ends his journey in the front hall and flops on the floor. "Rory Logan listened to his rabbit companion Hester and spiked the champagne trough. It was great last night but much less great this morning."

I chuckle. "Poor puss. I'll get the recipe for Ciara's rescue pill. That sucker worked like a miracle cure."

"I'd appreciate it."

"Ye should stay here and rest up." Sloan toys with the long tuft of black fur that tips the wildcat's ears. "No sense both of us feelin' like we got run over by a truck. We'll visit the witches and come home in a few hours."

"Ye won't go off and have one of yer grand adventures without me, will ye?"

"Not a chance. I feel almost as chewed up as you look. We need a down day."

"Or two," Manx agrees.

Gran chuckles and hugs Sloan. "Don't worry about yer wee man. He can stay home with me, and I'll have him up and about quick as a wink. You go now. Get yerself sorted."

Sloan zips up his jacket and holds his hand out to stack with Tad, Dillan, and me. "All right, let's get gone and see what the Blarney girls think they can do. Since I know where Sarah lives, I'll take us there. Tad, ye'll be our backup travel in case things go downhill at some point."

"Whatever ye need. I have nowhere to be and nothin' better to do than watch witches perform an anti-mocker exorcism on ye."

Sloan scowls. "Yeah. Thanks."

"Hey, Irish." Emmet opens the driveway-facing door on a quaint eighteenth-century stone cottage and leans out onto the top step. "You look better than you did last night but still look like shit."

"And feel worse."

"Well then. Keep up the front."

Sloan clasps palms with my brother and follows him inside.

The murmur of feminine voices cuts off inside the house as Sarah and two girls meet us at the door. Sarah reminds me of a hippie Cinderella, but instead of bouffant hair and blue ballgowns, she wears a ponytail and colorful peasant skirts.

"Welcome." Sarah gestures at the two girls standing with her. "These are my roommates and sister witches, Yasmine and Erika, and behind them are Seamus and Paul."

Once we have our coats and boots off and take care of the greetings and introductions, we move inside, and the guys all shake hands.

"I appreciate everyone coming together on such short notice," Sloan says.

"Yes, thanks for helping us." I squeeze Sarah's arm. "And thanks for letting us invade your home."

"Not a problem. The others are on their way. They should arrive within five minutes or so. In the meantime, we'll get ye set up and settled."

Sarah leads us down the hallway toward the dining room. They've removed the chairs and draped the table with a glittery green and silver tablecloth with a forest scene. Wide, ivory pillar candles line the buffet, and white tendrils of incense smoke rise from glass burners hanging from the ceiling. The mixed scents of tallow and lavender fill my sinuses.

"Have ye done this before?" Sloan asks.

"We've never removed the hex of a festerbug precisely, but hexes work in similar ways. This one has taken root inside ye fer some time. It won't break on the first try."

"Understood," Sloan says.

I nod and see the curiosity in the gazes of Seamus and Paul. "We got the first festerbug out of him back at the end of October when we took on the dark witches. Apparently, it nested, and he incubated a brood."

Everyone manages to keep any reaction to themselves, which I appreciate.

"The first thing we need to do is ensure the young are all out," Sarah says. "Then we'll start working on the damage they've done in the three months they've been inside ye."

That strikes me from left field.

It didn't occur to me that they've been doing anything inside him other than getting ready to hatch. I don't even want to think about that. What if they hatched a month ago and have been hurting him all this time?

"It's fine, Fi. Breathe, *a ghra*."

I swallow and close my eyes. "You're not supposed to be soothing me. You're the patient."

"It's fine."

I meet his strong and steady dark gaze and nod. "Yeah, it is. We've got this."

He winks at me and shifts to speak to Sarah. "What do ye need me to do?"

"Unbutton yer shirt and lay flat on yer back on the table. Undo yer belt and open yer pants. If neither of you objects, I'll need to access yer abdomen to position the crystals. The locations have to be very precise, and I need to connect with yer intestines and organs within fer this to work."

"You do you, girlfriend," I say. "You can go as far south of the border as you need to. Anything to fix him."

The girls spend the next couple of minutes speaking softly to one another and placing crystals while I chat with Sloan and try to cheer him up. "So much for a quiet weekend with the grandparents, eh?"

"I'd much rather be there than here."

"No doubt." I brush my hand over the ebony shadow of his buzz cut and smile. "But pretty ladies, playing around near your junk...that's fun too, amirite?"

He rolls his eye and chuckles. "No. Yer not right."

Emmet comes back from the kitchen with the brawny ginger, Seamus...I think he's Yasmine's boyfriend. "Dude, we found a straw," Emmet says. "It's pretty nasty but try to get some of this down your gullet."

"How do you know it's nasty?" I ask. "Did you test it?"

Emmet shrugs. "Maybe a little. Consider me the royal taste tester. I can't have my brother from another mother suffering alone."

When he brings it closer, Sloan sniffs it and makes a face. "What is in that?"

"Best not to ask too many questions. Erika threw a few things together and voila, something gross for you to drink."

Sloan chuckles. "Yer really sellin' it, Em."

"It's a gift. I'm thinking of being a product spokesperson if policing doesn't pan out."

"Yer a lock."

"Enough horsing around, you two." I wiggle the straw by his mouth. "Plug yer nose and drink up. If the ladies think it'll help, we're all in."

"Says the one who *doesn't* have to drink it."

"Right?" Emmet winks at me.

Sloan does as he's told and finishes off with a wince and a groan. "Okay, that was bad."

I smile. "If you want to talk disgusting potions, you should try Dora's red detox vials."

"Pass. My insides have been assaulted enough."

"True story."

The doorbell rings and six more women flood in and join the mocker party. "Okay," Sarah says. "Three times the power of three is the best we can do without a full coven. Would everyone who's not a Blarney witch please step into the living room, so we have room to work?"

"Okeedokee." I bend and kiss Sloan's cheek. Taking my lucky peridot Patty gave me, I slide it into Sloan's hand and close his fingers around its smooth surface. "Be a good patient and remember what Doc says, 'Tough times don't last, tough people do.'"

Sloan chuckles. "Who are we to question the wisdom of a woodland weasel?"

"Exactly. Feel better, broody. We'll be close."

His smile is forced, but I know I gotta go and let the witches do their thing. Turning sideways, I sidestep my way out of the now crowded room. "Good luck, girls. May the Force be with you."

"How many fingers am I holding up?"

Sloan gives me a look from where he's sitting on Sarah's table. His long legs are dangling loose as he shakes his head. "Yer ridiculous. What does that have to do with anything?"

I step between his open knees and snuggle in against his chest. "Nothing. I say whatever comes into my head when I'm scared."

"Only when yer scared?"

"Or bored or mad or drunk or in an assholish mood."

His chest bounces against mine, and he kisses the top of my head. "I feel much better, thanks. Now, if it's all the same, I'd like to do up my pants and get off the girls' table."

I ease back and give him the space he needs to button up his shirt and tuck himself back together. When he's fit for the front cover of any magazine with an ounce of taste, he takes my hand and pulls me into his embrace.

"Ye don't need to look at me like I might keel over at any moment. I'm much improved."

"Keeling I can handle. I hope you're not going to burb a beetle anytime soon."

"Yer gross."

"*I'm* gross? I'm being real. What happened in that porta-potty trailer is gross. What happened in your tummy and insides for the past three months is gross. I think not wanting that to happen again is perfectly normal."

"Fer yer sake or mine?"

"Both. Either. Your pick. Moira and her dark witch bitches deserve to suffer for this."

He takes my hand and tugs me toward the door of the room. "Let's be thankful the worst of it is over."

"It might not be," Sarah cautions as we join the group in the living room. "I'd like to say we cleared it away, but we only cleaned up the mess. The hex remains and will rear its ugly head until we find the woman who cast it and the reversal element she used."

"What's a reversal element?"

Sarah gestures at the loveseat sofa, and Emmet hops up to give us a place to sit. "A spell of this type has four or five working parts to make it as effective as it is. There is the intent of the witch, the building blocks of the spell itself, the binding elements, and a catalyst item or ingredient that activates it and brings it all together."

"What are we missing?" I ask.

"When Moira's coven infected Sloan, their intention was malevolence and revenge. The building block was the fertile festerbug. The binding elements would be the spell they cast plus any potions or natural ingredients they used in their ceremony— we should be able to figure that out by searching through spellbooks. Then there's still a catalyst item that set the entire thing into motion."

"You need to know what that catalyst ingredient is?"

Sarah nods. "For us to be certain this spell dies a final death, yes. Hexes are tied to something like a boat anchored to you. We need to know what anchors it to Sloan so we can pull up the anchor and release the boat once and for all."

Okay, that makes sense. "So, we track down anyone left from Moira's coven and find out."

"Moira and her top ladies are either dead or reside on the other side of the faery glass," Sloan says.

Sarah smiles. "I hope they're enjoying their new life with their dark prince."

"Do you think the ladies of the coven who were spared and returned to their lives here will talk to us?"

Emmet frowns. "Weren't they the ones whose powers were wiped? I can't imagine they're our biggest fans."

"They got off easy if ye ask me." Sarah heads toward the little office across the hall. When she comes back, she holds up a piece of notepaper. "I kept a list to check up on them. It should be pretty easy to track them down."

"Easy is never as easy as it sounds," I say. "What do we do if we can't find them or they refuse to speak to us?"

She hands me the list, and I scan down the lines of the page. There are more than a dozen names here, and with the three the dark prince took back with him to the fae realm and the ones who were killed...

"How many covens were involved in Moira's Samhain plot, do you think?"

Sarah pulls out one of the chairs and sits. "We figured two, but when I started tracking them and looking into where they lived and who they associated with, I think it might be three. Dublin's a big city. The population of empowered folk there is higher than a place like Kerry or Blarney."

Toronto has three times more people than Dublin.

I wonder how many witches are under High Priestess Drippy Face on the Guild council. Garnet says she counts the amassed power of her sect as her own.

That's how she sits so close to Nikon.

"The good news is," Emmet snaps his fingers in front of my face, "with that many people involved, there should be someone still around who knows what happened."

"Or not." Yasmine flashes Sloan an apologetic smile. "While our workings are vastly different to what they might do in one of those covens, they're still witches. If they're like us, coven business is private. Ye don't go off tellin' other witches the spells ye cast."

Dammit, that makes sense too. "Okay, so if we can't get the information from them, what's next?"

Sarah frowns. "We could trek off to the faery realm and ask the Unseelie prince if ye can have a chat with Moira."

I shiver at the thought. "Hard pass. May we never have to deal with him again. That man gave me the creeps."

"Me too." Emmet lifts his hands over his head. "'Six-foot-seven or over seven now. I haven't had my twigs pruned in a while.' Who says shit like that?"

"Someone with twigs growing out of his head."

Sloan stands and checks his stability before straightening. He catches me watching him and winks. "Let's not borrow trouble. We'll take the names of the witches that the Goddess Mother dealt with personally and start there. We'll track them down and encourage them to tell us what they used to tether this hex to me."

I grin. "I think it's cute you think you're coming. Nu-uh. We'll *poof* you home to rest with Manx as you suggested and check in with you later."

Sloan juts his chin and scowls. "The ladies fixed me up fit to fight. I'd much rather keep busy findin' answers than sit around at home not knowin'. Besides, with yer penchant for disaster, it's best to have yer back even when things seem straightforward."

Emmet grins. "I'd argue, but he's not wrong."

I process what he's saying and put myself in his designer shoes. I don't like where that takes me. Stupid logic.

Pointing my finger, I make sure I have his attention. "Fine, this is how it'll play out. We go back to Gran's, and you eat her get healthy soup, and check-in with Manx. If you still feel fighting fit in an hour, we grab Manx, Dillan's cloak, and are off to Dublin after lunch."

Sloan nods. "Fine. I accept yer terms."

CHAPTER EIGHT

After lunch, I slip into the spare room to change into clothes that have more give in case chaos ensues. It's funny. Dressing for the probability of mayhem has become more important to me than style these days.

I shimmy out of my jeans and my cowl-neck sweater and pull on a loose tunic and my new stretchy cords. When I turn back to the door, I find Sloan watching me. "Society frowns on men lurking in the shadows to watch women undress."

"Not women. Only you."

"That's called stalking."

"There's no helping me. I'm obsessed."

I pull my hair free from the collar of my top and strike a pose. "How could you not be? As Dillan would say, I'm fucking fabulous."

"No argument here."

I hug him, and when his smile fades and it looks like he's going to get serious and somber on me, I press my fingers to his lips. "You're going to be fine. I'll pull one of Patty's purple horseshoes from my ass if I need to, but we'll get you cured. That's the only way this plays out."

"But if it doesn't…"

"No. It's the *only* way this plays out. I don't want you entertaining any other option."

"There are things I need ye to know if we can't fix—"

"Then you don't need to worry because I *will* fix this. End of. Focus on the prize." I open the bedroom door and drag him out behind me.

I'm not talking defeat.

As the Carpenters sang…"We've only just begun."

Kerry to Dublin is more than three hours by car so it's a bonus that Sloan and Tad each have the wayfarer ability to *poof* us where we need to be. Today's witch-tracking team is me, Sloan, Emmet, Sarah, Dillan, and Tad.

Manx still felt like something the cat hacked up on the rug, so we left him with Gran and promised we'd stir up trouble again tomorrow so he could join us when he feels better.

We decide to begin at Moira's row house.

Before she pledged her fealty to the Unseelie prince and he took her to live with him behind the faery glass, Moira Morrigan resided in a historic brick building located a block away from Trinity College in Dublin.

When we arrive at the curb, Emmet stares up at the front porch and chuckles. "The last time we were here, Gran was on fire. She blew that power transformer with lightning, and once we got inside, she bitch-slapped Moira into next year."

"Which I guess is now this year," Dillan says.

"Right you are, brother," Emmet agrees.

I nod. "She took Sloan's kidnapping very personally and was even more pissed because Granda's ex was behind it."

"Granda picked the right girl," Dillan says. "Gran outwits and outclasses Moira a thousand times over."

"A badass both in and out of her apron," Emmet adds. "Gran's the real deal."

Sloan smiles. "She is at that. Now, shall we try to focus on the problem at hand?"

"Focus? Us?" I chuckle. "Yeah, the Cumhaill kids have been known to lose track of the bouncing ball."

"It looks like someone's home." Emmet points at a window on the second floor.

I shift for a better view. "What's our plan of attack? Should we send Bruin in or have Sarah test the wards, or Sloan could try to *poof* us all inside battle-ready, or—"

"We could knock," Tad suggests, his brow creased. "Occam's Razor, Red. Most often the easiest solution is the right one. If the goddess took their powers, these women aren't witches any longer. If she's been gone three months, that might be a new tenant in there or a squatter."

I make a face at Tad. "Aren't you Mister Logical? Fine. Knocking's good too."

I jog up the stairs with the five of them behind me, step into the covered porch of her entrance, and knock on the purple door. The skin on my knuckles singes on contact, and I shake out my hand. "Son of a witch bitch, that hurts."

"Let me see." Sloan catches my wrist mid-shake and scowls at the red blisters bubbling up to the surface. "I'm going to go out on a limb and say not a new tenant or squatter. Yer sure all the witches lost their powers?"

Sarah frowns. "The ones we caught who were involved in Moira's plot of madness did, aye."

"Nature abhors a vacuum." Dillan pulls up the hood of his Cloak of Concealment and scowls at the purple door. "Methinks there's a new witch bitch in town."

Sloan's lips move with the mumbling of his healing spell, and the burning pain recedes. When I can think again without my cranium cramping, I take a closer look at the front door. "Sarah, can you sense anything from the warding?"

Tad and Emmet shift in the ten-by-four-foot enclosed porch

to let Sarah come forward. She raises her hands to hold her palms parallel to the slab of purple and frowns. "I can tell there *is* warding, and I vaguely recognize the signature but couldn't tell ye where I've dealt with it before."

I'm not sure if that's good or bad.

Sloan finishes healing my knuckles and kisses them before releasing my hand. I flex my fingers. "Thanks, babe."

"I have you, *a ghra*."

Dillan selects a wooden-handled umbrella from the stand in the corner of the covered porch. He knocks again, this time loud and clear.

No one answers.

Rude. I decide to take the direct approach. "Hello...Dublin witch lady, we hear you in there. It's polite to answer the door when people come knocking."

Nothing.

I shrug. "Okay, McNiff, we tried Occam's Razor. That was a bust. Who wants to blow the door?"

I do. I do. Bruin flutters around in my chest. *I love letting loose against the witches.*

I smile at my bear's excitement. Who am I to deprive my boy of true joy? "Could everyone back out onto the steps, please? Bruin feels feisty. He wants to be the one to huff and puff and blow this door down."

"Do ye not think that's a bit excessive?" Sarah asks.

"Nope. Some new witch has moved into Moira's place. She's ignoring our polite attempts to have a face-to-face, so we're taking it up a notch."

Tad snorts. "I think an eight-foot grizzly bashing in the front door might be considered taking it up several notches."

"Fine, it may have escalated by multiples, but after what they did to Sloan, I'm not feeling very patient."

Sarah blinks and shakes her head. "Don't say I didn't warn ye."

I respect Sarah's all "harm to none" and nicey-nice but now is not the time. When I think about Sloan doubled over the sink last night groaning as he hurled up bugs, I figure a broken front door is a small price to pay.

When the coast is clear, and everyone has shifted down onto the steps, I release Bruin. He swirls around me once and materializes in the enclosed porch.

"The door is warded to burn on touch, buddy. Be quick."

"Och, I'm not worried about touching it long enough to get my paws singed. I'm going to send this slab of metal sailin' like a piece of paper in a windstorm. Watch."

I step to the side as he rears onto his back paws. When standing on all fours, my grizzly boy's head comes to my chest. When he rears up on his back legs like this, he towers over me. With a roar, he throws his weight forward, and the door crashes into the house—frame and all.

I marvel at the splintered and broken lumber. "The warding on the door held but the framework of the house was no match for you, buddy."

"What the feckin' hell? Who do ye think ye are?" A brunette woman rushes into the room, her hands poised, magic building in her palms. "Get out of my house!"

She looks familiar, but I can't quite place her.

Honestly, I don't care who she is. She's a witch, and she's here, so she's in this. "This is Moira Morrigan's house, and we know for a fact that she's currently out of town."

The brunette witch narrows her gaze on me, and our first meeting clicks for both of us at the same time. "Yer the meddlesome eejits who stole my shillelagh and trashed my pub!"

Emmet barks a laugh. "Crap. Well, this is an unfortunate coincidence."

It is. There's no way she'll help us.

There's also no way she was part of Moira's band of maniacal witches on the eve of Samhain. She was working at her pub and likely spent all night dealing with the aftermath of our snatch and dash.

She's only a Dublin witch who's taking advantage of the power vacuum and moved into Moira's house.

"Technically, it was my friend Patty's shillelagh, not yours. It was cursed for bad luck, so we did you a favor by returning it to him. You're welcome."

Sloan throws up a shield to counter the bolt of magic she chucks at my head. "I don't think she's in the mood to thank ye, Fi."

A buzz of magic is building somewhere close by, and I don't want to be around when it's all powered up. I point at the door. "We dropped in to check on things while Moira's gone. You know…water the plants, feed the cat, that sort of thing. I guess you have everything under control. Bye for now. Blessed Candlemas."

Bruin dissolves and takes his place inside my chest while the six of us beat feet back outside and off the property as quickly as we can.

When we get clear of the whole disaster, Sarah looks over at me and frowns. "Are ye still sure bashin' in the door was the way to go?"

I shrug. "If you want to make an omelet, you gotta be able to stand cutting the onions."

Sloan blinks at me and chuckles. "Yer whacked. It's break some eggs."

"Cutting the onions is where the pain point is. Breaking eggs is easy, amirite?"

Dillan and Emmet both nod.

"It's too bad she knew us," Emmet says. "That could've gone much better."

Tad has a hand against his stomach, busting a gut. "If ye want the help of witches, it's best not to trash their pubs and knock their doors off the hinges."

I shake my head. "Hey, don't point fingers. You were a participant in both of those misadventures."

Emmet laughs. "Did you see her face? Hilarious."

"Bruin knows how to make an entrance," Dillan brags.

I pull Sarah's witch list out of my pocket and show it to Sloan. "You went to school here. Are any of these addresses close? Where do you want to start?"

Sloan eyes the list and points. "This one's not far. Let's start there."

"Are we *poofing* or walking?" I ask.

"Walking. It's really not far."

The six of us strike off down the road toward the lights on Grafton Street, Tad still laughing as we go.

Dublin in February is dark, cold, and wet. I pull up the collar of my coat and adjust my gloves. Blech. "I'm trying to decide if Toronto weather is better or worse this time of year. We're darker, colder, but much less wet."

"Snow is sorta wet," Emmet says.

"It's also pretty."

"Yeah, and it's a different kind of cold," Dillan adds.

I nod. "Our February is less chill your bones and more freeze your boogers inside your sinuses."

Dillan scowls at the gray sky. "Yeah, in Toronto, it's too cold to be wet in February...unless it's one of our province-halting ice storms."

"Also horrid," Emmet agrees.

"And also pretty," I add.

"It's best just to hate February," Emmet says.

"I think all Torontonians hate February. I can't think of one thing I like about February...except the extra 'r.' I like that they snuck an extra one into the word."

Sloan looks at me like I'm a few bricks short of a load.

I ignore the look and prop my fists on my hips like a super-hero. "So, where are we going, slick? Lay it out for me."

Sloan tilts his head. "What is it? Ye've gone weird."

Have I?

I'm a little amped after breaking into Witch Pub Lady's house. Well...Moira's house. "Why do you think Witch Pub Lady moved into Moira's? Do you think she knows we sold Moira out to Keldane? What do you think Keldane has been doing with them all this time? More importantly, do you think he's had his twigs clipped recently?"

Dillan's giving me the crazy eye, and I start feeling my face. "What? Have I got something on me? Why are you looking at me like that?"

"You feeling okay, baby girl?"

"Yeah, why?" I pat the front of my coat and shrug. "Everything seems in order. Maybe it's you guys who are out of order." I get a flash of Jack Nicholson in my head and point at my brothers. "You're out of order. You're out of order. You're all out of order."

Sloan grabs my arm as Tad waves away the people staring at me.

"The truth? You can't handle the truth!" I shout.

"Okay, what's happening?" Emmet asks. "Fi? Did you lose your marbles somewhere back there?"

I look back at the sidewalk behind us. "I don't think so."

Sloan frowns. "We need to get her somewhere warm to have a look at her."

"I'm great!" I tip my head back and set my smile free to shine up to the heavens. "My skin is vanilla icing, and my blood is cream soda."

"Well, then." Dillan looks at Sloan. "Nothing to worry about now, is there?"

Sloan puts his arms around me, and we shuffle and waltz until we stop in a roadside bus shelter. With the wind blocked, the air is warm on my cheeks, and the noise of the world is muffled. "Mmm, you smell like French toast and caramels." I lean forward, but he moves before I can lick his face.

"Is this some kind of flashback drunk from your dad's whiskey shots, McNiff?" Emmet asks.

"Teeling is powerful but not magical. It's just booze. It can't do this."

Sloan leans close and looks into my eyes, so I look into his too. "The witch must've done something to her."

"Could touching the warded door give her a contact high?" Dillan asks. "Fi, take off your gloves and show us your hands, baby girl."

I pull off my glove and wave my fingers at my brother. "There's nothing wrong with me. My skin is vanilla icing. Here, Dillan, lick me and see."

"I'm good, thanks. Big lunch."

"Tad, lick me."

I shove my palm out for him, and Sloan glares. "If you lick my girlfriend, I will junk-punch you back into last year."

"Well, someone has to lick—whoa! Did you see that?" I stare out the window of the bus shelter at the street beyond.

"See what, Fi?" Emmet asks.

"I just levitated that pickup truck."

"What pickup truck?"

I point. "That one across the street full of gold. Watch. I'll do it again."

I press my hands on the bus shelter's clear plexiglass and focus on the red Ford F-150. The bed of the truck is heaped with gold bars, glowing in their radiance. "Do you see? How am I doing this? I have a new power."

"You have something," Emmet says. "A truck full of gold must be really heavy. Maybe you should sit and rest."

I shake my head. "It's not heavy. I'm magic-filled."

"Magic-filled?"

"I'm the Twinkie of the fae realm. Instead of goopy cream, I'm filled with magic."

"And cream soda," Dillan says.

"Yes! You know. You understand." I try to struggle through the crowded shelter to hug my brother. "I knew you'd understand, Dilly-bar."

Dillan arches a brow and scowls at Sloan. "Do something. Fix her."

Sloan growls. "This isn't anything in my wheelhouse."

"So, who's wheelhouse is it?"

He grunts and rolls his eyes. "Everyone grab hold of me. Tad, throw up a veil of privacy. We're not traipsing through the city with her like this."

When we finish *poofing*, we're not in our glass bus box anymore. We're in a fancy entrance to a hotel.

"You two. Have ye got her?" Sloan asks.

"We've got her," Emmet says, "but dude, you totes just *poofed* us into the lobby of a hotel."

"It's an empowered safehouse hotel."

"Like the Continental Hotel in John Wick?" I say, looking around. "Is Keanu here?"

"I don't think so, luv." Sloan strides over to the front desk and says something, and the wrinkly old man picks up a phone.

"Is that man a Shar Pei shifter?"

"I don't think that's a thing," Dillan points out.

Abandoning that, I grip my brother's shirt and prop up on my tiptoes. "Emmet. Psst, Emmett."

His eyes widen like green moons. "Yeah, Fi. What's up?"

"I need to tell you something."

"What's that?"

"Today's your birthday. Congratulations. What do you want for your birthday? I'm going to give you one wish."

He blinks at me and smiles. "If you have another F-150 filled with gold, I'd be okay with that."

I pat my hand on his chest. "Done. As soon as I get outside, I'll get you one."

I strike off toward the door, but I don't get anywhere. I look at my feet, but they're not moving. "Am I moving?"

Dillan frowns. "Right now, you mean? No. You're standing in a hotel lobby."

"I need to move."

"That's a great idea." Sloan points at the elevator. "Let's all move into the lift."

I sigh and sit on the floor. "I don't want to go in there. I want to go outside."

"In a minute. First, I need to talk to someone upstairs."

Lifting my feet in the air, I wave them around until someone grabs my heels. "Fine, but I'm tired. You pull me."

CHAPTER NINE

I'm floating. I'm not sure how or why, but I'm definitely floating. I open my eyes and reach toward the ceiling fan. My arm stretches long like it's made of elastic, but I still can't touch the ceiling. "This is weird even for me."

"Yes, it is," Sloan says beside me.

I twist and reach out for him to grab hold of me and pull me in. "Why am I floating?"

He smiles, but there's no sparkle in his eyes. "Yer not floating, luv. Ye reacted to the witch's warding, and your blood gases have altered."

"Altered into what? Helium? Am I a freaking helium balloon now?"

"It might feel like that, but yer not. Yer as solid and bound by gravity as ye've ever been."

"I don't like it."

"I'm not much of a fan, myself. Tad took Emmet and Sarah on a bit of a quest for ingredients, and now they're mixin' ye up an antidote. Kaija expects ye to make a full recovery within minutes after ye take it."

"Who's Kaija?"

I might be altered, but I don't miss how he hesitates when I ask. "A girl I knew when I lived here for college."

I point my finger but can't make it stay pointed at his chest. "Knew biblically by the guilt on your face. So did you date or simply have sex?"

"Hard to say...more the latter. We never really defined anything beyond the obvious."

I sigh. "Now she's the one that got away."

"Hardly. She's not the one for me."

"Yet you bring me here when I'm loopy on witch warding? What does that mean?"

"It means she was close, and I was fairly certain she would know how to help."

"And she did."

He nods. "She did."

"Then why are you acting so guilty?"

He purses his lips and sighs. "All right, full disclosure. Kaija is a dark fae succubus. I hesitated bringin' ye here because I knew if she didn't feel in a charitable mood, her price fer helpin' us would be...very singular. As it turned out, she *wasn't* feelin' charitable, and I wasn't sure what else to do, so I agreed to her terms."

Even through the bubbly sensations of floating, a wave of nausea hits. "Oh, Mackenzie, tell me you didn't have sex with the succubus to save me."

His eyes widen. "*Me?* No. I would never...not with us together. Yer brother volunteered."

"Which brother?"

"Dillan. He was quite set on takin' one for the team. Why would ye think it would be *me?*"

I pull myself over to his chair, and it's like trying to sit in someone's lap in a pool. I keep floating away. "I hate this. Hold me on your lap so I can hug you."

"I am holding you. Yer not floating."

"Good. Hold tighter."

"Yer not mad?"

"Mad that you pimped Dillan out to a succubus instead of sleeping with her yourself? Hells no. This is like a lottery win for him. We won't hear the end of it for months."

The door opens, and Emmet steps in, holding out a plate with a cookie. "Eat this and Kaija says you'll be as good as new in five minutes."

I take the cookie and sniff it. "How much do we trust this woman's grasp of magic remedy?"

Sloan nods. "Eat the cookie, Fi."

I do, and it's not bad—a little gritty—but not bad.

It doesn't take long after that, and I feel the weight of my body settle on Sloan's lap. "Yay! I'm not a balloon animal anymore."

"Is your blood still fizzing with cream soda?" Emmet asks. "Because I want my truck full of gold before you lose all your power. It's my birthday, and I'm holding you to that."

I shake my head. "It's not your birthday, numb-nuts. Your birthday's in July. What the hell are you talking about?"

Emmet throws up his hands. "I knew it. I should've gotten it on video. I bet you don't even remember being a magic-filled Twinkie."

I look at Sloan. "Tell me this is him making shit up to freak me out."

Sloan chuckles. "Sorry. Ye had yerself a little adventure all yer own, and there were multiple witnesses."

I press my head against his chest. "Perfect."

When I'm confident my body is working as it should be, I let Sloan lead the way into the outer suite. We're in a hotel. I remember that much, but the space is large, and I figure this must be either the penthouse suite or something like it. The walls are painted a pale gold throughout the suite, and the furniture and accessories display all the most brilliant, reds, blues, greens, and silver.

It's very bohemian.

Kaija is lounging on an area of overlapping floor rugs when we exit the back rooms. She's sharing a charcuterie board with Dillan, and yep, he looks like he's having the time of his life.

Why not?

The woman is breathtaking, with a warm, East Indian skin tone, long, chestnut hair, and stunning turquoise blue eyes that glow like they're backlit. She's wearing a flouncy see-through robe with a black bra and panty set beneath and doesn't seem the least bit self-conscious about being in a room with six other people.

I hate her immediately.

"Fiona Cumhaill, this is Kaija Muhari," Sloan says, as stiff and formal as ever.

I force a smile and try not to let my bitch out. "Thank you for helping me. I'm sorry we interrupted your day."

She winks, lifts her wine glass, and makes a seductive show of how delicious the swallow is as it goes down. "My door is always open. Mac knows that."

"Mac?" I turn and smile at Sloan. "All righty then. Are we ready to leave? Lots to do. Witches to find."

"Dillan was telling me about that." She sits up. "He mentioned yer searching for the tether for a hex on ye. Come here to me, Mac. Let me see what it is."

She crosses her legs and pats the rug in front of her. The motion makes the robe fall open—not that it was hiding much in the first place—but hello, talk about a room with a view.

Tad looks like he might need to excuse himself. Dillan is grinning ear to ear. Emmet is studiously studying a painting across the room. Sloan seems bizarrely unaffected.

"Do ye think ye'll be able to sense it?"

Kaija bites her bottom lip, and I draw a deep breath. "Oh,

Mac. When will ye learn there's nothing I can't sense when it comes to what drives a man?"

Would it be bad manners to throat-punch the woman who cured my witch poison and is offering to help save my boyfriend? It would, right?

Asking for a friend.

Sloan looks at me, and I read the question he isn't asking.

I roll my eyes. "As long as she's probing you and not the other way around. Her telling us what we're looking for and cutting out the city-wide search for exiled witches would be helpful."

He squeezes my hand and leans close to brush his lips to my ears. "I am sorry, *a ghra*. I promise I'll make this up to ye ten-fold."

"Yep. You sure will."

When he pulls back looking worried, I get a grip. "Go. See what Kaija's special skills can tell us. I want you better so I can take you home and get to the ten-fold part."

"I look forward to it." He steps onto the rug and sinks to sit cross-legged and match her pose.

Without her saying another word, he holds up his palms, and she mirrors the gesture. They both fold their middle fingers over the other person's hand, and she smiles. "I see ye haven't forgotten. That's sweet."

"Stick to the script, Kaija," he says. "I'm not here to flirt with ye."

She arches a sultry brow and closes her eyes. "Fine…but that snipe cost yer friend here another round of payment."

Tad groans. "Cumhaill. I'm sure yer tired. I'm happy to tag in—"

"Not on your life, McNiff." Dillan grins. "I'm the banker. Called it. Go ahead and set your snark free, Irish. You've had a shitty couple of days. If you need to vent, I'll pay the price no argument."

Save me.

Kaija grows still for a long moment, then opens her eyes and frowns. "Do ye know who cast the spell?"

"Specifically?" Sloan asks. "No, they cast it in the other room and came into where they held me to force me to swallow the bug."

She frowns. "That's too bad because it was tethered to the witch directly—by her DNA to be exact. To remove it, ye'll have to find the primary caster and have her reverse it."

"What if she's dead?" I think of all the women who fell at the Ring of Rath.

"She's not. If she were dead, the tether couldn't retain its hold on him."

"What if she lost her powers?" Sarah asks. "Many of the women involved were stripped of their magic."

Kaija shakes her head. "Same thing. The tether would've dissolved in either case. Whoever the witch was, she's still alive and still actively a witch."

I growl and rake my fingers through my hair. "Dammit. Why couldn't this be easy? Why couldn't it be an eye of newt moment and be over?"

Sloan releases Kaija's hands and shrugs. "That which doesn't kill us makes us stronger, I suppose."

I snort. "Now you sound like Doc."

"Wisdom of the woodland weasel." He grins. "Dillan, Kaija, off ye go. We have places to go and witches to find."

"Vagenius," Dillan repeats for the twentieth time. "Kaija said I was a vagenius and told me to be sure to drop in anytime I'm in Dublin."

I cringe and shoot my brother a look. "Can we not discuss your sexual mastery with such zeal? It's grossing me out."

Dillan laughs. "Hey, Irish. Did she ever tell you that you're a vagenius?"

I spin and point so fast, the soles of my shoes squeak on the hotel lobby floor. "*No!* You don't get to ask that." I swing my pointer over to Sloan. "You will never answer that. Please, guys, can we not talk about her? I get that she's confident and gorgeous and sexually expressive, but it was all I could do not to wrestle her to the ground and pound my fists into her perfect face."

"Since when are you jealous?" Emmet has his arm slung over Sarah's shoulder.

"Since never. I don't know what it is, but I want to tackle her onto those carpets and go primal."

Sloan chuckles. "She's a succubus, *a ghra*. Yer reaction likely had less to do with how ye feel and more to do with the pheromones she releases. Yer also a confident, gorgeous, sexually expressive woman. A primal response to her is perfectly normal."

Emmet looks at Sarah and smiles. "Did you want to rug-wrestle her?"

Sarah shakes her head. "I didn't approve of anything she wore, did, or said, but she certainly didn't bring me to a boil like she did yer sister."

Huh. I wonder if that says more about Sarah or me or our relationships. I push that out of my head. "Okay, enough about the succubus. She has now entered the discarded wasteland of the taboo subject we shall not discuss."

Sloan nods. "Understood. Back to the problem at hand."

Dillan opens his mouth to say something and Sloan smacks him in the gut. "Not another word. Yer sister's had enough."

Pulling the paper out of his coat pocket, he gestures to a city map mounted to the hotel wall between the double doors. "We have an address here, here, here, and here. Tad, you take Emmet and Sarah to these two addresses, and I'll take Fi and Dillan to these two."

"Splitting up is a good idea." I study the map. "More ground in less time."

Sloan nods. "Everyone keep yer phones on."

Maybe it's the dreary weather, or me being whammied by witches, or my boyfriend being hexed, or that same boyfriend having a past lover who is, by all accounts, the queen of sexual partners, but I'm in a mood as miserable as any I can remember.

I want to find the two witches on our list and make them tell me some good news.

We deserve a little good news, don't we?

"Up there." Sloan points up a walkway that divides two small stone houses.

"Are you sure we're in the right place?" Dillan asks. "It feels like we're trespassing into someone's backyard."

We turn the corner, and I point. "Purple door."

Dillan frowns. "What exactly does them having a purple door mean?"

Sloan stops and knocks. "It could be a symbol of open-mindedness. Purple is known to be a color of intuition and awakening the subconscious mind."

I roll my eyes. "Or it just means a witch lives here."

The door swings open and though I don't recognize her, the woman who answers seems to recognize us. "What are ye doin' here? Haven't ye done enough?"

I shrug. "Robin McCaster?"

"Ye know I am."

"We're on follow-up duty for the Goddess. Checking in."

She locks the screen door between us and crosses her arms. "Well, I don't have any magic if that's what ye want to hear. I've lost my friends, my gifts, and my purpose. What else would ye like to know?"

"Which coven were ye in?" Sloan asks. "Was Moira yer coven leader or were ye in one of the others?"

"What does that have to do with anything?"

Even feeling off from the witch poisoning and meeting yet another one of Sloan's ex-lovers who happened to be stunningly gorgeous and talented, I sense the discomfort of the evergreen shrub beside me.

I lean over to touch the browning bush growing beside the house and give it a little boost. Poor thing is struggling. "Just routine questions, Robin. And the answer about who's coven you were part of is…?"

"I was in Moira's coven."

Awesomesauce. I brighten and get a little more into this. "Then you recognize Sloan from the time your sisters kidnapped him and hexed him with the festerbug."

She shrugs. "Maybe. Hexes weren't my thing."

"Oh? What were your things? Dark magic reversal spells that kill white witches? Torturing innocent people by poisoning their water supply and turning them into mutants? What gets you off, Robin?"

Sloan frowns at me and points at another dying bush farther from the door. "That boxwood looks sad, Fi. How about ye take a moment?"

"Yeah. Fine. Whatevs." I leave the men to talk to her and rub my chest. *Bruin. Are you okay? I'm feeling weird and strangely want to rip everyone to shreds.*

The growl that echoes inside my mind gives me goosebumps. *I'm with ye, Red. Shredding sounds good.*

That can't be good. I rub my hand over my forehead and groan. I can't catch a freaking break today.

Okay, hang in there, buddy. I'll try to figure out what's wrong. I don't think I should let you out until we have control of this. We don't want any magic-induced homicides.

Says you.

Shaking out my shoulders, I roll my neck, trying to ease some of the tension. Is it wrong to hope a mugger jumps me? I really could use an outlet right now.

"Yo, Fi. We're done here, sista. Good to go."

Awesome.

I finish fixing the boxwood and pat his little green fringy bits. "Be well, dude."

Joining the other two mid-stride, we head back to the street. Sloan stops on the sidewalk and shows me the list. Two names are highlighted now, Robin, and Caitriona, from the other team's list.

"Yeah, so? What does that mean? What did we learn?"

"It means that when we asked her to list the women from her coven who survived, there was only her and one other and they're both devoid of power."

"How is that possible? Kaija told us that if they were dead or powerless, it would break the hex's tether."

Sloan nods. "So, if the person we need to undo the hex on me isn't dead or powerless she must be..."

I groan as my mental caboose finally arrives at the station. "One of the witches Prince Keldane claimed as his Unseelie orgy playthings."

"And took behind the faery glass into the fae realm."

"Well, shitballs."

CHAPTER TEN

The six of us return to Gran's and Granda's home—a.k.a. the Irish Shire. Sloan *poofs* us into the front hall, and we meander from the front of the house, past the massive tree that grows through the thatched roof at its center and into the part of the home built into a hill.

My grandparents sit close on the couch, sipping tea in front of the telly and watching the Six One news.

I love how amazingly normal that seems.

We fill them in on what we learned about needing to access the witches in the fae realm, and I wait for their reaction. The lack of response doesn't bode well for us, I'm sure.

After a long moment, Granda sighs and shifts to the front of his seat. "I have a firm grip on the magic and the fae creatures of this realm, and *I* can't wrap my head around what life on the other side of the faery glass might be like. How do you possibly think you'll manage?"

"If it's even possible for ye to travel there," Gran adds.

I push back at the anxiety twisting in my belly. "You don't think we can get there?"

"Och, I have no doubt there are ways," Gran says. "My point is the lands might not accept yer presence. We're wholly human. Even gifted with fae magic, that doesn't mean druids are in any way fae."

"I get that. Maybe if we're quick, it'll be okay. We'll pop in, find the witches, get them to release the hex, and leave."

Granda frowns. "I don't think popping and zipping have any bearing on whether or not the lands will accept ye. Lara's right, yer not fae. We're not meant to travel beyond the veil."

"Keldane took Moira and the other two witches," Dillan offers. "The lands must've accepted them."

Granda frowns. "Them bein' there is less about travelin' and more about bein' the prisoner of the evil they unleashed. I would bet, if they're still alive, the lands are takin' their toll on them either physically or mentally."

"Karma's a bitch."

"It couldn't have happened to a more deserving bunch," Gran agrees. "That doesn't mean it's safe for you."

Granda's brow pinches. "Moira and her followers aren't the point of this conversation. If ye want answers about who can go to the fae realm and how that happens, yer better to ask someone *from* the fae realm."

I look at him, wondering who I could—"Oh, Patty! You're saying Patty might know and I should ask him."

Granda nods. "Or the Queen of Dragons."

"Right. I think of her as old and scary, but dragons were originally from the fae realm, right?"

"They were."

I stand and nod at the group. "Okay, I'll take a quick trip to the new dragon lair. I told Patty I'd come to say hello, so that works out."

"Since yer headed there," Granda says, "one of the local farmers lost a bull yesterday. He dropped it off an hour ago. If ye want to deliver it to the dragons, I'm sure the queen and Patty will appreciate the visit as much as the offering."

"Will do." I turn to Sloan. He's sitting on the loveseat looking a little worse for wear. "Are you coming with me or staying here?"

"While I don't like ye going to the dragon's lair yerself, I also respect that Patty and the queen uprooted their lives and relocated their lair and twenty-three dragonborn young because too many people knew their location."

"So you're staying here."

He nods. "I think it's best. I'm a little wilted after our day in Dublin anyway. You find out what ye can. I'll rest and be ready to venture off when ye return."

"Sounds like a plan. Granda, do you think I'll be able to take something as large as a dead cow with me? I've only ever taken myself and one person—a normal-sized person."

"It's magic, *mo chroi*. The size and weight of the passenger have no bearing on things."

"If you say so." I kiss my guy and leave him to rest. "Get unwilted. I'll be back ASAP."

Sloan winks and flashes me a supermodel smile. "I'll be here waitin' with bated breath."

Part of me doesn't want to let him out of my sight. What if he has a turn while I'm gone? What if he needs me and I'm stuck in the time warp of the dragon lair?

Still, the sooner I go, the sooner I'll be back.

Aren't I supposed to be gaining footing as a druid power, working toward my destiny? Yes, I am. "Okay, Granda. Do you mind showing me where the dead cow is?"

Granda sets his teacup on the coaster and extricates himself from the couch. "At yer service, milady."

Granda is right, as usual. I materialize with the rigid bull into a torch-lit cavern which is both similar to the last dragon lair and at the same time, very different.

The last home of the Dragon Queen of Wyrms was a series of caverns and passageways carved into the stone beneath the Cliffs of Moher. This lair has a sandy floor, packed soil walls, and to my left, a pool of water encircled entirely by stone.

"Fiona, ye made it!" Patty strides over to meet me. "Welcome to our new home."

"Thank you. It's quite impressive."

He grins and points toward the bull. "Let's take care of yer delivery, and I'll give ye the tour." He turns back the way he came, cups his hand to the edge of his mouth, and shouts, "Kids, Fiona brought ye a snack. Come say hello."

The vibration of the ground beneath my feet is much more apparent on soil than it was on the stone at the other lair. I watch the direction he called, waiting with anticipation for the stampede to begin.

A thunderous explosion behind me has me spinning and letting out a shout of surprise. The air fills with glistening scales as first one, then a second, and two more dragons breach the pool of water.

Their powerful exit from the pool sends a misty spray through the cavern. I blink as cool sprinkles land on my face.

The four wyverns shake off on the swimming hole's sandy edge while the others come running and slithering and flapping from all directions.

I wonder if it's me they're stampeding for, but it quickly becomes clear it's the bull, so I get out of their way.

Dart is the exception. He rushes to me and rubs his face against my chest, purring. I hug him and point at the food. "Get your share, buddy. I'm not leaving right away."

He tilts his head, and I nod.

"Go on. I don't want my boy hungry."

Dart whips around and runs to join the others, whacking a green wyrm dragon out of his way with a flick of his mighty, spiked tail. When he stops rolling, his brother snorts and pushes back in undeterred.

The dragons are getting bigger but not as quickly as I once worried. I suppose that with ancient species, nature doesn't force them to grow to adulthood overnight.

One of the wyverns finishes eating and flipper-hops his way back into the water. He does a slick barrel roll along the surface, then dives and is gone.

"I love that the wyverns can swim in this lair."

Patty's grin is infectious. "Och, aye. This lair has something for everyone. At night, the wyverns are allowed to go out into the waters and strengthen their flippers. The wyrms dug an extensive warren of tunnels so they can explore without the worry of being discovered, and Her Graciousness allows the Westerns to use one of the tunnels that run close to the surface to stretch their wings on overcast nights."

"So things are working out here. I was worried. I felt awfully responsible for you all having to move."

Patty waves that away. "Best thing that happened to us in centuries."

"Second best." The queen slithers in to join us. Scarlet scales catch the flames of torchlight and reflect the flickering dance. It makes it look like the queen dragon herself is on fire. "The very best thing that has happened is Fiona quenching my heart's true thirst and making all this possible."

I drop my chin and give the dragon queen a small bow. In truth, that was Baba Yaga, but I delivered the basilisk seed, so I played my part. "My pleasure, Your Highness. I'm glad things turned out the way they did."

"As am I." She swings her head and smiles at the frenzied massacre of the dead cow. "Whether it was the Fates, or the Goddess, or the magic of the universe itself, I believe you were meant to come into our lives, Fiona macCumhaill. I am pleased to include you as part of our family."

Wow. "I'm honored to be included."

The three of us stand together and watch the dragons feed. Unlike when we first started supplementing the dragons' feedings back in October, the dragons aren't ravenous.

They're still ferocious eaters, but I'm not afraid that I'll get blood-splattered and be mistaken for food and not their Mother of Dragons.

"Oh, I was asked to speak to you about two young druids who would like to dedicate themselves to dragon care. They're twin brothers and heirs of the Nine Families. From the few times I've spoken with them, they seem to be brave, upstanding lads."

"And they wish to revive the lost art of dragon care," Patty says. "Isn't that lovely?"

"I said I would mention it and put you together with them if it's something you're interested in. They'd be starting from scratch, but I can speak to Pan Dora about how they should proceed in their studies."

The queen looks at me and nods. "I think it's a fine idea. My children will need care at some point. It's best to prepare. Isn't it exciting to revive a lost art with a new generation of dragons?"

"It is."

The three of us stand and admire the massive horde of scales, wings, and flippers for a while longer before Patty breaks the silence. "How's yer man, duck? Did ye have any luck with the witches?"

"Some. They eased him a bit and are confident they can eliminate the festerbug problem, but the hex is set. The witch we need to break the hex's hold on him is currently living as a captive of the Unseelie Prince Keldane."

"The eerie male with the kindling fer hair?"

"That's him."

Patty scrubs his chin and strokes his silver chinstrap beard. "One of those ladies he claimed as his prize is the one ye need to set Sloan free?"

"That's the gist of it. What I need now is for you to tell me how to get into the fae realm so I can find them and end Sloan's suffering."

He blinks at me. "Ye want to go behind the glass?"

"I have to get her to release the hex."

"And if she doesn't?"

I shrug. "She has to. Since she made Sloan's life depend on it, that's what has to happen."

Patty cants his head and pegs me with a gaze so full of sympathy it hurts my heart. "Fi, ye know I love ye, but—"

I shake my head. "No buts. Please, Patty, I swore to him I would do everything I can to fix this. I won't let him down."

"Do ye have any idea what it's like in the fae realm?"

"Absolutely none."

"Do ye understand the species and customs well enough that ye can keep from gettin' yerself killed?"

"Not at all. I told Granda I'd fly under the radar, pop in, and zip out as quickly as possible."

Patty tugs on his beard again and frowns. "I don't like it, Fi. Not one bit."

"I get that, and I agree. It sucks hairy rhino testicles, but it's what Sloan needs to survive. Do you know how to get me into the fae realm?"

Patty nods. "Gettin' ye in isn't the problem. I can open the door, but I can't go with ye. I belong to this world now. I chose a life with Her Benevolence and washed my hands of the other realm. The lands wouldn't accept me back even if I were crazy enough to try to join ye."

"You know how to get me there. That's a start. So, hypothetically, you open a door to get me there. Can you open another door to get me back?"

He frowns. "That's the next problem. You think it's difficult to judge time from here to the world outside, and the two flow at constant but different rates.

"The fae realm makes the time jumping here seem like child's play. There's no rhyme nor reason when compared to time here. How will I know when to open the door? What if yer in trouble and ye need to escape?"

It's hard for me to brainstorm when I have no idea what I have to work with on the other side of the glass.

"Is there a magical key or golden ticket I can take with me that will power me up enough to open my way home from the other side?"

Dart rushes back from the bloody bull buffet and moves in to rub his snout on my chest. "Oh, hells no, buddy. You have half a slaughterhouse on your face. You're not rubbing that into my jacket."

Patty chuckles and points at the pool. "Wash up, boyo."

Dart hustles off, makes a running leap, and bellyflops into the pool. He swishes his face in the water a few times and rushes back, dripping wet. Patty flicks his hand, and a large chamois appears.

He tosses it to me, and I wipe Dart's face.

"So, back to my golden ticket question. Is there anything I can take with me that will allow me to trigger the door to open from the other side?"

Patty nods. "There is, but it's not a golden ticket. It's a royal blue ticket, and I doubt Her Most Protectiveness will allow ye to take him with ye."

I finish wiping Dartamont's face and turn to meet Patty's gaze. He tilts his head toward my dragon boy, and his words click. "Dart? He's my way back home?"

"Dragons in this realm possess an untold amount of magical energy. If he were in the fae realm—the source of his power and heritage—he would be that much stronger. He might be able to help ye open a doorway back."

"I forbid it," the queen snaps. "I'll not put one of my little ones in harm's way."

Her hostility doesn't affect me because I'm in full agreement. "I wouldn't either. There must be another way. We need to figure out what it is."

By the time I get back to Gran and Granda's, it's late, and everyone has gone to bed. I find my toiletries bag set out in the bathroom, so I wash up, brush my teeth and let myself into the spare room.

My shield warms against my back the moment I close the door behind me. It's not the tingle of a warning of danger or the burn of needing to brace for a fight. It's a message for me to take notice of my surroundings.

I slide my hand into my pocket and pull out my phone to access the light. The illumination is sudden and jarring.

"Och, Fi. Why'd ye do that?" Manx gripes, blinking sleepily at me from the foot of the bed.

I wince, and my eyes adjust. "Sorry, my shield says...oh, *nonononono.*" I rush across the room and turn on the bedside lamp. When I brush his cheek, Sloan's skin burns hot against my palm. Oh, gawd...there's a weird black veining spreading up his chest. "Sloan? Wake up."

"*Sloan?*" I say louder.

"Wake up, hotness."

He doesn't.

With my phone still in my hand, I flip through my contacts and hit send. "Tad, I need you."

"Fuck off." The line goes dead, and my screen blanks out.

I curse and call back. When he answers this time, I jump in. "Don't you *dare* hang up on me, McNiff. I need help!"

"What?" he stammers. "Shit. Sorry, Fi. I wasn't awake. Where are you? What do you need?"

"I'm in the spare room at Gran's. I need to get Sloan to

Wallace's clinic. Please tell me you've been to Stonecrest Castle and can *poof* us."

"Yeah. Let me find my trousers..."

"In the kitchen," a woman mumbles in the background.

"Right." Tad sounds more awake by the moment. "Okay, I've got trousers. Give me two minutes to gather myself, and I'll be there."

I hang up and rush to open the bedroom door.

My screech swallows the squeak of the hinges as I jump backward. "Holy crap, Gran! You scared the bejeezus out of me."

"What's wrong?" Gran pats her heaving chest, looking breathless. "I heard ye say ye need help."

I turn back to the bed, my heart hammering against the base of my throat. "It's Sloan. He was like this when I got back. I can't wake him up."

Granda shuffles in looking half asleep, followed by Dillan, who despite the crazy patch of hair sticking out in the wrong direction, looks remarkably alert. "Is Nikon or Tad coming?"

"Tad's here." Tad jogs in from the hall. "Forgive me for intruding into your home, Lugh. I figured this was an emergency."

"No apology necessary, son. Our boy needs to be at Stonecrest Castle."

Tad rushes forward and places a hand flat on Sloan's chest. "Who's coming?"

"We all are." Gran shuffles forward and takes Granda's and Dillan's hands. I wrap my arm around Manx and grip Tad's arm when he reaches out to make contact with the others. When he turns his attention to focus on Sloan, I feel the signature of his gift build in the air.

A moment later we're in Wallace's clinic. It's dark, but Dillan gets the light, and we all blink against the brilliance of industrial lighting bouncing off stainless steel.

"I'll get Wallace." Manx races off on all fours.

"Thank you, puss." I barely have the words out when Sloan starts to convulse. Dillan curses and rushes to roll him on his side. I hold his head so he doesn't hurt himself on the steel table. "It's okay, babe. I have you."

Tears run hot down my cheeks as the seizing seems to go on endlessly. "Can anyone stop this?"

"I can." Wallace rushes in. "You two keep holding him. I'll be right there to help."

Dillan and I safeguard Sloan for as long as it takes for his father to grab the crystals he needs and a couple of vials from the medicine cabinets.

"All right, son. Let's see what we can do to make ye feel better, shall we?" Thankfully, the moment his father starts working on him, his body runs out of steam, and he falls still. "That's right. Yer where ye need to be now. All is well."

Janet sweeps in, her robe billowing behind her like the cape of a superhero—or in her case a supervillain. "Ye did right bringin' him here. Now, I'd like ye all to leave."

CHAPTER ELEVEN

Our group shuffles out of the clinic to allow Wallace to tend to Sloan without distraction. Once we arrive in the outer waiting room, I reach the far wall and boomerang back to face Sloan's mother. "There's no way we're leaving while Sloan's life hangs in the balance. The fact you'd use your son's ailing condition to try to force a wedge between him and people who love him is a dick move."

Janet's gaze narrows on me, and a chill runs the length of my spine. "Ye think ye have a say in this? Ye've known him less than a year. I gave birth to him and have raised him fer twenty-seven years."

"But you don't *know* him," I blurt. "You have no idea who he is and who he's becoming."

"I'm his *mam*. I know him better than anyone else."

Her gaze lands on my grandparents, and the hairs on the nape of my neck stand on end. "If that were true, you'd know how much it hurts him when you focus on his money over his happiness. Did you honestly think suing him for control of his fortune would do anything other than nail the last spike into your coffin?"

Janet stiffens, her glare turbulent. "I'm sure ye've been right there paintin' us as the villains and fillin' his head with lies, ye wee bitch."

Gran and Granda both shout and move to intervene.

I raise my hand. "It's fine. It's not the first time she's called me that."

"Had I known that," Gran snaps, "I would've handled things differently."

I shake my head. "Don't let her upset you, Gran. I've dealt with bullies and haters before. I'm immune. What upsets me is that it hurts Sloan and she doesn't care."

Janet grunts and rolls her eyes. "Yer tellin' me how I feel about my only child, are ye? Wallace is wrong. Yer not young and opinionated yer delusional."

I hold my hand out to block Granda from stepping in. I know they have issues with the way Sloan was raised, but they need to take a number and move to the back of the line.

"I'm not delusional, and to the point of your accusation, I don't paint you as the villains. We don't discuss you. We're building a life, and you're not part of it. He bought a house. He's building a social network. You're missing out on all of it because you refuse to see him as a person."

"He refuses to see yer a talentless hack who's after his inheritance."

"You don't even *know* me. What have I ever said or done that makes you think I give two shits about his money?"

"That's what women like you are always after."

I throw up my hands. "Who the hell do you think I am, lady? I've put my life on the line for him a dozen times, and I'm about to do it again. If you think that's hyperbole, it's only because you don't have a clue about what he's facing. The only way he lives through this is if I get the DNA of the witch who hexed him. That witch is in the fae realm. Are you going to go? No? Then don't talk to me about loving him."

Janet's glare is as cold and piercing as an ice dagger through the eye socket. "Get out of my house!"

Gran shifts between Janet and me and widens her stance. "If it were in Sloan's best interest fer us to leave, we'd go without a fuss, but it's not. We're here for him. We'll stay for him regardless of what kind of histrionics ye care to unleash. Now Fi, get in there and see what Wallace needs to save him."

I'm happy to take the out and leave the tension of the face-off with Janet. I find Wallace sitting quietly at Sloan's hip, staring at his son. My footing falters as I approach, and I have to force myself to accept how badly the hex has affected him. The rich brown of Sloan's complexion has drained to a chalky tan and those black spider-web lines veining their way across his stomach are now up to his neck.

Oh, broody. Look what they've done to you.

It's hard to look, and yet, I'm afraid to look away.

Wallace hasn't taken his eyes off him to acknowledge my arrival. Sloan's father suddenly doesn't seem so intimidating and indifferent. He's hurting, and it's plain to see the love he keeps hidden too well.

"I'm sorry to interrupt." I give him a moment before I approach. "How is he?"

"Not well, I'm afraid." Wallace takes a moment and clears his throat. "Maybe if I got to him sooner I could've done more."

I stiffen and ready for the attack, but it doesn't come. In the spirit of the moment, I choose to think he wasn't taking a shot at me and simply made a clinical observation. "Sloan was adamant he not be brought here. He thinks you'll twist it and use this against him for your lawsuit."

The sound that escapes his throat is pained. "Things have gotten so fouled up. Janet's been angry and hurt about him walking away. I know she blames you, but that's not fair. It's our fault too."

I fight the urge to correct him and say that it's *all* their fault. That high road is a tough one to navigate.

Adulting is hard.

"When will you know more about what he's facing?"

He lifts his shoulders in a weak shrug. "When the crystals finish doing their cleansing. Until then, we wait."

I grab a stool from beside the medicine cabinet and take a seat opposite his father. Collecting Sloan's hand in mine, I squeeze it. "Hey, broody. I'm here. We're all here...waiting and worrying and loving you."

I brush my hand over his cheek and swallow against the emotion clogging my throat.

"Ye genuinely care for him, don't ye?"

I smile. "I love him...but don't say anything to him. We haven't spoken the words yet, and the first time I say that out loud shouldn't be to his father."

Wallace chuckles. "No, I suppose he'd like to be the first to hear it. Does he love you in return?"

I chuckle. "He's been there longer than I. He knew he wanted this and pursued me for months. I wanted to stand on my own while I learned and grew as a druid. I held him at bay as long as I could. He's hard to resist when he puts his mind to something."

"I didn't realize it was his doing."

"One hundy percent." I lift his hand against my chest and hug his arm. "Despite what you think, I don't care about his money. Your son is thoughtful and brave and supportive and sweet and one of the smartest, most talented people I've ever met. You can be proud of him for that. He's amazing."

"Sadly, I don't think we can take much of the credit."

I shake my head. "He's principled and driven like you. He's fierce in battle and stubborn, like Janet. He may have learned about the gooier parts of life and love from my grandparents, but there's a lot of you two in him."

"That's generous of ye to say, Fiona."

"It's true. Yes, I realize from where you stand he outshines me on many levels, but I have a lot to offer too. We enjoy one another, and we're excited every day to spend time with each other. When the dangers of the world rear up and attack, he's glad I'm the one at his side, and I feel the same. Surely, you remember what it was like to fall in love."

Wallace looks at me, and I read the worry and exhaustion clouding his eyes. "It wasn't like that for Janet and I. Ours was an arranged marriage joining two powerful druid families. The feelings we built as a couple came much later and over a lifetime of working together as partners."

Well, that explains a lot. "I didn't know."

"No, I don't suppose ye did. There's likely a lot ye don't know about our family and us."

Even though the words sound critical, his tone doesn't make it seem like he means it that way. "I would like to get to know your family. Not only for my sake but Sloan's. He may not discuss what's happening between you, but I know it hurts him. He doesn't want to hurt you, but he's determined to explore being the man he sees himself being."

"He can't become that man here?"

I shake my head. "From what he's said, no. He doesn't think so."

"Why? We can give him things, open doors for him, ensure his future."

"He doesn't want that. He feels a million expectations pressed upon him here. Some he embraces...others he doesn't. He wants to open the doors of his life and ensure the future he ends up with is the one he chooses."

It isn't my place to have this discussion, but Sloan and his parents don't talk to one another. Or, I suppose, don't listen to one another is closer to the mark.

A knock at the door brings our attention around to Emmet. "Hey, sorry to interrupt."

I smile and hold out my hand. "Thanks for coming, Em."

He squeezes my fingers and kisses my forehead. "Dillan texted us, and Sarah thought she might be able to help. Is it okay if she comes in and lends a healing hand?"

Wallace looks confused, so I catch him up. "Emmet's girlfriend Sarah is a white witch from Blarney. She and her coven were the ones who cleared him of the little blue bastards and perked him up the other day. Because it's a witch hex, we found witch magic helps to counter it."

"It would." Wallace shifts his attention from me to my brother. "She's fine to come in and try. I'll step out for a moment and get properly dressed. It's going to be a long night."

"Wallace?" I reach and catch his wrist across the exam table as he turns to leave. "If I may say something without overstepping?"

"What is it?"

"You might want to take Janet with you and try to calm her a little. She's upset and brewing for a fight. It won't do Sloan any good to have everyone tearing at one another. I'd hate for her and Gran to throw down. It would hurt Sloan terribly if he found out."

He nods. "Yes, it would. I'll do that."

―――――――

Wallace and Sarah switch positions in Sloan's care and once Janet exits the outer room, my family floods in to check on our fallen warrior. I give Gran and Granda some time next to him and soak up a few strong hugs from my brothers.

"Thanks for being here, guys." Emmet hands me off to Dillan, and I bask in brotherly love.

"There's nowhere else we would be when you need us, Fi." Dillan eases back from our hug and chucks my chin. "Calum texted. He says if you need them here, Nikon will bring them in a snap."

I look at Sloan and sigh. "There's nothing they can do. The answer to this problem is in the fae realm. There's no sense in them sitting here and feeling helpless like the rest of us. What I need to do is figure out how to use the witch DNA to break this hex."

Emmet brightens and reaches deep into his pants pocket. "Ask, and ye shall receive, sista. Sarah's coven has been working on that since we left. This evening they finished this and are pretty sure it's your answer."

He hands me the oddly shaped gemstone, and I run a finger over the iridescent surface. As the warmth of my skin trails across the uneven surface, the opulence seems to swirl and react, following my fingertip.

"Well, that's cool. What is it?"

Emmet shrugs. "No idea. All I know is they said you need to cover the stone's surface with the witch's DNA. You have to immerse it wholly."

I chuckle. "So what, I walk up to a witch that we sentenced to a life of imprisonment in the fae realm and ask her to lick my stone?"

Dillan snorts. "I suggest you don't use the term 'lick my stone.' That sounds rude."

"It doesn't have to be saliva," Emmet adds. "Considering the audience of who you'll be asking, I think blood is likely the way to go."

I can envision how that will play out. Sadly, I didn't bring my battle knife and thigh sheath Kevin bought for me. Birga might be overkill, but she's always an option.

I close my fingers around the stone and feel it warm in my

palm. It's bursting with witch magic, and I hope it's everything they believe it will be.

"Okay, so we're one step closer. Patty says he can get me into the fae realm. The only problem is getting me out. Once we have that sorted, we'll be ready to go."

"The sooner, the better," Sarah looks up from where she's working over Sloan and frowns. "The damage the festerbugs initiated is extensive. I can stabilize him right now, but to do it, I'll have to put him into a magically induced coma."

I cover my mouth and try not to freak out. "You better wait and speak to Wallace. He might know something we don't or have a different plan. The last thing I want to do is decide without his input."

Sarah nods. "That's fine, but we need a decision."

I can't believe we're at a point where I have to decide whether we should put Sloan into a coma to slow his decline.

How did this happen?

Three days ago we were happy. Other than him having the odd stomachache, we weren't worried about anything.

I'm still struggling with that when Wallace returns, and I inform him about what Sarah suggested. He examines the cleansing crystals he set up and frowns. "I hoped for better results with these. What exactly would ye do to put him in a state of stasis?"

While Sarah and Wallace speak, I zone out and spend a moment with Sloan. "I have to go, hotness. Gran and Granda and your parents are here with you, but if we're going to beat this, I have to leave you for a while. Hang in there. Don't you dare leave me."

I bend over his still form and hug him. "Wish me luck, Mackenzie. I have a feeling I'm going to need it." As I release his hand, my fingers catch on his bone ring. Something inside my gut lights up. "I'm borrowing this. I'll give it back as soon as I return. Promise."

With my path before me clear, I sit up, press my palm against his heart, and draw a steadying breath.

"All righty then, let's getter done."

I'm up and crossing the clinic when Emmet and Dillan step forward. "Ready when you are," Emmet says.

I shake my head. "Not this time, boys. You know I love you as backup, but Patty warned me this has to be a quick in and out. I have a better chance of not being detected as a wholly human interloper if it's only Bruin and me."

"Hells no!" Dillan says. "That ain't happening. If you're forced to go behind the faery glass and face a world none of us knows anything about, you're certainly not doing it alone. Stamped it. Blackball beats them all."

I frown. "You can't blackball beats them all when it comes to real-life issues."

Dillan shrugs. "Tough noogies, I already did. Besides, if you're talking about stealth and finding the quickest way in and out, that's ranger territory. You need me. My cloak of concealment was made for exactly this purpose."

He has a point.

I hate the idea of him coming and being in danger.

Dillan pokes his finger into the end of my nose and scowls. "I know that look, missy, and that's bullshit. I'm the big brother here. I have seniority, and I will decide what danger I am willing to face."

I'd argue, but I won't get anywhere. With Emmet, I can usually make him see reason—Dillan is too stubborn to reason with once he's locked horns.

"Fine. You, me, and Bruin. It'll be quick and dirty, and no one gets hurt."

"Do I get a chance to get in on this?" Emmet asks.

I shake my head. "You need to get back to Toronto because you have a shift in the morning. It doesn't do any of us any good if our druid life gets you boys fired."

Emmet hisses. "Fuck that, Fi. There's no way I'm watching the two of you go off to the fae realm while I sit here with my thumb up my ass."

"Then don't watch," Dillan says. "Or better yet, don't put your thumb up your ass."

Emmet rolls his eyes. "If I get fired so be it. I wanted to be a cop to serve and protect. I can do that as a druid too. If I get canned, maybe Garnet has a job opening he needs filled. He pays better than the PD anyway. I may not turn into a lion, but I can turn into a kangaroo."

Dillan pegs him with the look. "You turned into a kangaroo for one day three months ago. That doesn't make you a shifter for hire."

"It's something to offer, a skill to put on the table."

Dillan shakes his head. "You're reaching."

Emmet's brow furrows. "Don't dismiss me as an effective part of the team."

I can't stand the look of rejection on Emmet's face. I know he's felt slighted and left behind since the night we all assumed our intended powers in the Hill of Allen.

He tries not to show it, but I know it hurts him.

"We would never dismiss your contributions to the team, Em." I brush his arm. "Your support as a buffer has ensured more than one win for us, your diversions are unmatched, and you're always there when we need you. I think what Dillan means is when up against an unknown offensive force, he doesn't want to see you get hurt. I don't either."

Emmet's expression falls, and the hurt in his eyes sears my soul. "So that's it then, I don't offer an offensive benefit so I get benched? I have to say, Fi, I'm surprised...and fucking disappointed."

Dillan curses. "Don't be like that. What happens if we get into a donnybrook with a horde of fae and you have no active powers of offense? The universe didn't give you a weapon. It won't be like here when we can have Tad or Nikon snap in with backup."

Emmet isn't listening. He flashes the two of us his middle finger over his shoulder and storms out of the room.

"Maybe we're wrong," I say, watching him go. "Maybe he should come. Three Musketeers, right?"

Dillan shakes his head. "We're not wrong. He might be pissed at us for a while, and we might have to kiss his ass for the next month or two, but at least he'll be alive. Him staying here is the right call."

As much as I want to run after Emmet and make things right with him, I need to go if I'm going to save Sloan. Patty told me the time warps are brutal between realms.

Dammit. I hate this.

I scrub my fingers through my hair and curse. "Okay, we'll make it up to him later. We gotta go. Tad, I need you."

CHAPTER TWELVE

To honor the secrecy of the dragon lair's location, I have Tad *poof* us back to Gran's and Granda's house. Dillan needs to grab his cloak, and if we're going to spend the next day or two in the Fae realm, I need yoga pants and a sports bra instead of underwire.

"Are you two sure you don't need me?" Tad asks.

"I'm sure." I finish my text to Patty and hit send. "Wherever our access point to the fae realm is, Patty said he could take care of it. We'll be fine."

Before Tad *poofs* out, I hug him. "Thanks for tonight. You came through for us in a big way, and I appreciate it."

His smile is awkward and genuine. Two emotions I don't think I've ever seen when dealing with Tad. "Good luck, Fi. I'm sending you both all the good vibes I can. Bring back that witch stone and save your boy. Sloan is a tightly-wound, straight-laced pain in the ass but after all these years, I'm starting to like him."

I chuckle and squeeze his arm. "I won't tell."

"Good because I'll deny it."

Tad leaves my brother and me alone in the dark house, and the two of us get our hustle on to get ready for our quest. We decide to take nothing but what we're wearing. Our weapons are internal, and with Bruin, we're well-covered.

"Do you think we should've said goodbye to Gran and Granda?" I scan the space for one last check. "I feel bad about *poofing* off without talking to them first."

Dillan pulls off his shirt and bends to grab a fresh one from his duffle bag. "What do you think they would say to us about going to the fae realm alone? There was nothing to be gained by having a family argument about the insanity of what we're about to do."

"I still feel bad."

"Then write a quick note before Patty gets here. Tell them we love them, and we'll be fine, and we don't want them to worry. Tell them we'll be back as soon as we can, and we'll be careful. And tell them to make sure Emmet's okay."

I hear the regret in Dillan's voice and have to look away, or I'm going to cry. Instead, I hurry into the kitchen, grab the notepad and pencil Gran uses for her shopping list, and write down everything Dillan told me to say.

By the time I finish our note, Patty's whistling for us from the living room. "Hello the house. Are ye here, Fi? Are you ready to go?"

"We're here." I meet up with Patty and Dillan in the living room and point at the front hall. "What's the weather like in the fae realm? Do I need a jacket? Should I wear sneakers or my winter boots?"

Patty chuckles and waves his hand. He doesn't activate his leprechaun magic often, but when he does, I'm always impressed by how much power a wee man contains.

With the flick of his hand, my clothes morph, and instead of wearing black yoga pants and a navy hoodie, I'm now wearing a forest green tunic with brown leather pants, bodice, and matching boots that come up to my knees.

When I look at my brother, he's wearing the boy version of the same outfit.

"We look like twinsies," I say.

"No offense, Fi, but we look like two of Robin Hood's merry men."

I laugh. "I'd rather look like one of Robin Hood's men than Maid Marian any day. S'all good."

Dillan swings his cloak around his shoulders and latches the brooch clasp below his throat. "So, this is what the kids in the fae hood are wearing these days, is it?"

Patty looks us over and gives us an appraising smile. "It'll do the trick in a pinch."

I slide the witch stone and my phone into the leather pouch on my belt. "Okay, so we're dressed, we have our witch-spelled hex-stone, and we look the part. Now, all we have to do is figure out how to get there and get back."

Patty holds up his finger. "I figured out the answer to our timing problem on how to get you home once yer there."

From the pocket of his vest, he pulls out a small, golden sand timer. "Wear this around your neck. I set the sands to give you twenty-four hours here. It won't feel like that makes any sense there but trust me. When the last of the sands run out, you need to be in the spot where you first arrive. I won't have much control of where you land, but when I pull back the veil, it will at least be in the same spot."

I check with Dillan, and that seems simple enough. "And on the off chance that we miss our window? What's our backup plan?"

Patty frowns. "Try not to let that happen, but if chaos keeps ye from making the rendezvous, ye'll have to hang around that spot and watch for the air to shimmer. From this side, I'll try every hour for as long as my magic lasts."

I draw a deep breath and check with Dillan. "Are we ready to do this?"

Dillan pulls his hood up so the shadow falls and his face is hidden inside his cloak. "I was born ready. Let's go find us some witch bitches."

All righty then. I turn my attention to Patty. "Okay, where do we find our access point to slip behind the faery glass?"

Patty grins. "Why at the end of the rainbow, o' course."

As it turns out, there aren't any rainbows at five o'clock in the morning. Patty portals us from Gran's house into the dragon lair and escorts us to where he keeps his massive pot of gold—which, in truth, is an above-ground pool that he's filled with coin. He says he's not worried about having Dillan there because if he escorts him in and out, my brother will have no memory of where the lair is.

It's a magic thing, so I don't question it.

While we wait for the sun to rise so Patty can call us the rainbow, Dillan and I get a little dragon downtime.

"You're getting big, dude," Dillan says to Dart. "Not like *Godzilla: King of the Monsters* big, but bigger than the last time I saw you."

Dart seems to approve of Dillan's comments and struts his stuff, swinging his scaled and spiked tail like a powerful club as he prances around us.

Pfft, pfft, he lets out a couple of throaty huffs and lobs some baby fireballs. The fiery globes shoot into the giant cavern of glittering gold where Patty stores his treasure. They get great hang time, but what goes up must come down, and they crash, sending up a spray of coins.

"Yes, yes," Patty says, "yer a fierce and magnificent beast, Dartamont, but if ye'd be so kind as not to melt me gold, I would appreciate it."

Dart tilts his head and offers Patty what I suspect is an apologetic smile although he still looks pretty proud.

I kiss his scaly snout. "You're a good boy, Dart. Patty loves you enough to forgive a little melted treasure."

Patty chuckles. "The keyword in that sentence, Red, is a little. Ye weren't here when he and his Western siblings started a fireball contest and nearly turned my treasure trove into a smelting factory."

I make a face at Dart and chuckle. "Okay, well, you have to be careful. Patty might not miss a couple of melted ingots, but he doesn't want his treasures to be running like golden rivers through the lair."

I'm still scrubbing my fingers over the three scaly horns on Dart's snout when the air of the lair lightens and colors come streaming in from the heavens.

I tip my head back and search the dirt and rock ceiling high above us. "How is that possible? Where is the rainbow coming from?"

Patty chuckles. "Yer aware that everyone livin' in this lair is a magical, mythical creature, aren't ye?"

"Yeah, I get that."

"So how hard do ye think it is fer us to pipe in some natural lighting?"

"Not hard, I guess."

"If we can pipe in natural lighting, why can't I call a rainbow to my pot of gold?"

I'm not even going to try to figure that out. Patty is a leprechaun, and a leprechaun's pot of gold is at the end of the rainbow.

That's how things are, I guess.

"Now what?" I gesture at the beaming light cutting the darkness. It bends in an elegant arch of red, orange, yellow, green, blue, indigo, and violet, reaching in from somewhere high above to focus its end in Patty's pool of gold.

"Now take yer brother's hand, close yer eyes, click yer heels together, and make a wish as ye jump into the colorful beam of light."

I see the amusement twinkling behind his spectacles and peg him with a withering stare. I drop Dillan's hand like it's a hot rock. "Seriously? You're picking now to bullshit me?"

Patty barks a laugh and doubles over at the waist. "Och, I'm sorry, Fi, but it was too rich to pass up. Humans are so gullible."

"Yeah, yeah, yuk it up, shorty." I shake my head at Dillan, but okay, the Man o' Green totes had me going there for a minute. "Any time, oul man."

Eventually, Patty gets control of himself, and the laughter ends. He swipes his stubby fingers under his glasses and collects the tears that brimmed his glassy blue eyes. "Och, it's been a long time since I enjoyed a good hard belly laugh. Thanks, Red. Yer one in a million."

"Glad you're having fun. Now, how do we cross the veil between the realms?"

He shrugs. "Walk into the light."

Dillan frowns. "You know that's not usually a good omen for a long, healthy life, right?"

Patty doesn't respond, so I take Dillan's hand and close the distance to the rainbow. As we draw close, the air grows warm and tingles against my skin. Mmm...and it smells like cotton candy.

When the two of us get to the brightest point, I squeeze Dillan's hand. "Glad you're here, bro."

He chuckles. "Wish I could say the same."

With that, we step into the ray of the rainbow.

Piercing the veil and transporting into the fae realm isn't the same as transporting with wayfarer, immortal, or Moon Called magic. Not only does it leave my limbs weirdly tingly, but it also makes me light-headed. Like the fun buzz between the fourth and fifth drink when your favorite song comes on, and a hot guy invites you onto the dancefloor.

The euphoria doesn't last.

A split-second after we step into the beaming ray of the rainbow, I'm rammed from behind. Knocked off balance, I lurch into Dillan, and we crash to a sudden stop on the packed dirt of the ground. My shoulder blade lights up where I take the hit, and I pivot to flip off the semi-truck that ran me over.

Only it isn't a truck.

"Dart! What are you doing here?" I panic for a second until I find Dillan behind me and I can breathe again. Bruin flutters in my chest, and I relax a little more.

For better or worse, we're all here.

"Come out and join the fun, buddy."

I release my bear, and he materializes beside me. "What happened, Red?"

"We failed to stick the landing, but we're here, and we're whole, and that's what matters most."

Dillan grunts and untangles his leg from my arm. "What exactly were you expecting to happen if us being whole is the benchmark of success?"

I roll onto my knees shaking my head to see if the buzz will clear. "Nothing specific. With no frame of reference, I hoped we didn't get puked out at this end looking like we belong in a Salvador Dali painting."

"Us not looking like melting clocks is a win, I guess."

"It all went according to Hoyle, except for the stowaway." I cast a stern look at my baby dragon. "Your dragon queen mama will be so angry with both of us. I don't even want to think about it."

Dart pushes his snout against me, and I can't help but scrub his scales and snuggle him in.

"I love you too, dude. I understand the impulse to step out and make your own decisions, but no one wants you to get hurt. Events around me tend to go bad very quickly."

Dart stretches his wings wide and prances around us in a circle. With his head high and smoke coming out his nostrils, he's pretty damned impressive.

"Yeah, I get it. You're a badass."

Dillan looks around and brushes bits of debris off the ass of his leather pants. "Okay, we're not in Kansas anymore."

I follow Dillan's wide gaze and my jaw drops. "Holy crapamoly. Look at this place."

"I'm looking." Dillan turns in a slow runway circle. "It's hard not to."

My brain is cramming to take it all in. The swirling pastel pink and mango sky reminds me of a beautiful Bellini cocktail. A spongy copper-colored moss covers the ground, and the trees and bushes are the most stunning array of greens I've ever seen.

"It's so...magical." I always thought my grove was the most magical place there could ever be, but it's obvious now that it's a wonderous vessel for magical creatures, but their heritage realm is magical in every aspect.

A little mauve and gray animal is hovering in the air, curious about our arrival. He flits his feathery antennae at us, and I smile. His upper half looks like a purple, fuzzy squirrel, his bottom is smooth like a fat slug, and he has gray bat wings.

"Hello there. You remind me of my Ostara rabbits back home." I take a step closer and reach my hand up to rub a finger on his belly when my shield flares.

I withdraw as he spits glowing purple goo.

"Whoa." Dillan pulls me clear of the spit zone and the steaming and withering plants that got hit. "Did not see that coming. Venom-spitting glow bugs. Got it."

I frown at the other creatures stirring and flying around us. "They can't all be bad. Our fae are lovely." I point at what looks like a large golden hummingbird. "There, that guy looks nice enough."

We watch as the bird zips this way and that, sticking his chunky beak into strange-looking flowers.

My shock over the venom spit eases.

"See, he's nice. We just had a bad start—Oh!" I shout as a jagged vine whips into the air, lassos the bird, tightens its grip and bashes the poor dude on a rock.

"Harsh," Dillan says.

"Me no likey."

Dillan turns us to go in the other direction. "Let's do this and get gone. Take a visual snapshot of where we are for when we need to get back here."

I survey the land and am thankful that, if nothing else, we arrived in the fae realm version of a secluded garden without a dozen people watching us materialize.

Part of my pessimistic fear was that we'd suddenly appear in the middle of a Renaissance sporting event. The horses would be thundering toward one another with the knights holding lowered lances. We'd materialize, the horses would rear, the crowd would gasp, and we'd be busted.

Thankfully, we're merely in a garden at dusk.

Other than killer creatures it's innocuous enough.

"Seize them!"

Our heads snap as one. There's movement in the garden, not far from us and moving in fast. My shield flares hot, and I curse. "My bad, guys. Sorry. I jinxed us."

CHAPTER THIRTEEN

The command to capture us still rings in the air as the thunder of hooves bears down on us. An incoming force of centaur guards is navigating manicured hedges, marble fountains, and wooden arbors. Men with cloven feet, hairy chests, and massive ram horns curling against the sides of their heads are racing at us.

I scan the area, searching for an escape. "Dillan?"

Dillan bolts through a bush on our left and I gesture for Dart to follow. My beloved blue boy grins and makes chase, his little wings fluttering as he gallops off.

I think he thinks this is a game. Whatever works.

I'm almost to the opening in the bush when I glance back. Bruin isn't on the move. My bear is standing his ground, snarling at the incoming security team.

"Buddy, let's go."

"I'll hold them. I've been itching for slaughter for days."

Yeah, I've felt it. There's no time to argue. He's sure and can spirit out if things get to be too much. "Love you, Bear."

I follow the sound of Dart crashing through branches and catch up as quickly as I can. The foliage is dense, and as we go deeper into the wooded area, the leaves grow sharper, and the branches scrape with jagged thorns.

I try to avoid getting diced, but there's no way around it. It's dark in here, and we're going too fast to be careful.

I release the glamor on my fae eyes, and the illusion burns away. My nocturnal vision kicks in. *"Tough as Bark,"* I mutter as tendrils of greenery claw at me, wrapping themselves around my arms. "Okay, I officially hate these plants."

Dart seems to agree. *Pfft, pfft.* He hisses out a few fireballs, torching the groping plants. A high-pitched squeal follows and the vines recoil.

"Good boy. They didn't like that."

Dart grunts and lets out a couple more *pffts* of fire.

"Dillan, where are you taking us?" I snap a branch twining around my wrist and growl as three more take its place.

My brother doesn't respond. I don't know if he's too far ahead to hear me or too focused on what he's doing to answer.

Then, I hear Sloan's voice in my head as clearly as if he's standing next to me.

Yer a druid, Cumhaill. Think like one.

Oh, right. Know it all.

I raise my hands as we press forward through the scrub, connecting with the natural world around me. *Command Plants* isn't a spell I have much experience with, mostly because the plants at home don't actively try to strangle me, but it's not beyond my abilities.

With as much respect as I can muster for the razor-leafed strangle weed trying to slice me open, I command it to retreat and give us room to move. While I'm at it, I focus on encouraging growth behind us to conceal our path and make it more difficult for those guards to follow us.

The response is sluggish, but there is improvement.

I'm here, Red, Bruin says into my mind as a gust of wind announces his arrival back with the group.

"Great. Take point. See if you can get a big picture of where we are and when this greenery nightmare will end."

On it. He's gone in another heartbeat, and I focus on Dart. Several vines are twining around the base of his wings, but they don't seem to be able to cut his scales.

Good. I don't want my boy hurt.

"How's it looking up there, ranger? Are we there yet?"

"Uh...yep, we've gone as far as we can."

His tone is strained, and it sets off warning bells. I grab Dart's wing and pull him back, pushing past him to take the lead.

When I break clear of the greenery, I understand why Dillan sounded weird. He broke free of the trees and is standing at the edge of a clearing.

He's not alone.

Opposite him stand a dozen centaurs holding spears glowing with magic. The weapons are leveled at us and buzzing with potential energy ready to discharge.

Awesomesauce. "Well, that's not intimidating at all."

"Right?"

"Who are you?" the lead centaur shouts, stomping a furry black hoof. He's a massive brute with wild black hair twisting down his ribs. His braided beard is a little Jack Sparrow for my taste, and the extensive inking across his cheeks looks like someone got carried away on a drunken dare.

I check out the gold and burgundy sash he wears and assume the sigils covering it mean he's the man in charge of this bunch. "Who sent you here?"

I lift my palms and force a smile. "No one sent us. My brother and I got lost in the woods. If you point us toward the nearest pub, we'll be on our way. We don't want any trouble. We're just poor, weary travelers."

The centaur growls. "Siblings lost in the woods, are you? What are your names?"

"I'm Hansel," Dillan says. "And this is my sister, Gretel. We meant no harm, honestly. We were taking a basket of goodies to our grandmother's house and got turned around. We saw a white rabbit and followed it off the path and to his hole. That's when you found us and took chase."

If I weren't standing in front of twelve piss-your-pants scary hairy men with hooves, I'd laugh.

"You. Female," the leader grunts, pointing. "Come out of the shadows. Let me see you."

I do as he asks and his gaze narrows on me. I'm used to the assessment of how I look with my body armor engaged and my fae eyes glowing an eerie ice-blue. I await the tightening of his face and the recoil that follows.

It doesn't happen.

Instead, he arches a brow and flashes me a seductive grin. "It seems your sister is the one blessed with the looks in your family. Has she a mate?"

Hubba-wha?

"She has." Dillan snaps, his voice husky. "A giant man, very jealous, very powerful. He's expecting us. We should go before he's angered."

The moment Dillan shifts his weight, the guards tighten up on their weapons and ready to fire.

"What is the name of this very powerful mate?" the guard asks, assessing me. "I know most males of power in this land. If I respect his claim, I shall let you go. If he is a lesser male, I shall claim you for myself and share you with my friends."

There's a rousing chorus of grunting over that and my stomach twists. I waggle my finger in the air. "While sharing with your friends is nice—hard pass."

"His *name*, female," the black centaur shouts. "Answer me or I'll sate myself regardless."

My mind reels as I try to think of fae males of legend. All I come up with are gods who may or may not be alive or Thor. Wrong pantheon.

I don't know the fae lore well enough to hazard a guess on who would live on this side of the faery glass.

Sloan would know. Damn. I wish he were here.

"His name!" the centaur shouts.

"Keldane!" I freeze as the word trips off my tongue, but it's too late, so I go with it. "The Unseelie Prince Keldane is my man... and yeah, my brother speaks the truth. He won't be pleased if you keep us any longer. He *is* expecting us, and he's not a forgiving man."

"You are one of Keldane's females?"

I nod. "Yep. Part of the harem. We met on the eve of Samhain. It's been a whirlwind ever since."

The ebony guard seems to consider that for a moment before he drops his chin. "I am aware Prince Keldane brought several females from the human realm on the eve of Samhain. I wasn't aware any of them still lived."

I tense. *They're dead?* They can't be. If they were dead, Sloan wouldn't still be suffering under the hex.

"Well, obviously I still live."

His gaze narrows. "I don't believe you."

"You don't believe I'm alive?"

He shakes his head like a horse, and his long, ebony mane flows wild in the light of the rising moon. "No. I don't believe you are the claimed female of Prince Keldane. Tell me about his mighty member."

"I'm sorry, what?"

He gestures between his front legs. "His member. Everyone in the realm knows the rumor. Tell me if they are true."

I blink and catch Dillan's gaze, dumbstruck. "You want me to describe Prince Keldane's junk to you?"

He dips his chin. "Arynstalt has had relations with the prince on more than one occasion. He shall know if you lie."

I follow his tilted head toward the centaur down the row. He's brawny, with a brown and black speckled rump and a metal bar through his nose. He arches a bushy brow at me, and I feel like he measures me up as competition.

Ew, no…but that *does* make me wonder about him.

I tilt my head, considering the mechanics of how his stallion half would get the job done. Keldane is tall but—

"Gretel," Dillan snaps, pegging me with a look. "Now is not the time, dear sister."

"Right." *Squirrel.* I send him an apologetic shrug. "Sorry, thoughts of Arynstalt and the prince distracted me."

Dart shifts behind me, getting impatient.

"Back to Keldane's mighty member." I look at Arynstalt and try to read what he's waiting to hear. "Wow, where do I begin… well, you all know the rumor…"

"Enough stalling. Take her."

Two centaurs start forward, and I curse. I call Birga to my palm, and Dillan calls his dual daggers.

Bruin lets out a menacing growl.

Dart grunts behind me. *Pfft, pfft, pfft.* Three fireballs lob toward the line of centaurs.

The world goes to hell.

The arching flames of Dart's fireballs spook the centaurs, and they rear. Their magical spears discharge and bolts of magic shoot at us from all angles.

Game on.

Bruin meets a charging centaur and sets his Killer Clawbearer groove free.

Dart sends off another lobby of fireballs, and one catches a centaur's mane. The hairy warrior breaks out in a wild whinny and aims his weapon to take us down.

There's no cover from the incoming fire so we scramble and dive. I return Birga to her resting place within and focus on not getting hit.

Magical bolts of power sizzle in the air as they blast past. There are so many. They're coming from everywhere at once.

Bruin tackles me to the ground, his massive frame twisting as a bolt of magic catches him in the shoulder. He lets out a murderous bellow and rolls over the copper moss beside me.

A chilling shriek of fury rends the air. At first, I think it's Bruin, but it's not—it's Dart.

My heart thumps against the inside of my ribs as everything around me erupts in scales. There's a loud *whoosh, whoosh* close to me and I grip a massive log that divides me from the ensuing battle.

Only it's not a log.

Straightening to stand, I run my hands over the rough surface and follow the line of blue scales to my right—three spikes at the end of a tail. I flip my gaze the other way, winding all the way around and up the back of my protector and—

"Holy hell!"

Dillan's eyes are as wide and round as the rising moons. "Dart got really big, reeeeally fast."

My boy is massive. "He's ready for *Godzilla: King of the Monsters* now."

"Yeah, he is."

Mind blown. The queen of dragons is huge. I pictured that as full-grown. Dart is almost twice her size—and he's pissed. He roars, and instead of little warning fireballs, a streaming blaze shoots from his mouth. The heat is unbelievable, and the hiss and crackle of the flames are deafening.

I shield my eyes from the brilliance of the flame. It drives the centaurs back. I can't see if they retreat or fall back, but for the moment it doesn't matter. There's no getting through Dart's defensive line.

"A protective little bugger." Bruin squats back to rest on his haunches beside me. "I don't think he much cared for ye getting shot at."

The centaur that caught fire drops to the ground with a heavy *clunk.* "The attack seems to have worked him up a bit."

Dillan snorts. "Worked him up? He completely Hulked out. Dayam, I'm glad he's on our side."

"You and me both."

"Preach," Bruin says.

I snort, hearing my mythical spirit bear talk like us.

Dart finishes with his flamethrower impression and goes over to sniff the crispy centaur. Carefully, he picks up the charred guard between his front teeth, flips him into the air like a piece of popcorn, and snaps him out of the air.

The juicy crunch that follows is seriously disturbing.

I make a face, marveling at the innocent smile on Dart's face as he chews. "So, will he Bruce Banner back down again, or is his super-sizing permanent?"

Dillan shrugs. "I think we have to wait and see. At least you're off the hook about Prince Keldane's junk."

I look at my brother. "What the hell was that about? What are the realm-wide rumors about the man's Johnson and how did it work with him and that centaur guy? I mean...inquiring minds want to know."

"Honestly, I'm willing to let that die its last death if it means we can get the hell out of here."

I stroke a hand across Dart's tail and survey the area. "I think we're good, buddy. You saved the day."

Dart swings around and drops his head so I can snuggle it against my chest, only now his snout is as big as I am and I have to reach with both my hands to rub the spot around his three horns.

It doesn't matter.

Whether he's four feet or forty, he's still my blue boy.

"The sun's getting real low." Dillan pats the frill of Dart's neck collar. It flares off his neck like the plated shield of a triceratops and is both cool and scary. "You did good, dude. Real good."

Dart lets out a heartfelt purr, and it vibrates in my chest as if I'm standing close to a speaker that's blasting bass. As he soaks in the love, magic tingles in the air, and he shrinks back down into his normal form.

"Well, that's amazing."

Dillan scans the clearing. "And handy. Do you think that's on-demand or solely inspired by protective instincts?"

"I guess we'll figure that out as we go. In the meantime, we have witches to find and blood to shed."

Dillan nods. "Busy, busy. Pitter patter."

CHAPTER FOURTEEN

B ruin brushes his snout against a patch of spongy moss to get the blood out of his coat and spirits off to get an aerial lay of the land. We need to find Prince Keldane so we can track down Moira and her coven sisters. A town would be good, or a castle, or even a group of people we could talk to.

While Bruin's gone, Dart reaps the rewards of his barbeque efforts and tops up on the delicacy of charred centaurs. It's too bad we can't send a care package back to the dragon lair. There is a lot of centaur going to waste.

Bruin returns from his intel gathering in good spirits—battle always puts a spring in his step. "A mile or two that way, there's a gated town or back the way we came through the brush, there's a fancy house on a span of land that could be considered a palace."

I consider the options. "Going back onto the grounds patrolled by the centaurs who already attacked us is a bad idea. Let's try the town."

"Agreed," Dillan says. "Besides, a mile or two isn't far to double back when it's time to catch our window out of here. How's our time?"

I pull out the sand timer from where it hangs on a chain around my neck. "How long do you think we've been here?"

"Half an hour? Forty-five minutes tops."

I frown at the sand. "Well, if that's the case, we gotta hustle. I'm guessing we've lost a quarter of our time."

"Shit. Okay." Dillan raises his wrist and taps his watch. "I'm setting an alarm to notify us when we're getting close. If forty-five minutes ate up a quarter of our time and we have to walk two miles to the town and back, that will take up another quarter. We've got two hours of fae time to get this done."

"Wow. Okay then, let's get moving."

We set off at a steady clip, and it's not long before there's a flow of overhead traffic headed in the same direction.

"This town must be hopping," Dillan says. "If everyone is buzzing in that direction, there has to be a reason, amirite?

"Makes sense. What do you think they are?" I point at the fae people flying above our heads.

"Gnomes," Bruin says.

I picture the Travelocity gnome and the gnomes in Mrs. Graham's garden across the road. Totes not the same. "I didn't know gnomes could fly."

"Naturally, they can't, but they're a technologically creative population and long ago realized with their small stature, having magically powered wings was beneficial."

"So their wings aren't real?"

Bruin swings his massive head to eye the flying fae above. "Their wings are real in the way that they're attached to them and flap and allow them to fly. They simply aren't appendages they're born with."

The four of us walk along the edge of the clearing, staying out of sight when possible. Still, it's impossible to go completely unseen with a massive grizzly bear and a jazzed dragon as part of our party.

By the time we arrive at the manned gate of the town, my skin is heated from our pace, and I'm parched. I'm looking forward to arriving at whatever establishment this town considers its watering hole.

Tipping my head back, I scan twenty feet above my head, taking in the size and scope of the city entrance. The gate is made up of two huge doors constructed of bound and tethered logs, lined up, and carved to a dangerous point at the top.

I search the door, looking for a knob or knocker or something that tells me what to do next. The only thing I see is a line of four iron plates with thin slots. They're aligned one above the other along the seam of where the two doors meet.

One is two feet off the ground, the second two feet above that, and so on. I get the feeling that's important but am not sure why.

"Are these peepholes?" I bend to look into the one at four feet and frown when I can't see anything. "Where's the sliding eye panel for the guy who grunts, 'Who goes there'?"

"Not sure." Dillan's hood is up and he's frowning at the gate the same way I am. "This is my first fae rodeo."

I give up trying to figure it out and pound the door with the meaty part of my clenched fist. "Hello? Is anyone working the door? We're in a bit of a hurry."

When no one answers, I knock again and sigh. "It's hard to get good help these days."

Three more gnomes zip overhead and Dillan frowns. "So, what, we're penalized because we don't fly?"

Rude. I knock a third time and frown. "We need to get inside, find a pub, and share a drink with the locals."

Dillan nods. "I'm all for that plan, but how exactly do you expect to pay for a round in a fae pub?"

"Dammit. Good point." I pause to think about that for a moment when someone shoves me from behind. He's a slim, straggly-haired, pointed-eared guy with a long nose that looks like a humiliated zucchini. "What's your issue, dude?"

"Stop the hold-up, bold pup? Close your mouth and get yer gold up."

I glare at the pushy rhymer. "We already knocked. When someone comes, we'll getter done."

"Make haste. Make haste. No time to waste."

"Yeah. We're with you on that, but there's nothing to be done about it if no one answers the gate."

"Not true. Pay your due or let me through."

I frown. "Pay who what due? No one answered."

"Step aside, Red," Bear says, glancing over his shoulder to the three other locals bustling up to the gate. "Maybe watch and learn is the best course of action here."

I shrug and step to the side. "Have at it, Dr. Suess."

The rhymer pinches a gold coin between his fingers and slips it into the four-foot slot. When he releases it, a little Tinkerbell ring goes off, and the door opens. He flashes me a snide look and slips inside, turning to watch the door close with us on the other side.

"All righty then. Pay your due or let me through."

Dillan chuckles. "It makes sense once you have context."

"Right? Now, all we need is some coin."

I make a sweeping hand gesture toward the next in line, signaling for them to play through. Each time someone goes inside, we watch and learn. It's a simple system, but the door closes quickly. There doesn't seem to be time for the four of us to get inside.

"Dart and I can get in," Bruin grunts after the fourth person gets inside. "He can fly, and I can spirit my way in."

I scowl at the spiked palisade. "I don't want my boy trying to fly over that wall. In this form, he's still learning. Maybe we talk to someone out here and don't need the town."

Next to arrive is an excited elf couple.

"Hello. I'm Fiona and we're new to—"

They frown at me as the man reaches up and puts his coin

into the slot and then stands in the way of the gate closing until his lady is inside too.

"So, it's not one coin for one person. They both went in."

A pug-nosed hairy man with mossy green skin is hustling along the path in bare feet. He's breathless when he stops to retrieve his coin, so I take advantage and speak with him.

"Excuse me, sir. My brother and I are new to the area and forgot our coin purse in our other leathers."

The man looks up from his pocket pillaging. His nose is emitting a slimy string of snot and with a practiced swipe of his tongue, he cleans that up and swallows.

Gross.

Once I stop my throat from lurching I swallow. "I'm Fiona. Could you spare a coin to get into the city?"

He bares a set of crooked teeth, and the foul stench of rot almost knocks me down.

"That's fair. How about taking us in as your guest?"

He pulls out his coin and turns away. After slotting his coin, he pushes the gate open and then promptly slams it shut.

"Friendly crowd," Dillan says.

"Very welcoming."

"You'll have to excuse, Grunter," a gnome says, landing beside us. "When he gets excited he can't focus on more than one thing. He was likely so keen to get to the cantina he barely registered your conversation. Also, he didn't understand a thing you said. He doesn't speak Common."

He—or no, maybe she—has a bushy tuft of bright purple hair, a rosy-cheek child's face, and a warm smile. Ahh, the two-foot coin slot makes more sense to me. "What's so exciting that Grunter and the others are racing into the city?"

"One of the Unseelie princes is coming. Word has it there will be a slaughter."

"A slaughter. Wow, that is exciting."

"Och, I love a good slaughter," Bruin says, grinning. "We need to get in there before we miss the action."

"Which prince is coming, do you know?" I ask.

"Keldane, I think."

Dillan brightens. "Is he bringing his harem for the bloody event, by chance? You know, setting the mood."

The gnome blinks. "I wouldn't know."

Before we lose her—and I'm pretty sure it's a her—I get back to the problem at hand. "We're not from around here. Is there any way you could help us get inside the gate? Do you have a coin for the wall we could use to pay our due?"

She props her tiny fists on her hips and rolls her eyes. "Not from around here for certain. Payment isn't mandatory. If you don't have a coin, you stick your finger in the slot and give it a wiggle. The sentry trylle will make you do something to earn your passage, but nothing too terrible."

I grin and eye the coin slot at six feet. "It sounds like we're trick-or-treating."

"I wouldn't know."

"All righty then. Thanks. We'll see you inside."

The gnome pushes off the ground and flies off in a buzz.

"Stick my finger in and give it a wiggle, eh?"

"Name of your sex tape," Dillan coughs into his hand.

I roll my eyes. Reaching slowly for the slot, I give my shield time to weigh in if this is a bad idea. When nothing happens, I stick my finger in and give it a wiggle.

Sticking your finger through a hole when you don't know what's on the other side is remarkably unsettling. Maybe I'm traumatized by having five older brothers, but I'm anticipating someone biting it or shocking me or doing something that will make me jump and scream.

The gate simply swings open.

I shrug. "That seems remarkably anti-climactic."

"And yet, it doesn't matter. We're in."

Bruin leads the way into the town, followed by Dart and me, then Dillan. When we get inside, Dillan closes the gate as we saw the others do.

"Let me get a look at you." The man on sentry duty is almost as wide as he is tall. He's wearing a Zorro mask that looks more like a raccoon bandit mask against his round beady eyes. "A little light on donations today, are you?"

"We are."

He's looking at us, and it's as if something dawns on him. "First time in the realm, is it?"

"It is."

"I can smell the reek of first-timers a mile away."

Rude. We might have worked up a bit of a sweat fighting centaurs, but we certainly don't reek.

His hand is the size of a snow-shovel, and he scratches his chin. "It's been a lotta years since a baby dragon came through these gates. What do you want for him?"

"Excuse me?"

"Is he up for sale, barter, or trade?"

I step closer to my boy and gauge whether this man is shooting the shit or if he wants to take possession of Dart. "He's not a thing to be bartered or sold. He's a magnificent creature with thoughts and will."

The rotund bandit holds up his leathery palms. "No need to get defensive. It's my job to evaluate marketable goods as they enter the city."

I take it down a notch and try to relax. "All right, my mistake. Dart isn't marketable goods."

The door to the gate opens and three more fae come through. Two more gnomes fly overhead.

"Wow. Prince Keldane killing people draws a crowd."

The gate sentry nods. "Of course. There will be betting and specialty drinks made, and the bards will come to record an account of the event. It'll be one to remember."

"Just not for the poor sucker getting slaughtered," Dillan says. "Who is he, anyway?"

The man shrugs. "It hasn't been released yet, but I don't want to get there too late and miss everything."

Dillan sweeps his hand through the night. "Then lead the way, sir. We're not the kind of people who would make a new friend miss a good slaughter."

"You are required to perform a task," he says.

"What should it be?" Dillan asks. "The gnome we spoke to mentioned you decide what we do based on your mood."

He grins. "It's the best part of working the gate."

Dillan holds his hands open to his sides and looks around. "So, what then, a dance? If you have some apples, I can juggle. The baby dragon can fire off a few flaming spitballs for your entertainment. What's your pleasure?"

The round little man looks from us toward the town and back again. "I don't know but let's make it quick. We're going to miss it."

Dillan shrugs. "Well if you're in charge of the tasks, let us escort you to the pub, and we'll call it even. We'll get there faster, and you can tell your friends about hanging out with the baby dragon, the bear, and the strangers."

"That's not a very good task. When I write out my report, my supervisor will think you got the better of me."

Dillan scrubs a hand over his jaw. "What about...oh, I know. Is there anyone at the pub who you'd like to impress? Maybe there's a lady you've noticed, and you're nervous about speaking to? I can give you some pointers and help you out. You know...smooth the way for you."

"You'd help me with Pilar?"

Dillan flashes him a winning smile. "I will. I'm quite successful with the ladies. I can hook you up, can't I, sista?"

"For sure. When we get to the pub, we'll get you sorted out with the fair Pilar." Having no idea what kind of guy he is or who Pilar is, I think it's crazy to promise to get the guy hooked up, but honestly, the prompting got things moving, so I go with it.

The five of us leave the gate and head deeper into the little town. It soon becomes apparent that this isn't like a human town. Instead of houses, there are small mossy cottages with lopsided windows, massive tree trunks with oval doors, and phallic-looking mushrooms the size of my SUV with chimneys and little white fences.

While I've always been proud of Toronto for embracing diversity, the citizens of this town range in size, shape, and color on a scale that surpasses my city.

There are eight-foot-tall men with horns and cloven hooves chatting with tiny winged friends sitting in the palms of their hands. It's awesome.

Not everything is different though.

The moons shine like two cool globes above us, the crickets chirp their high-pitched melody in the grass nearby, and the smell of pub fare grows stronger as we close the distance to the center of town.

"How often does an event like this happen?" Dillan asks.

We must be getting close now because more and more people are milling around in the streets. There is a hum of chatter building, the excitement of the impending slaughter becoming quite a crowd favorite for a night out.

I take in the line of carriages and wagons and find the different creatures tethered to tow them fascinating.

"This is the first one in a long while, but a couple of months ago there was quite a lot of excitement when some human females escaped the Unseelie Court and tried to hide in the stables during the Yule feast. That night, Keldane offered a reward of gold and chickens to the person who found his missing females, and after that, there was a killing."

I stop watching the locals walking past and focus on our guide. "Women escaped from Keldane's harem?"

"Briefly. The miller's son, Jeremy, had his paramour in the stables for a private tour of the hayloft. They discovered them and won the prize."

Dillan nods. "A good night for Jeremy all around."

"It's not every day you earn yourself gold and chickens."

"No siree." Dillan obviously enjoys this story more than he should. "I can't remember the last time I earned myself gold and chickens, do you, Fi?"

We arrive at the cantina, and I scan the crowd. I doubt we're going to get inside. The place is packed.

"Outdoor seating only," the barmaid calls, pointing at a dozen sawed-off logs with some makeshift tables set up between them. Torches staked along the outer perimeter and the glow from some of the luminescent fae species light the patio area. "I'll send out an ale wench, but it's mead, ale, and bread only. I'm not serving food out here."

We take our seats, and I make a face as my fingers stick to the surface of my log. There is sap seeping up from the rings of the newly hewn stump.

"I take it the patio seating is quite fresh."

Honestly, I don't care how much sap I'm sitting in if being here gets me to Prince Keldane.

I pulled the small sand timer from beneath my leather bodice and assess how much time has passed. I might be crazy, but I'd swear there is more than there was the last time I looked. Patty said it would be crazy. If it's going to jump back and forth, I need to keep closer tabs on it.

The time may be flying, but I'm not having fun.

For the first time since we got here, I worry about letting Sloan down. What if we don't get the witch's stone back to him in time? I hate the thought of him suffering. I hate the idea of him lying there in an induced coma.

We need to find out if Keldane still has the witches with him and if so, where.

"We didn't get in." The gateman looks at the main entrance, deflated. "I knew I should've left earlier."

Dillan waves that away. "If you left before we got there, you wouldn't have secured us to get you hooked up with Pilar. Which one is she anyway?"

The gateman throws a thumb over his shoulder toward the pub's entrance. "She'll be inside working the crowd. You don't put your best girl on satisfying the people outside. We'll get Margle or Shen."

"Well then." Dillan stands back up. "We need to get you inside. If it's my task to hook you up with Pilar, we can't hang around outside with Margle and Shen. Come on."

Our rotund masked gateman balks at the idea of heading inside, but Dillan is tough to dissuade when he gets rolling. "Hold our table, Fi. I'll be back. I gotta get a swipe right going here."

"Good luck."

A haggard-looking elf comes out with a basket of bread. I don't think they've invented bread knives in the fae realm because the pieces are pretty much torn to bits.

"What'll you have?" She looks from me to Bruin to Dart. She doesn't give my boys a second glance. Maybe in the fae realm, mythical bears and dragons are everyday customers at the cantina.

I raise my palms. "Nothing for us thanks. We're new in town and haven't got any local currency. We heard there was going to be excitement tonight and joined. When are you expecting Prince Keldane to arrive for the slaughter?"

The girl's eyes widen as my question settles between us and I wonder for a moment if it's like me with Kain Harry Potter and Prince Keldane is their He-Who-Must-Not-Be-Named.

"Hello?" I wave my hand in the air. "Is he coming? Someone mentioned the Unseelie Court. Is that a castle around here? When are you expecting him to arrive?" The woman seems frozen until she lets out a little squeak and rushes back inside the establishment.

I chuckle and scrub a hand over Dart's snout. "She's a little skittish, don't you think?"

Bruin sniffs the air and growls as his head cranks around. My shield flares simultaneously, and I know what my bear will say before he opens his mouth. "He's behind you, Red."

Of course, he is.

For a split second my mind wars between ducking under the flimsy table, hoping he hasn't noticed me, and grabbing the reins of this clusterfuck and confronting him.

I didn't mean to cross paths with him.

I wanted to lurk in the shadows and follow him home or figure out where he lives so we could infiltrate and get to Moira and her coven sisters...or whoever is still alive.

"Had a run-in with my court guards, did you?" he asks, behind me. The Prince's voice is as deep and cold as I remember. The moment he speaks, the excitement seekers relegated to outdoor log seating scramble to get outside of the slaughter splash zone.

I gird my innards, stand, and face him.

He's bare-chested again and wearing the same black leather slicker covered in raven feathers as he was the first time we met at the Ring of Rath.

I force myself to meet his eerie gaze.

Simply looking at him triggers my fae sight.

My vision flares as the core malevolence within him registers. It's consuming and terrifying. It's like a heat signature. Only instead of being orange-red from thermal energy, it registers the aura of a person.

Keldane's aura is a dark void of green and black.

The backdrop of darkness makes his opal skin and his thicket of silver and grey twig hair look ghostly pale.

My reaction to him is visceral, I can't control that, but I can control how much he sees. I push my natural response to him way down deep and channel inner confidence I don't feel. "Do you own a shirt or is the whole exposed nipple thing a statement of style?"

He grins. "I told you I would see you again, little one. In truth, I thought it would've been before now. Do you feel the pull of the unexplored potential between us?"

"I sure don't. That's not why I'm here."

He steps right up to me, and I'm too caught up in his gaze to step back. As much as it curdles my stomach contents to admit it, something about his scent draws me in.

"Wow. You are seriously tall. Your twigs are a lot longer than the last time. No time for pruning lately? Too busy with sex and slaughter?"

His smile is half nice and half I'm going to rip your throat out if you make any sudden movements. "A male must have his distractions."

The heat of my shield is scalding me where I stand. There really should be an off button. I am fully aware of the danger and where it's coming from. Not burning like I'm a lit human match head would allow me to focus on what to do about it. "Did you know I was here or is this serendipity?"

Again with that cruel smile. "A bit of both. There I was, filleting the staff members who displeased me this week—"

"—as you do—"

"—and then *boom*, my workroom is invaded by singed centaurs raving about being attacked by a dragon and a red-headed witch from the human realm."

I raise my finger. "Not a witch."

He dips his chin and frowns. "Do you realize how rancid burnt centaurs smell? It tainted the air in my private space."

"I'm sorry I killed your men. I didn't know they were yours and they made me uncomfortable talking about claiming me and passing me around to their friends. I wasn't on board with that."

He glances toward Bruin and Dart. "When they reported a dragon attack, I admit I expected more."

I pat Dart's head and send him a smile, hoping to keep him calm. "You, of all people, know rumors get out of hand. I wasn't here ten minutes and heard a few about you."

He arches a mossy brow, and I curse myself inwardly. I really don't want him questioning me about that. Why did I bring his junk into this?

"Yes, well, the classes do enjoy a salacious tale."

"I'm sure."

Dillan trundles from the cantina with a tankard in his grip and a smile on his face. When he sees Keldane and I standing off, he curses and sends me a worried gaze. "Seriously. I was gone, like, five minutes."

Keldane glances over as if my brother is a bug for him to squash. It sets off my ire. "Don't get any ideas. My brother and my animal companions are off-limits."

"Well, you owe me lives. The males you killed in the skirmish were of value to me."

I frown. "I gave you lives on Samhain."

"I suppose that's true, but that was because I'd been summoned under the lure of certain promises." He moves to round the table to get to me, but I shift to keep the flimsy chunk of wood between us.

"Don't let us keep you from your plans. You have a crowd gathered. You came for a slaughter. Have at it."

His mouth curls in a creepy grin as he chuckles. "I wouldn't think you'd be so enthusiastic. Are you a masochist by any chance?"

I hear what he's saying and groan. "Oh, *I'm* the one you came to slaughter?"

"Now you're catching on."

"But everyone knew you were coming here for the big event. How'd you know I'd come here?"

"You told the guards."

I think back, and yep, that was probably a mistake. I look at the expectant faces in the crowd. "All right, we're canceling the slaughter. Sorry. There was a miscommunication. No new party drinks and bard tales tonight."

Keldane shakes his twiggy head. "Never disappoint the crowd, female. They came for slaughter, and they shall have it." Keldane looks around. "You and you, into the street. Fight to the death. The victor will receive two gold and a chicken."

Huh...again with the gold and chickens.

The two men get up reluctantly and are swept toward the street by an excited crowd. "Now then, little one. Tell me why you sought me out?"

CHAPTER FIFTEEN

The haggard-looking ale wench returns with a tray of drinks and baskets of food. Apparently, the manager will serve food outside if that's where the prince sits. Lucky me. Behind her rushes a large man carrying a real table. There's a whirlwind of activity, and a moment later, I'm seated in a cleared and private patio with the Unseelie Prince Keldane.

He picks up one of the tankards and gestures for me to do the same. My stomach growls long and loud, and I realize I haven't eaten or slept in over twenty-four hours.

"To mysterious females." He raises his mug.

I raise mine in agreement. Sure, if mystery keeps him wondering and me breathing, I'll go with that. "Do you mind if we eat? It's been a long couple of days."

He gestures to the tray, his rings catching in the light of the moons. "Help yourself. I don't eat in public."

I think about that and sigh. Yeah, I suppose a man like him has enemies. I look at the food, and the poisoning plot of every movie ever comes back to haunt me.

Dammit. I'm soooo hungry.

I should've had a bite of centaur back at the clearing.

"What does your shield say?" Dillan looks at the food with a hopeful expression. "If you were about to be poisoned, your shield would warn you, wouldn't it?"

Good one, Dillan. I sift through the saucy meat piled on the silver platter and hold it to my nose. It's greasy, but I'd liken it to pulled pork. I sniff it, then pause when I open my mouth.

Nothing alarming happens, so I pop it into my mouth.

Dillan's studying my every move, and when I give him the okay and grab for a chunk of bread, he grins and joins me.

Keldane is sitting back, manspreading like you read about, his gaze narrowed. "You're a suspicious little thing. I respect that. Tell me why you've come, or I'll assume it's because you've succumbed to your wanting of me."

I choke and have to swig a mouthful of ale to force down my food. Thankfully, I think I mask my reaction fairly well. "No offense meant, but it's nothing like that. The witches we gave you that night hexed my friend. He's dying, and the only way I can save him is to determine which of the three women it was and have them break the spell."

I take another long drink and assess his reaction as I swallow.

The tangy bite of the ale takes a little to get used to. I can live with that. What's worse is that it's warm. I call *Icy Palm,* and my spell chills the tankard and the amber contents within.

"This friend of yours. Why did the witches hex him?"

I don't want to tell an Unseelie Prince that Sloan is a Keeper of the Shrine for magical relics so I go another direction. "He offended Moira. She tried to coerce my grandfather, he and I broke her spell, and he dumped her rather unceremoniously back at her home."

"He should have killed her," Keldane says. "Dead witches cast no hexes."

"Hindsight. To kill or not to kill, amirite?"

Keldane frowns. "Always kill."

I pass the cold ale to Dillan and shrug. "Lesson learned. Write that down."

Dillan gives me a wary glance, and I understand his apprehension. Keldane isn't just a bad guy. He's fundamentally immoral. He kills people for fun. He won't help me out of the goodness of his heart.

I'm quite sure he has no goodness in his heart.

While I try to work out what to say next, I play with the sand timer around my neck. There's next to no sand, and I don't know if that's because I'm running out or if it'll fill back up again. "Where are the three women you took the night of the Samhain festival?"

"The three women you offered up to me, you mean?"

Technically that was Sarah and not me, but yes, I was there and am complicit. "Yes, them."

He flicks a hand through the air. "Disobedience is punishable by death. They disobeyed me. They are dead."

"All three of them?"

"Yes."

"When did you kill them?"

Keldane looks over his shoulder and shouts into the shadows. "Stortan, when did those three human witches die?"

A man steps into the torchlight of the patio area and my jaw drops. He must be ten feet tall. A giant maybe. He stops at the table next to ours and clasps his hands against his abdomen. "The eve of the Yule festival."

Keldane shrugs as if that's the end of that. Dillan casts a sideways glance. Yeah, I know. They can't all be dead, or the hex on Sloan wouldn't still be tethered to him.

"You're sure they're dead?"

He sits forward and frowns. "You bore me with questions I already answered. They thought to escape. They were recovered, and they were killed."

I scowl at the sands escaping the timer. I don't have time to fish around for answers and solve a puzzle. "There is something wrong with that account of things, Prince."

"You doubt my word?" he snaps, leaning close.

The dark green aura around him ebbs black as his anger rises to the fore. "You call me a liar here, in front of the people of the lands?"

I shake my head. "I would never. Let me explain." I tell Keldane about the festerbug hex and what the white witches said about the caster's tether. "If all three witches were truly dead, the tether would dissolve."

His gaze narrows. "Either you lie, or someone else has."

I shrug. "Not necessarily. Moira was a powerful woman. Perhaps they were able to mask the truth. If the witches are believed dead and discarded, maybe they glamored their death or used their magic to heal and get away, or someone found one of them and helped them recover."

"They were my property. No one in these lands would take from me what is mine. Would you townsfolk?"

There's a rush of hurried responses from the crowd, everyone swearing their oath that they would never dare take anything from Keldane.

Sadly, I believe them.

I sit back and frown. I don't have time for this. "Who declared them dead and where were their bodies taken?"

Keldane stands up so abruptly, his stump tips backward and thumps on the ground. "Come with me, female. I've had enough of your questions and accusations."

I rise but more out of jumping into a defensive posture than following Keldane's orders. Still, when he casts a backward glance, he seems pleased that I'm on my feet.

"Bring your brother and your pets too."

Dillan seems as reluctant as I am to follow.

"Where are we going?" I ask.

"To the burial mounds to hunt for bodies."

Superstition is a funny thing. I grew up in a Celtic community my entire life. Even the most level-headed, modern Celt knows better than to piss off the faeries. Before I knew about fae magic and empowered species, I knew a dozen things never to do if I wanted to stay on their good side.

First off—don't call them faeries out loud.

When Da told us stories about growing up in Ireland, he always referred to the Fair Folk or the Good Neighbors. After all, Them That's In It are never far away, and you never want to piss them off or get in their way.

Next off—never disturb a faerie mound.

So, when Keldane takes us to the burial mounds of the fae realm, I'm really freaking sure I don't want to step in the wrong place. The legends are clear. You don't walk on them, build on them, or disturb them.

The flat ground between the mounds is called the faery trod. You can walk there, but keep moving and never set anything down that will be in the way, in case a member of the fae community—visible or not—needs to pass.

Dillan and I are clear on these basic lessons. Bruin is likely aware, but Dart won't understand. My baby dragon is a little clumsy having not grown into his adult body yet and is forgetful and excitable.

"Bruin, if you don't mind, will you come with Keldane and me into the crypt? The door to the mausoleum looks small so you have to hitch a ride. Dillan, you stay here with Dart and make sure he doesn't step anywhere he shouldn't."

Dillan doesn't look happy, but I think he understands my reasoning. Bruin, Birga, and I can fend off the Unseelie prince if he gets out of line. My baby dragon needs somebody to watch over him.

"Yeah, fine. Be quick. This place gives me the creeps."

I cup Dart's chin so I have his complete attention. "You stay right here, buddy. Dillan is in charge while I go away with this man. I'll be right back, and I don't want you walking on any of the hills. Do you understand?"

Dart grins and nods enthusiastically.

I'm not sure he does, but I give him the benefit of the doubt. "Okay, good boy. I'll be back soon."

Keldane's massive bodyguard doesn't look pleased about any of this. I'm not sure if he looked forward to my slaughter, isn't a fan of burial mounds, or has his own thing going on, but he's tense and seems jumpy.

I'm surprised the Unseelie prince put women from his harem into the royal family crypt. He seems more apt to flick his wrist and tell his men to dispose of a body.

Likely after he desecrates it.

When we arrive at the crypt's entrance, he pulls on the long handle and moves the heavy door to open our way. The stench of stale air and damp rot hits me like a gust of wind in the face. Gross.

I need to ask Da to get me some of the nose rub that the detectives and coroners use when dealing with a particularly stinky crime scene. I twitch my nose as my sinuses burn and try to breathe through my mouth.

Keldane leads the way. I'm glad he does because honestly, if I had to go first and he was looming in behind me, I don't think I'd be able to do it without freaking out. He's a scary guy. The idea of being trapped in the stone tomb with him is enough to make me crumble.

As we step inside, the first thing I notice is the already lit torches. The second thing is we're not alone. Movement to my right has me adjusting my stance to place my back against the stone wall.

A hunched woman with straggly lip twig hair and clawed fingers shuffles out from the shadows. She moves quicker than I expect and when she looks up, a bright spark of intelligence glitters behind her eyes. "My Lord, always a true horror to see you. What brings you to the tomb?"

Keldane makes no indication whether her greeting was appreciated or not. It's not that I disagree, but I'm surprised he allowed the comment to go unchallenged.

It *is* a horror to see him.

"There are questions about the three witches brought here some time ago. I want to see the rotting corpses and make certain they are as dead as I was promised."

The woman goes to the cabinet by the door and pulls out a clipboard. "Three witches, you say? One moment. I'll check your page. Business or personal?"

"Personal. They were part of my harem. New additions. They didn't survive the learning curve and washed out during the probationary period."

The old woman chuckles while scanning the page. "So many of them do. Timeframe?"

"Stortan believes it was the eve of Yule."

"That long." She flips back a couple of pages, and it's a wonder to me there have been so many additions to the list of dead in two months. Then again, if Keldane is an example of the people in his royal family and court, I'm sure the turnover is very high.

"Here we are." The crone points at a line on her record sheet. "December twenty-first. Gender: female. Race: human. Discipline: Wiccan practitioner. Quantity: three."

Keldane straightens, looking vindicated. "As I expected."

"Do you mind if we see the bodies?" I ask.

Keldane stiffens. In the close space of the crypt, he seems impossibly large and looming. "Do you challenge my word? If so, it's very opportune we are here. I will end you, and she will add you to her list."

I raise my hand. "I have it on good authority that at least one of these women is still alive. Either you or I have been misled. I simply want to be sure. Lives depend on it."

He arches a brow. "Yes, they do."

The threat hangs in the fetid air between us, but I don't back down. Sloan depends on me, and I won't let Keldane bully me into returning empty-handed. Maybe all three are dead, and the Blarney witches and Kaija were wrong.

It's easier to make sure here than to have to come back.

I meet Keldane's eerie gaze and stand my ground. "Please, this is important. The three bodies, where are they?"

The woman makes no move to answer me. Instead, she looks at Keldane for instructions.

I've pled my case, so I wait. Keldane is a powerful man who knows his mind. If I were him and I believed somebody deceived me, I would want to know the truth.

After a long moment, he dips his chin. "Where are the bodies, Yaya?"

Yaya? This is his grandmother? He's making her work in the crypt? That's all kinds of weird.

Keldane's grandmother traces a clawed finger along the line of her report, then starts toward the door. "Follow me. Try to keep up."

I gulp a deep breath of fresh air as we exit the crypt. The bitter tang of death still rides the back of my tongue, but at least I can breathe. "I don't suppose you have any gum?"

Keldane frowns but doesn't acknowledge my question.

The witches being buried out here makes more sense. I didn't see how he would include them in the crypt.

We follow Keldane's yaya through the maze of faery trod paths and end up three hundred feet away from the stone mausoleum. It's close to a stand of trees, and when she points at a mound of settled earth, I meet Keldane's gaze.

"May I?"

He tilts his head toward the ground.

I take that as him giving me approval. *"Move Earth."* I hold my open palms toward the mound, and the earth begins to shift and move off the little hill. It's the work of a moment to uncover the bodies below.

It's been less than two months since these women were reportedly killed for trying to escape Keldane's harem. I know enough about crime scenes to understand the bodies won't be so badly decomposed that we won't recognize them.

As much as I regret this is where they ended up, logic reminds me of what they did and that I was ready to kill them myself that night. They called Keldane to the Ring of Rath, and they made promises to him they didn't keep.

When the dirt shuffles away enough for us to identify the women lying there, I curse.

There *are* three women, but Moira isn't among them.

CHAPTER SIXTEEN

"So where is she?" Dillan asks when I get back to him and Dart. "She slipped away from Keldane and found a body to take her place so she could get free of him?"

"Looks like it."

"Who helped her?"

I cast a leading glance toward the jumpy giant. "I have my suspicions, but it's irrelevant. We need to find Moira, and whoever helped her, they won't admit it and help us."

Dillan scans the skyline and frowns. "Dammit. We don't have time for this."

"No. We don't."

"On the plus side, it looks like getting blood from Moira isn't going to be a problem. Keldane looks pissed."

"I can't even look at him. The darkness and rage in his soul are so strong that it's too much for my fae sight."

"I'd suggest glamoring it and giving yourself a break, but it's still the dead of night, and your sight is helpful."

I sigh. "I know. I'm fine. I can take it."

Keldane storms past us and heads for the carriage. "I will end her a hundred times over."

"Not without us." I chase after him. "I need her DNA, remember?"

Keldane rounds on me, and I shrink back, the fire in my shield burning as if my skin has burst into flame. "Don't try me, female."

Stortan gets the door to the carriage open a split-second before Keldane launches inside. "Drive."

Before we have time to react or catch up, the weird fae creatures they're using as horses shriek. A moment later, the carriage roars out of sight.

"I think we missed our ride," Dillan says.

I rub a hand over the pressure in my chest. "I'm not sad to see him go, but how will we find her and get there before Keldane?"

"Finding her isn't the biggest problem on that list. She has a two-month head start and can glamor. There's no way we'll be able to locate her within the next hour."

"It feels like someone has parked a cement truck on my chest. What does a panic attack feel like?"

Dillan brushes his hands against my arms, looking worried. "Release Bruin. Maybe that will ease the pressure."

I do, but it doesn't help.

As panic sets in, I bend at the waist and prop my hands on my knees. My breath is coming in gulps, but I can't seem to breathe. "I can't fail Sloan. I can't lose him."

Dillan wraps himself around me and rubs my back. "Breathe, Fi."

My brother's advice is a simple statement of concern, but his words hold power. The tingle of magic he sends into my cells helps open things up so oxygen can once again flow into my lungs.

After a long moment, I straighten and wipe the moisture from under my eyes. "Okay. Tears and panic help no one."

"Even heroes lose their shit. You're still you."

I nod. "I can be me later. Right now I need to save Sloan. What's our plan?"

Dillan straightens and scowls at the burial grounds.

"Ye need to track the bitch," Bruin growls. "Maybe scry for her? Or divine? Or *Detect Magic*."

"Do we have time for that?" I pull out the sand timer.

Dillan leans in and frowns. "We're not going to make Patty's window unless we head back now."

"I can't go back empty-handed."

"Then we're here for the duration of the quest, and we'll figure out our door home once we've got what we came for."

The idea of losing our sure way home is terrifying...but there's no way around it. Dillan's right.

"Patty said he'll continue to try for us and we have Dart here now. We have options."

Dillan nods. "Then our first step is finding the bitch."

"Agreed." I think about the options. "*Detect Magic* won't work without a way to tether the search to her. Same with scrying."

"She'll likely have wards up to avoid being tracked."

"True story."

"If she's tethered to Sloan, could you scry for Sloan using something of his?"

I twist the bone ring on my thumb and wonder if this is why my instincts told me to bring it. "That's a good idea. Moira likely shielded herself, but I doubt she'd think about her tie with Sloan."

Dillan nods. "Then that's where we start."

Since we don't have a map of the area and I don't have enough experience to scry with a mirror or water, we move on to creating a divining rod. It's a spell I can cast with confidence, and I've had good results.

Dillan and I comb the stand of trees in the darkness with our phones held out with the flashlights turned on. He finds a forked branch of an oak tree. I pull up the text from Sloan that he sent me back in the summer and modify the words to suit.

"Okay, so let's assume we have the spell sorted out. How do we travel? I agree with what you said earlier. I think with her head start, she's long gone by now."

Dart throws his head back and grunts. Before I have a chance to ask him what that's about, his metamorphosis begins, and he's sizing up again.

"Dragon-on-demand. Good to know." I shuffle back with Dillan and Bruin to give our blue boy space.

When he finishes his transition, he makes a show of flapping his wings and lays his head on the ground in front of us.

"I think he's suggesting we fly Western." Dillan laughs and waggles his finger at Dart. "Do you see what I did there? Western...he's a Western."

I laugh. "I do...and it's an amazing idea, but he's never flown before. Are you sure you're ready, dude?"

Dillan frowns. "Very good point. How about you take a spin in the air around the burial grounds and get a sense of your power before we decide?"

Dart huffs and rolls his eyes but humors us.

He crouches low to the ground, his muscles bunching with power held in reserve, and then, effortlessly, launches straight up into the night.

My jaw drops as he opens his wings to stretch across the blanket of sky. He carries himself in a graceful, swooping circle and lands in front of us with a *whoosh* of air and a rumble of the ground.

"Wow. You killed that, dude," Dillan says. "You're a natural."

Bruin chuckles. "Ye understand that fer him, it *is* natural, aye? He's a dragon. Flyin', fightin', and flames are what they do. Remember how much easier it was to connect with yer druid magic in Ireland than when ye returned to Toronto, Fi?"

I nod. "Yeah. I could feel the ambient magic in the air, but it wasn't enough for me to do what I knew I was capable of doing until after we cleared the shield blockages."

"Well, it's like that fer the wee dragon. He's a fae creature, and here he can connect with everything he is and will be. It's like being set free to claim the power that's been beyond his reach all his life."

That makes so much sense.

I lean forward and hug one of the horns on his snout. "You're amazing, buddy. Whether it's here or there, big or little, you're amazing."

Dillan waggles the forked branch. "So, let's get this chunk of wood spelled and find Moira before Keldane does."

I take the branch and hand him my phone so I can read it but hold on with both hands. "After he finds her wouldn't be all bad either, as long as we have access to her before he disposes of her."

"Before would be better," Bruin says. "After means we have to deal with him again too."

"Great point." I look at the situation with restored urgency. "Let's getter done."

With a swipe of my finger, I wake up my phone and grip the stick we're using as a divining rod, and cast the spell.

Branch of oak, I cast this charm
Find the witch that did Sloan harm
Where Moira hides, you shall see
and feel the pull to guide me
Protection spells hinder you none
We find the witch, and this is done.

The moment I finish uttering the words of the spell, I feel magic tingle against my palms. I reclaim my phone and tuck it back into my leather hip pouch. Then I make sure I have a good grip on the divining rod so I don't do an Emmet.

I snort, just picturing it. There will never be a time that memory won't make me laugh.

With care, I grip Dart's neck frill and scramble up onto my dragon.

Bruin dematerializes and takes his place within me.

Dillan climbs up Dart's neck and joins me in standing there, looking for where to sit and how to hold on. "What if we sit here between the spikes on his spine and wrap our arms and legs around them as though hugging a tree?"

I assess the other options and honestly don't see a better idea. His neck is too broad for us to straddle and his wings are going to be flapping...

"Let's go with that." I take the first spine and get settled, wrapping my arms around to the front with the divining rod clutched in my hands. "Okay. I'm good."

"I'm good," Dillan shouts behind me. "Nice and easy, Dart. Let's not dump the passengers."

If someone told me a year ago that I would become a guardian of nature, wield fae powers, and make mythical and magical friends, I would've thought they were cray-cray. But here I sit—riding a freaking dragon!!

I *lurrrve* my life.

Guilt strikes me the moment I think that. I haven't forgotten about Sloan, and I'm wholly committed to saving him, but it would be an utter shame not to rejoice at this moment.

I'm riding a dragon.

As the pull of the branch leads us on our search, I stomp my boot against his left or right shoulder. I keep my face hidden behind the spike to cut down the wind, but with my cheek against the rough surface, I search the sky and the moons, all the while my heart racing.

I'm riding a dragon.

When the branch starts pointing downward, I realize I don't have a signal for that. "Go down," I shout, but the whistle of the wind racing past swallows my words.

Closing my eyes, I focus on my gift of animal communication and try to remember what Gran did when she connected with Dart. She said it was easy, but we've never been able to communicate that way.

Maybe with his magical connection with his surroundings bursting with power, he'll hear me.

Down, buddy. We're getting close. One of the key components in performing any kind of magic is intention. With that in mind, I focus all mine on connecting with my beloved Dartamont and repeat my message.

Down, buddy. We're getting close.

The communication that comes back to me is less about words and more emotions. He understands, he's happy to have me communicate this way, and he loves me.

The warmth and unending devotion he feels for me are pure and deep.

I love you too, buddy. So much.

He circles a dense area of trees for a little before he finds a spot big enough to set down. The landing is graceful for a first attempt and I send him a huge rush of admiration.

Amazing. I'm so proud of you.

When Dillan and I have both slid onto the ground and settled, he shifts back to his normal size. I watch to see if it looks painful or difficult for him, but it doesn't seem to. I think it's simply a magical transformation.

I'm glad. I don't want him to hurt.

When the magic settles, and Dart is in his junior form again, I bend to wrap myself around his neck. "Now I can hug you. Great job, getting us here."

When I straighten, I release Bruin. "See what you can see,

Bear. The divining rod is pulling for us to go that way."

On it.

As he rushes off, Dart, Dillan, and I venture off on foot.

"This is the most involved game of Hide-and-Seek we've ever played," Dillan says.

"True. Let's hope we have a better ending to this than the last time we played."

Dillan makes a face. "Yeah, let's hope."

A tingle in the air brings my attention to the sand timer around my neck. I pull it out from where I've kept it tucked under my shirt and watch as the last of the sand seeps to the bottom of the twenty-four-hour hourglass.

"Well, that's the end of that." I'm both disappointed and worried about not getting what we need and making it back in time to meet Patty's deadline.

It wasn't enough time.

Still, how much time does Sloan have? I don't know.

The wind picks up around us, and I smile as Bruin takes form. "There's a cottage up ahead. Very well hidden. Very remote. Very heavily warded."

"That sounds about right." I release my spell on the divining rod and set it on the ground. "I don't suppose anyone knows anything about taking down witch wards? My last exposure didn't go that well."

Dillan chuckles. "No shit, my little magic-filled Twinkie. Although Sloan's threat to junk-punch Tad was hilarious when you asked him to lick your vanilla icing."

I roll my eyes. "I was blood gassed."

"Maybe or maybe you were letting your freak flag fly."

Acknowledging him will only make things worse. "What are our options here?" We tromp through the forest, and the beginning of foreboding and fear take root in my gut. "She has a repulsion ward running. Do you feel it?"

Dillan's clenched his jaw, and he's glaring at the woods ahead of us. "Yeah, I feel it."

Not wanting to get spelled into a frenzy, I stop our approach. "If we can't get close to her, we can't get her DNA to cover the witch stone."

Bruin grunts. "What are ye suggestin', Red?"

"We need to talk to her. Maybe we can reason with her or maybe once she realizes we found her, we can trade what we know about Keldane for what we need."

Dillan nods. "It's not a bad idea. I get the feeling that self-preservation is one of Moira's top priorities."

"Let's use that to our advantage."

I check in with everyone, and we all seem to be on the same page, so I call, "Moira. It's Fiona Cumhaill. We need to talk."

The forest remains eerily quiet, so we wait. When nothing happens, I send Bruin back in to be my eyes. "If you can get close enough to speak to her, tell her I have news—news about her coven sisters, what's happened in Dublin, about Keldane, whatever it is she wants to know about.

Bruin dips his chin, but before he spirits away my thumb gets itchy—like, really itchy. "Hold up, Bear." I stare down at Sloan's bone ring. "The ring of true sight is stinging my finger. I think it has something to say."

Dillan shifts his stance a few steps closer and calls his daggers to his palms. "What's it saying?"

I twist the ring on my thumb and sense its discontent to be dealing with me. "I think it's reminding me that I have no claim and it doesn't belong to me."

"Is that relevant to something that's happening now or simply a tantrum of some sort?"

"Not sure." I close my eyes and focus on the energy the ring brings to our connection. "I wish with all my heart Sloan was well enough to be part of this journey, but he's not. Help us find the witch we need to cure him. Then you'll be back where you belong."

I wait to see if it's going to respond to me, but when nothing comes, I press on. Keldane will be anxious to find Moira and could be here any moment. As well, every moment we waste is time that Sloan suffers and declines.

"Moira! I know you can hear me. If you want to live, you have to speak to me."

The ring seems to settle because the stinging ends and the magic it holds activates. I blink as my sight flares, trying to focus as my vision adjusts.

I've been a passenger to what the ring shows Sloan. I've held his hand and had the privilege of seeing Pip crying on the boughs of a fir tree or the truth behind glamors of deception.

It occurs to me now that I only saw what it allowed me to see. The magic of true sight is much more powerful and involved than I thought.

Standing in this forest, staring at a little fairy tale cottage forgotten among the trees, Moira steps outside and the whole truth reveals itself.

"Holy crapamoly."

CHAPTER SEVENTEEN

"Hello, Moira."

The dark witch stares at me from behind a barrier of magical wards that have illuminated to reveal the extent of her protective shield. The spellcasting arches up and caps her and her cottage beneath a glowing dome of power.

Inside the protective bubble, she stands next to four snarling and sneering harlequin Danes—or at least that's the closest animal I could use to describe them. They have the physical frame of Danes, a rack of antlers coming off their heads, and a mane of plated armor covering their massive shoulders and chest. Their eyes are black voids, but when they look at me, their gazes flash to a glowing red.

"Welcome to the nightmare for the rest of my life."

Dillan chuffs beside me. "What's black and white and red all over?"

"Us as soon as the power bubble drops."

"Uh-huh, that's what I'm thinking."

Moira has always glamoured herself to appear young, sexy, and sleek. I've torn down the illusion before and exposed the witch behind the mask, but it wasn't something she wanted the world to see.

Her standing here looking rough and aged seems off.

"Does she look a little cray-cray?" I whisper to Dillan.

"You mean because of the Einstein hairdo, the wild, wandering gaze, or the drool?"

She's not drooling, but the rest is true.

"Maybe her tango with the Prince of Repugnance was too much for her, and she snapped. She betrayed the goddess, mutated innocent people into fae monsters, and led three covens to their death. It's not a stretch to go from cracked to completely broken."

"I'll give you that. She already had bats fluttering around in her belfry. Spending months with Keldane could've pushed her over the edge."

That's what I think too. "So, we gain her trust and have her stand down so we can get close enough to get her DNA on the witch stone."

Dillan snorts. "Is that all? Sure. No probs."

Her gaze stops roaming through the trees as she tilts her head and studies me. "I know you, don't I?"

Doesn't she recognize me?

I remember Granda's warning that humans living too long in the fae realm would pay the price mentally and physically. Is that what happened? Maybe it wasn't all Keldane. Maybe this realm is stealing her magical mental marbles?

"Yes, you know me." I'm about to ask her to remove the hex on Sloan when it dawns on me that reminding her she hexed someone I care about likely won't warm her up to helping me. It might make her leery about taking down the wards. "We were looking for you."

"Why? Who are you to me?"

"We knew each other in the human realm...before Keldane took you and brought you here."

At the mention of the Unseelie prince, Moira recoils. Her guardian beasts stiffen at her reaction, and a low growl rumbles through the forest.

"The twig man is a bad man," Moira shouts. "He does terrible, vile things."

"I'm sure you've been through a lot. You're a strong woman though. You survived and got away."

"I'm a great witch," she says, the words hollow of emotion. It sounds more like she's trying to convince herself than a statement of memory and fact.

"You are. You were the High Priestess of witches."

She looks around, her gaze blank. "How did I get here?"

"Last Samhain, you and your coven sisters performed a ritual to call Keldane through the veil to our realm on the other side of the faery glass."

She frowns. "I called him? Why would I do that?"

"More power, I expect. I don't know your motivation for certain. The point is things didn't go your way. You and your witches made vows to Keldane that weren't met, and he brought you back here as payment."

I omit the part about me and mine foiling her plans and allowing him to take her. If she doesn't remember us being on opposite sides, I'm certainly not going to offer it up.

"My witch sisters. Where are they?"

"Only two lived through that night."

Her expression twists and she pulls at her tangled hair. "Keldane had them killed. Now there's just me."

"Keldane had the two you were with here killed, yes. I'm talking about the two who survived in our realm—Robin and Caitriona."

"Robin and Caitriona. They live?"

"Yes. They're alive and living in Dublin."

"Dublin." She nods. "I remember Dublin."

"Of course, you do. It's your city. I understand what it's like to be at one with your city. It's a part of you, a source of strength for you to draw upon."

"Will you take me back there?" She grimaces and waves her fingers toward her head. "I feel like I could remember who I was if I could get out of this place."

"I'm sure it would help. You've been here too long. This realm isn't good for humans."

"You'll take me back?"

That wasn't the plan. I need her to lick the witch stone so we can get gone before Keldane finds us. Nothing more.

If I leave her here, she'll soon go mad.

If I take her, it's like forgiving her for what she did—I don't—but Mother Nature will strip her of her powers, so that's good.

If I leave her here, we'll travel lighter and faster.

If I take her, Keldane will hunt us until we escape this realm… and maybe even back to our domain.

I frown at the ethical versus logical war in my mind. In truth, the answer is obvious. If I leave her in this condition, I'd hate myself. It isn't who I am.

It wouldn't be right.

Dammit. Moira is no longer the evil bitch she was last autumn. I can't leave her here to die a Keldane-violent death.

"Yes, we'll take you with us."

"We will?" Dillan says.

I send him an apologetic gaze and sigh. "Yes, we will." Returning my attention to Moira, I gesture at the magical energy separating us. "Release the wards on your shield, and we'll go. We have to hurry."

"And tell the hellhounds not to eat us," Dillan adds, pointing at the splotchy black and white beasts at her side.

Moira giggles and waves her hand. As she speaks in tongues, the warding dome comes down bit by bit, and the murderous dogs disappear.

"They weren't real," I whisper to Dillan.

"Smart. They were an effective illusion."

"Yeah, they were."

Once the shielding is gone, Moira tugs at her tangled hair and pegs me with a crazy look. "Now we go to Dublin?"

"That's the plan...but first, I need you to lick my stone."

Ten minutes later, we're tromping through the dense forest, backtracking to the clearing where Dart was able to land in his full-size form. Once there, we'll try to figure out how to open a doorway. We think we'll have a better chance at success with him super-sized and calling on the magic of the realm here in his full form.

More power input means more power output, right?

I hope him accessing a portal door back to our world is as natural as his transition to adult size and spewing fire.

If not, we'll have to trek back to the centaur garden to wait for Patty to open one for us.

"I told you not to lead with lick my stone," Dillan whispers close beside me. He and I are bringing up the rear while Bruin leads the way and Dart and Moira are in between.

"I thought she looked crazy enough to go with it."

"Hey crazy lady, lick my stone."

"We had a rapport building."

"Apparently not enough of one for her to want to lick your stone."

"Why do you keep saying it? You're making it weird."

Dillan chuckles. "*I'm* not the one who made it weird. I say we tackle her and shove it in her mouth."

"And when she swallows it? Where are we then? I'm not waiting twenty-four hours to search for it on the other end."

Dillan frowns at me. "You're disgusting."

"Well? At least we found her and got her out from behind that warding. We could've been stuck there for days if she hadn't taken it down."

"True. That was good. Point to us for that."

"Now all we need is to get the witch stone immersed in her DNA and get back to Sloan."

I rub the heel of my hand over the tightness in my chest. As much as I want to believe that Sarah put Sloan into a magically induced coma and he's stable and waiting for me to fix this, part of me is panicked that no matter what happens here, I'll be too late.

"He's going to be fine." Dillan reaches between us to squeeze my hand. "He's strong and stubborn, and he believes in you. This will work out."

"How'd you know I was worrying?"

"You get a look on your face when you think about him. It's a pained look right now, but usually, it lights you up."

"Sloan says I'm easy to read."

"He's right."

"I love him, D. Like deep, adult, all-in love him. I think he might be the one."

He snorts. "No shit. The two of you are a lock—like Calum and Kev, and Aiden and Kinu."

It makes me happy that he thinks so.

I let that thought soothe my worries for a while as we finish the last of this leg of the journey and near the clearing. Morning light is gaining on the night and traveling is easier by the minute.

The lack of sleep is catching up to me, but the need to finish this quest is a strong motivator.

Hurrying a few steps forward, I catch up to Moira walking with Dart. "Do you have any idea how a dragon would activate a portal door to get us back to the other realm?"

Moira scowls at me. "You don't know?" Her ire fades as quickly as it appeared and her gaze glosses over with confusion once more. "We're still going to Dublin, right? You said we were going to my city."

I step over a pithy log and try not to disturb the bugs scurrying around inside. "We are. It will be faster if we open a door here rather than travel back to where we entered the realm—"

I wince as my shield lights up and my back starts to burn. "Heads up. Alarm bells are ringing."

Dillan curses and calls his daggers at the same moment Bruin roars and barrels toward us. I know from fighting with Bruin over the past months, he doesn't close ranks unless there's a significant force coming at us.

I call Birga and activate my body armor. "Dart, if you know how to open us an escape door back home, now's the time. If not, get ready for battle. The bad men are here."

Dart throws his head back and powers up to his adult size. His body expands in height and breadth, snapping back trees and forcing the forest to accept his presence.

Seeing his transformation—even for the third time—quickens my pulse and steals my breath. It's mind-boggling.

Distraction isn't my friend in a battle situation.

A bolt of magical energy hits me squarely in the chest and knocks me back. I groan as I slam into a tree trunk and bounce forward to land on my knees.

"Well, that sucked." I shake myself and reclaim Birga from where she fell. "Sorry about that, girlfriend. How about we go quench your thirst and even the score?"

The staff of my spear practically vibrates in my grip.

My ancient necromancer weapon wants blood.

Racing back to the group, I find Dart holding our ground single-handedly. He's risen, wings outstretched, and set a burning ring of fire as a perimeter around us.

While it's keeping them out, it's also keeping us in.

"Give the witch to us," a man commands from the other side of the wall of flames. "She's a fugitive and is the property of the Unseelie Prince, Keldane, and the Unseelie Court."

The power of magical persuasion vibrates in the air around us. With my armor up and my shield burning, I seem to be immune to the suggestion.

Dillan isn't. He strides forward and grips Moira's arm, tugging her toward the ring of fire.

I rush to block him, and he pushes through me as if I'm not there. I don't know how to break a magical suggestion and don't have time to figure it out.

Thankfully, I don't have to.

Moira lifts her arm and taps his forehead with two fingers. "Release."

Dillan's head snaps back as if she electrocuted him. When he straightens, he looks around, liberated from the fog of the command cast over us. "What happened?"

"You got will-whammied, and Moira zapped your brains. Are you all right?"

He frowns at the fire. "Other than being pissed, yeah. What are we dealing with now?"

"Keldane's fan club is here to claim his property. They caught up to us faster than I wanted."

"You knew he was coming for me?" Moira snaps. "You led him to me?"

"No. I found you first and tried to save your crazy ass."

"In the air," Dillan shouts, pointing at the sky.

Winged horses swoop in the air. They've found their way inside the wall of flames, and their riders are poised to fire their weapons at us.

"Incoming!"

Several riders dismount and plummet at us from above.

Crappers. I grab Moira and pull her out of the way.

"It's raining men," she says, eyes wide.

It kills my inner smartass that I don't have time to sing

Hallelujah, but magical weapons are firing at us. Dodging the *pew, pew* of the incoming assault, I stash Moira behind a tree and check her for injuries.

She looks unharmed. I'm of two minds about that. If she were bleeding, I would totally get my witch stone fix taken care of. As it is, that's not possible.

"We need to get out of here." Dillan is tucked behind a tree to my left and looks worried. "We're corralled in a ring of flames and are sitting ducks."

He's right. The tables have turned, and now our defensive blockade has us penned in. I could extinguish the flaming wall, and we could make a run for it, but we'd never get away with us on foot and them on winged horses.

I glance up at the swirly pink sky above. "I think it's time for another flight on Western Air."

Dillan glances at the circle of sky above. "Agreed."

"I have Moira. You cover us until I get her settled. Bruin, don't get left behind, buddy."

Dillan nods. "On one. Three…two…one."

I push off the trunk of the tree I'm using as cover and charge the two fae warriors between me and Dart's back.

The surprise on their face makes my day.

I come in fast and hard, swiping the lead man with the point of Birga's spear. He hisses and covers the opening of his belly with one hand while swinging a sword at my head with the other.

I duck the swing, spin out of his range, and jab the second man in the side with the blunt end of the spear.

The second guy is built like concrete, and instead of him buckling at the waist, the hit rattles up the staff and vibrates in my bones.

I don't have time to recover from the internal rattling before he grabs me by the hair and yanks me to the forest floor.

"Ow, fucking hell." My eyes sting as I get whipped around. My armor has saved me from head injuries a dozen times but doesn't seem to protect my scalp when my attacker goes caveman.

I'm still scrambling to reclaim my footing when Dillan rushes in and tackles the guy off me. The two of them hit the forest floor, grappling and grunting until Dillan calls his daggers and sinks the blades deep.

We don't wait for the downed to breathe their last breaths. The two of them are out of commission, and that's good enough.

Dillan rolls off his man, points toward Dart, and we're on the move once more. "You get her sorted. Bruin and I will cover you."

I grab Moira's wrist and close the distance between me and the mountain of scales that is my baby dragon. "Dart, I need you to lay flat while we get on your back, buddy. Then you're going to fly us back to that garden where Patty sent us through, okay?"

My boy grins, nodding wildly as the man clenched in his jagged teeth screams. With a flip of his head, he opens his mouth, and his opponent becomes a morning snack.

I wince at the bone-grinding *crunch, crunch, crunch,* and try not to judge the gleeful grin gracing Dart's lips.

Dragons will be dragons, I suppose.

Focused on Moira, I help her onto Dart's back and get her wrapped around one of his spine spikes.

Once she's seated, I take my spot.

Dillan races up Dart's shoulder and takes the third spike.

The moment I feel the power of my bear return to me, I stomp my boot on Dart's shoulder. "Okay, buddy. Go!"

CHAPTER EIGHTEEN

I close my eyes as the g-force of Dart's launch pulls at my body and tests my hold. It's amazing how strong he is in this form. I grimace as the pull of gravity threatens to break my grip. It's all I can do to fight to keep my fingers locked. My muscles ache from the strain...then it's over.

There's a split-second moment when the upward thrust ends, and it feels like we're falling. We're not. He levels out and pumps his wings, propelling us forward as though he's been flying like this his entire life.

I groan as my stomach lurches.

Who needs rollercoasters when you have a dragon?

When the world rights itself and my body adjusts, I open my eyes. There are still three winged horses with us, and their riders are readying to fire their weapons.

Dart maneuvers in the air to bat at them. The shift in position tosses us around, and I lock my grip around my opposite wrists to hold on.

He manages to flick one Pegasus with his wing and spit fire at the second. The one he hits with his wing topples end over end and loses his rider. The one he blows fire at bursts into a ball of flame and plummets toward the ground.

"Where's the third one?" I crank my head around like a panicked owl trying to see.

"I think they bugged out," Dillan shouts from behind me. "I don't see them."

I search for the third one for a few more heart-pounding minutes before I take Dillan's word for it and draw a deep breath. I don't see them either.

"Good boy, Dart." I press my cheek against his spike as I try to slow my heart rate. "You're a brave and talented boy."

This dragon flight is very different than it was a few hours ago in the dark of night. Ha! It literally is the difference between night and day. I chuckle, but the fact is, it's true. On this voyage, I'm not nearly as panicked that Dart will lose his shifted form and we'll plummet to our death. I'm not one hundy percent confident it won't happen, but more than I was before.

There's also a spectacular view of the fae realm.

Not for the first time do I wish Sloan were here with me.

Then again, if he were well enough to be here, I wouldn't be here in the first place. Funny how life works.

I'm coming, hotness. I have the witch, the stone, and am closing in on the way home to you.

When Dart starts his descent, my heart pumps a little faster. I only need to activate the witch stone with Moira's DNA and get home. It's almost over.

We sink, and the horizon rises as we glide below a line of trees. Dart lands with even more grace and coordination this time, and I unlock my hold around the spike I'm clinging to.

"You're amazing, Dart," I say as we scramble off his back and onto the coppery moss of the garden where this adventure first began.

"What have you done? Why are we here?" Moira scans the garden with a wide, horrified gaze. "You horrid little bitch! You said you were taking me home. You brought me right back to Keldane."

Okay, harsh. I raise my hand to slow her roll. "I brought you back to where our door home opens. This is where we arrived into this realm."

"In the garden of the Unseelie court. This is Keldane's backyard."

Crappers. "I did *not* know that. Wait a minute...you seem awfully lucid and nasty all of a sudden."

She looks at me and scowls. "I may be foggy on some things but what he did—the pains he inflicted on my sisters and me—that's impossible to forget."

"I'm sure that's true."

"Now you've delivered me back to him."

"Unintentionally, maybe, but not if the door opens and we get out of here before that happens."

Her eyes blow wide, locked on something over my shoulder. I spin and shriek. Bruin materializes as Keldane looms large and storms through the garden toward us. Moira scrambles behind Dillan and Bruin, and shrinks into a quivering mass.

I glance toward the trees and suck a breath through my teeth. We already know how a chase ends.

Been there, done that.

Every cell in my body burns to put distance between me and this vile excuse for a person, but running won't accomplish anything.

"Hello again, little one," Keldane says as he reaches us.

His deep, guttural voice grates at my sense of well-being. In most situations, I have an abundance of confidence, if not optimism. Keldane sucks the hope right out of me.

"Aren't you resourceful? My men said you beat them to the witch. Even with no knowledge of the realm and no acquaintances, you bested my search."

"It seems so."

"They also said you refused to give her up."

I hold up my finger. "Technically, they never identified that they were there on your behalf. They charged in and demanded we give her up and we defended ourselves."

"That seems to be your go-to disclaimer. You said the same thing when you killed six of my centaur guard."

"It was the truth then too. A girl has a right to defend herself, doesn't she?"

"Perhaps in your realm but this isn't your realm." He grips the leather-wrapped hilt of the weapon at his hip and snaps his scimitar free of its tether. The long, curved blade catches the light as he cuts the air between us in lazy, practice swings. "You disappoint me, little one. I thought you were smarter than to take me on."

I sigh. "I'm not taking you on. You knew I needed her and you left me behind at the cantina. We put our minds to finding her, and we did. Then, we brought her here. That has to count for something, doesn't it?"

While it's true I didn't know this was Keldane's home and technically we came to await a door opening to return home, there's no benefit in getting into any of that.

"If you are truly committed to aiding me, tell your dragon to stand down and give the witch to me."

I consider it. I want to.

Staring at her crouched and babbling behind Dillan and my bear, I curse. If she were the same Moira who I battled at the Ring of Rath, I would...but somehow she changed categories from evil bitch to battered, batshit victim.

I can't sacrifice a victim.

"I told her I'd take her home. This realm has taken its toll, and she's not the woman she was four months ago when you brought her here. Being here has bent her brain."

He clucks his tongue and frowns. "I'm disappointed, little one. I thought you smarter than that."

"It's not about intelligence. It's about compassion."

"You're wrong. She's manipulating you. The madness that invades the minds of mundanes in this realm takes longer than a few months. She's playing to your weakness. She's trying to avoid the months of torture I have planned for her."

I turn to assess Moira.

Is that true? Am I getting sucked in by a sob story?

It wouldn't be the first time. One way to find out. "If that's true, Moira, there are a few things you should know. The goddess was pissed about what you and the other witches did. She stripped everyone who participated in the Samhain murders and mutilations of their magic. If you go back, you won't be a witch anymore. You'll lose your powers."

I'm staring straight at the woman and see the dilation in her pupils. She rises to her feet. "You're lying."

"No. I'm not. I didn't think it would matter since you seemed out of it, but if you intend to go back and reclaim your life, that's not how this plays out."

That news registered just fine.

Her gaze locks on mine and the violent hatred and resentment there is as sharp as the comprehension of her situation.

Her outburst a moment ago wasn't her fear of Keldane breaking through the fog of madness. It was her true colors shining through.

"You haven't lost your marbles at all, have you? You intended to dupe me into taking you back home so you could resume your life."

She doesn't give it up, but I have her number now.

"There's another problem with that plan. Even if you could live life as a mundane woman once the goddess strips you of your power, your reputation is shot. The women in your coven are dead or disgraced, and another witch moved into your home and assumed your life."

Her gaze locks on me and narrows.

"Don't like the sound of that, eh? Yeah, the blonde woman who owns the Witch's Brew. She made herself right at home in your house."

Dillan chuckles. "Yeah, she moved in when your sheets were still warm."

I laugh. "Witches be bitches, amirite?"

Looking over to Keldane, I shrug. "My apologies, Prince. If you give me one moment, I will return your torture toy."

I reach over to take one of Dillan's daggers from his hand. Pointing the tip at her, I smile. "We can do this the easy way or the hard way. Saliva is easier for you, but blood is more fun for me. You choose because either way, we're done. I'm taking your DNA. I'm breaking your hex on Sloan. I'm going back to my life and won't give you and your fate a second thought."

Moira's lip curls and she raises her hands. "No. You'll die here for what you've done to me."

Before she can cast, I rush forward, tackling the old bitch to the spongy, copper ground. "Don't kill the messenger."

Moira is a lot stronger than she looks, but now that we're throwing down, I have a lot of pent-up hostility to unleash on her —for what she did to hurt Gran and Granda, Sloan, and all those innocent people she poisoned with fae prana.

She gets a lucky elbow to the side of my head, but I roll back, kicking her off with the momentum of our movement.

She has a hold on my hand with the dagger, but there's no way she'll disarm me. She may not be insane, but she's still nuts if she thinks she's coming out of this the victor.

With a kick of my legs, I roll over her and straddle her chest. Leaning to my hand with the dagger, I give it a strong pull. Swiping the dagger out of her grip slices her flesh wide.

"Blood it is."

Moira shrieks, kicking and squirming, throwing me forward in a wild attempt to buck me off her.

"Someone, help me pin her down."

My beloved warrior bear lumbers over and flops across Moira's body. She cries out, and we win the battle. Bruin grunts as he settles and grins up at me.

I can't help but chuckle. "Thank you, sir."

Now that I don't have to hold her, I shift to trap her bleeding hand and pluck the witch stone from my leather pouch. After forcing her fingers open, I make sure her blood gets on every surface.

"I'll never let you win," Moira growls. "He'll die a horrible death, and it will be your fault."

I force her fist to close around the stone with my left hand and punch her in the face with my right. "You already lost, Moira. You're just too stubborn to accept it."

Laughter bubbles out of her, and it's a crazy, maniacal sound. She may have played the part of one of the Looney Tunes characters, but she's definitely not all there.

I'm done caring. "You made your play and got the guy you called. You can't change your mind because the dark and powerful man you summoned turned out to be more dark and powerful than you expected. Hello...did you think you could woo him to be one of your minions?"

She grins. "You think small, Cumhaill. It takes daring and foresight to see what's coming in our world. I made a play to ensure my place in the new world order. It's no surprise to me that you don't understand."

"No. I do understand it. You had a great life with a lot of power, and you wanted more. It doesn't take daring and foresight to be great. It takes honor and courage."

Moira laughs. "You're as sanctimonious and self-righteous as your grandparents."

I punch her stupid face. "Thank you."

Before this bickering gets out of control, I dig at her fingers and force her to surrender the bloody stone. It must be thoroughly immersed because now it glows.

"Halle-fucking-lujah," Dillan says behind me.

"We're good to go." I dismount the witch and scramble to my feet. "I have what we came for. Keldane, she's all yours."

Moira busts a gut laughing and now I think maybe she *has* lost her marbles. "You sure about that little girl?"

She sits up with a smug smile and snaps her fingers.

The witch's stone grows warm in my hand, then hot, then molten. It sears my palm, and I drop it onto the moss in front of me. "Ow, *dammit!*"

I take a step back as the glow of the stone grows brighter, and a sharp whistle rends the air. To my horror, the whistle turns into a scream, and the bloody stone explodes like a miniature sun gone supernova.

I stare at the shattered pieces, and my heart collapses inside my chest. After everything we've done to break Sloan's hex, the magic fix obliterates itself into dust?

I stare at the tiny glowing particles as my fury flares.

"No!" I shout, shifting my gaze from the stone to the witch who destroyed it. "You bitch! What did you do?"

Moira's still laughing. "If I can't have my life back the way it was, you can't either. You ruined everything."

I stare at her, and the world recedes behind the thundering rush of blood pumping in my head. I am numb.

Keldane will torture her for months. Months.

That can't happen. Calling Birga forward, I adjust my grip, thrust forward, and gore Moira through the middle.

Keldane bellows behind me, and I turn to meet his heated glare. "You will die for that, little one. If not for your dragon, you'd be dead already."

I wink up at Dart and pat a hand against his scaly shin. "The

DNA on the witch stone was only one way to break the hex. Her being dead is the other. Sorry, not sorry. She dies, and Sloan lives. That works for me."

I meet Moira's gaze and see the satisfaction glittering back at me. She wanted this. She knew I'd leave her to Keldane. Knowing she'd die anyway, she chose death by cop—or at least death by cop's daughter.

Moira lays gasping on the ground in a pool of blood creeping across the fabric of her top.

Dillan and Bruin have closed ranks and are tense in their ready stances. I check the air by the purple bush and wish with all my might that Patty's door opens.

It doesn't.

Okay, we need to hold out until it does. No problem.

Dart cries out and shrinks to his normal size, his magic reserve used up.

"Oh, fuck," Dillan says. "Fi? What now?"

"Kill them," Keldane shouts. "Make it slow and bloody."

The centaurs take advantage of our dragon shield being down and move in hard.

"Bruin, help me protect Dart."

The hostile force is more than we can handle and more court warriors flood into the garden by the moment.

Damn. Shifting my position to give Dillan and Bruin my back, I glance over my shoulder. "I'm sorry, guys. It doesn't look like the good guys are winning this one."

Dillan flips his hood back and casts me an uneven smirk. "Don't sweat it, sista. There are worse things than dying a hero. The good news is the tether to Irish is broken. We win."

I chuckle, pulling my spear from Moira's belly to face the incoming horde. "Hells yeah, we win."

Dart lets out a sad whimper, and I back up my stance so I can rub his snout. "It's okay, buddy. You did great. I'm so freaking proud of you. You were amazing."

I blink against the sting in my eyes. Crying won't help anything, but it kills me that we'll die here and the people at home who love us will never know the whole story.

The battle explodes in our faces, and there's nothing to be done. I try to call a lightning strike, but it doesn't respond.

"*Earthquake.*" Nothing happens.

I take a knee and press my palm to the ground. Nature here isn't responding to my command the way it does at home. Maybe a direct connection will work. I focus my intent and try again. "*Earthquake.*"

The response is sluggish, but eventually the ground drops. It takes too long, and the centaurs simply leap the crevasse.

"*Wall of Stone.*"

Again, it's too little too late. Unlike this place magnifying Dart's powers, my druid powers seem stunted.

A centaur charges in from my left, his arm swinging and his blade slicing downward. I grip Birga with two hands and raise my arms to block the strike. He's unbelievably strong.

Focused on keeping that sword from coming down on me, I miss his other hand jabbing low in a stab.

The scrape of metal hitting the hard bark covering my skin is both good and not. I'm glad to have the protection, but it proves how skilled and determined they are to kill us.

"Your armor serves you well, female."

It takes all my strength to push off his sword and stumble back. Centaurs are really freaking strong. He chuckles, watching me, toying with me as if he's flirting.

I draw a deep breath, my lack of sleep catching up fast.

For each step he advances, I match the movement and retreat, looking for an out. The shift in position allows me to glimpse Bruin ripping through the opposing force, keeping everyone away from our very drained little dragon.

Another few steps put me in a position to check on Dillan.

Two warriors and a centaur are attacking him from opposing sides. He looks tired and overwhelmed too.

He's blocking and slashing, but one guy with daggers against two with swords isn't good. I watch as a strike gets through his defenses. Dillan doubles forward with a steel blade sticking out his back.

"No!" My world tilts, and I race toward him without thought or awareness. The only thing I know is that I have to get to my brother.

He drops to his knees and coughs blood.

I am steps away, my entire focus on forward momentum, when a centaur bucks and kicks me with his back hooves.

One hoof catches my chest and the other my shoulder. The force of the blow knocks me flying, spinning in the air until I crash like a rag-doll.

The world goes black.

I blink back to awareness, with dirt in my mouth and the sound of Dart whimpering in my ears. I focus my spinning gaze and find my baby dragon crawling toward me.

"No, buddy. Stay back." He doesn't understand that defending me will get him killed. He has no strength left.

"*Move Earth.*" I place my palm on the ground and use every ounce of energy I have to erect a dome of earth over Dillan and Dart.

"*Earth to Stone.*"

The sound of dirt crackling and packing to a solid sheet of protection around my guys is music to my ears.

I try to regain my footing, but my limbs no longer follow the commands of my mind. I swipe my fingers across my face and try to clear my vision. Blinking past the blood blurring my line of sight, I smile at the centaurs cursing the stone dome protecting my brother and my dragon.

It won't hold them off forever, but it's something.

With a guttural grunt, I force my body off the ground. My legs are sloppy, and my head spins, but I'm more up than down, so I call it a win.

"Bruin? Shall we go down fighting as one?"

"It will be my honor, Red." He dissolves from sight, and I feel the flutter of him taking his place. I swallow against a thick throat and take comfort from his strength.

Raising Birga, I meet the strikes of the next two warriors.

I'm no challenge.

I have nothing left.

One of the warriors knocks me left, then right. I stumble straight into the strike of the other. There's no defense. Remaining on my feet consumes all my strength.

"Leave her to me," Keldane snaps. Either the prince of doom is very far away, or my ears are ringing so badly my perception is whacked. "You took from me, little one. First, you stole the witch. Then you killed her. That can't go unanswered or unpunished."

My neck aches from looking up at him and I realize that I'm no longer standing. At some point, I fell onto my knees. "You would've killed her anyway. What does it matter?"

"It matters. I desired to make her suffer, to make an example of her. You robbed me of that and allowed her to escape her punishment."

I point at her corpse. "Have at her. Make her pay. You can still do terrible things...I won't even look."

He stalks forward, and I'm the helpless prey in his sights. A surge of magic hits me as he swings back his weapon and slices forward.

My mind is quicksand.

It takes time to process the stinging of my skin is his power negating my body armor. I follow his swing and watch in disjointed fascination as the blade of his scimitar scores my chest. The searing pain of steel piercing flesh sucks the breath from my lungs.

Bruin roars in my ears.

I press my filthy hands against the gaping wound, my hands suddenly slick and warm. The moss of the ground is spongy under my cheek, and I take pleasure in that.

The rush of blood thundering in my ears is getting tinny, and my vision starts to narrow. When I feel an icy chill seep into my body and start to take me, I know the battle is over.

I'm going to black out, and I won't wake up.

I love you, Bruin.

I love you too, Red. It was a good run.

Yeah, it was. I squint against the blazing orange of the sun and find Keldane staring down at me. He raises his scimitar to finish the job and...

The echo in my head morphs into that horribly annoying brain worm song by Chumbawamba—*I Get Knocked Down.*

Keldane turns, looking baffled, and I bust up. I'm not even sure it's real, but I don't care. Leave it to Emmet to break the tension of my death and make me laugh.

Classic.

I fight the darkness long enough to see my brother racing through the shimmering air of Patty's portal door. He's running in with Manx and accompanied by the Dragon Queen and twenty-two wildly excited dragonborn.

Yay team.

CHAPTER NINETEEN

I wake to the warmth of someone stroking my cheek. It's nice and peaceful, and it takes a moment for the morning fog of reality to burn off my mind. I breathe deep and take in the unmistakable manly scent of...*Sloan.*

My eyes flip wide as I gasp.

"Hush, *a ghra.* Yer safe as houses here with me."

"You're alive."

"I am."

I cup his face in my hands and blink, focusing my gaze. "You're really here, right?"

"I am. You did it. I woke up yesterday and have been waiting for you to come back to me so I can thank you. You did it. You took on the fae realm, and you saved me."

Right. I dial back my panic and let my surroundings sink in. I'm lying in bed in the spare room at Gran's house. Sloan is with me, and he looks alive and much healthier than he did the last time I saw him. "You're fixed?"

Sloan brushes his fingers over my forehead and sweeps my hair out of my eyes. The weight of the world clouds his dark and dreamy gaze. It's a look he wears often, but somehow, I know this look is for me.

My eyes sting. "Is it Dillan? Did he—"

My heart aches, and I'm about to burst into tears when Sloan shakes his head.

"No, luv. Emmet and what he's calling his dragon brigade found ye in time. They got ye all back through the door, and Patty did what he could before he flashed ye both to the clinic for Da to take care of ye."

"Dart? Is he okay?"

"From what I've heard, he overextended himself quite badly but will make a full recovery once he's fed and rests. The queen took him home. I think ye might be grounded from seein' him fer a bit. Emmet says she might eat the head off ye if ye show up too soon."

That makes me sad, but I get it. I expected as much.

"Patty will work on her. He'll explain it wasn't me. Dart blind-sided us by barreling through the portal door. He's stubborn and too brave for his good."

Sloan chuckles. "I wonder where he learned such behavior."

I stick my tongue out, but I know he's right. I'll have to be more careful about what I expose the dragons to. Kids pick up everything. They're too trusting and eager for adventure. "Bruin? Are you with me, buddy?"

There's no getting rid of me, Red. Yer stuck.

"I'm glad to be stuck. I love you."

How could ye not? I'm fuckin' fabulous.

I burst out laughing. "No argument." With roll call taken care of, my attention comes back to Sloan's dire expression. "If everyone is all right, why do you look so upset?"

"Why do ye think? Ye almost got yerself killed to save me, Fi. *Again.* That can't keep happenin'."

I snuggle in closer and close my eyes. "Seems like a good deal to me. There was no way I was going to stay safe and watch you die. I'll always fight for this."

He squeezes me against his chest, and I'm thankful he has no shirt on. His skin is warm and smells nice. "There's none of *this* to fight fer if yer dead, *a ghra*. It's plain mathematics. Two only works when you add one plus another one."

The pain and worry lacing his voice make me sad.

I don't want to be sad. I slide a hand down his chest and grin. "Math isn't my thing. I'm more of a natural science girl myself. You know, nature, pheromones, the law of attraction...or mhmm...phys ed. How about we work up a sweat?"

His chest bounces against my cheek, and he pushes me back. "You're recovering from being sliced open by a scimitar. You're not to over-exert. Da said it's bed rest until at least tomorrow."

"Who said anything about getting out of bed?"

"What part of *rest*, are ye missin'?"

I ignore his logic and wrap my arm around his shoulder to pull him over me. "Okay, I'll rest. You do all the work."

Seeing his face light up as he laughs almost makes up for him rolling off me and putting some distance between us. "If ye can't behave, I'll sleep in another room."

I shake my head and sober. "Please don't go. All I've wanted for days is for you to be with me, happy and healthy. I missed you. You scared me, Mackenzie."

"*Och*, well yer no better. I came out of my state of rest and knew by the look on Lugh's and Lara's faces that ye'd gone and done somethin' too brave fer yer own good."

I pat the mattress and lay my head on the pillow. "I promise to be good. Let me hug you a little longer, and we'll go find Dillan and Emmet and get me something to eat."

I hold up my finger to stop the argument. "I promise not to exert, but I must pee, and I want to see my brothers. Then I'll come straight back to bed. You can even *poof* me here if it makes you feel better."

He sobers and lets me snuggle back in. "I suppose the fifty feet from the loo to the living room to bed won't kill ye."

I shake my head. "If a deranged Unseelie prince couldn't manage it, I'm golden. What happened to him, anyway?"

"I wasn't conscious when Emmet arrived back and filled yer grandparents in on the details. Ye'll have to ask him. I was more concerned with what was happening here with Da workin' to save ye both."

I swallow against the thickness in my throat and fight the burn of tears. "When I saw that sword go through Dillan, I thought for sure I'd lost him. I couldn't breathe. It was my fault. He was there because of me—"

"Hush, now." Sloan kisses the top of my head and pulls me in for a hug. "If truth be told, ye were there because of me. Don't blame yerself. Ye did what yer prone to do. Ye put yerself on the line fer the people ye love."

I blink up at him and smile. "You think I love you, do you? That seems presumptuous."

"Downright cocky, aren't I?"

"Utterly conceited."

He chuckles. "Ignore me. I promised I'd never rush ye and I won't. Let's lay here and enjoy the fact that we're both alive. Then, when ye've had enough huggin', ye can let me know, and we'll get ye sorted out on those other issues."

With my face pressed against his chest, I smile at the steady thrum of his heart beating beneath my ear. "I don't know that I'll ever get enough."

"Consider me forewarned."

———

In fact, it's my bladder that makes the decision. After another five minutes, I give up our love-in to head to the bathroom. As I turn back to close the door, I see him lean against the wall and peg him with a look. "Don't stand out there listening or I'll never be able to pee."

Sloan laughs. "Yer so odd."

I close the bathroom door and growl. "Away with ye, Mackenzie. Stop bein' a creeper."

He knocks his knuckles on the door. "Fine, I'll leave, but if ye feel faint, send Bruin out to fetch help."

"Buh-bye. Go make me food."

"As ye command."

I finish in the bathroom, wash up, and check myself in the mirror. Lifting my pajama top, I grimace at the long, pink line running from under my left boob to my right hip.

Yikers, that's big.

It's a good thing Keldane wanted to torture me. If he weren't so keen on having his victims suffer, I'd be dead. Ironically, his despicable lack of soul is the reason I survived.

Life is full of lots of twisty turns.

I smooth out my top and decide not to worry about the scar. If there's one thing I've learned since discovering druid life, its magic makes miracles happen. Sloan has a lot of his father's healing talents. He's likely already working on an ointment or a salve to erase the scar.

After drying my hands, I open the door and shuffle out.

I'll never admit it, but Sloan's right. The trip from bedroom to bathroom to the living room isn't far, but I'm already winded and wondering if I'll make it.

"Hey, baby girl." Dillan meets me in the hall, coming from the living room. He's shuffling only minutely faster than me. "Some pair we are, eh?"

I laugh, but it hurts, so I stop.

He's tall, dark, and as handsome as always but I'll never get the image of him being skewered out of my head. I step into him and hug him long and close. "Gawd, Dill, I'm so glad you're not dead. I love you."

"I'm glad you're not dead too. Right back atcha, Fi. You're my heart." He kisses the top of my head and squeezes me with his muscled arms.

I close my eyes and soak him in.

"Thanks for the concrete igloo. Emmet said you had me barricaded well."

I don't want to think about him lying there bleeding. Instead, I want to celebrate the fact that we were both saved. "If Em hadn't shown up it would've been a concrete shrine. We cut that one way too close."

He eases back and nods his agreement. "I guess we're not as indestructible as we thought."

I speak the words Da has said to us a hundred times over the years. "There's always someone bigger and better prepared for the fight."

"Yes, Da."

I shrug. "By all accounts, we cheated death—again—and came out of it stronger than ever."

Dillan looks at us and smiles. "Stronger than ever, eh? Methinks you're reaching."

"Well, not now. We *will* be stronger than ever."

Something sad flashes in his emerald green eyes but it's fleeting and gone as quickly as it came. "Okay, I believe you. Now, go eat. I've gotta get going, or at the rate I'm old-man-shuffling, I might piss myself."

I laugh and wave a hand. "Good luck, oul man."

By the time I get to the family room, Gran and Sloan have a meal set out on the little puzzle table by the wall, and I'm set.

"Och, my girl." Gran rushes to hug me. "Yer granda got called away on Order business, but he wants ye to know how glad he is yer home and only slightly worse fer wear. He'll check in with ye when he gets back if it's not too late or in the mornin' if it is."

"That's fine, Gran. No sense him sitting around here waiting for me to wake up when there are issues to tend to."

Cue another round of hugs. "Are ye all right? Can I get ye anythin' else?"

I scan the spread of food, and my stomach growls its approval. It's her homemade chicken pot pie with garden veggies and a heaping pile of cooked spinach on the side.

Yum. "This looks perfect, Gran. Thank you."

Gran waves that away and kisses my forehead. "Yer far too brave fer yer own good. Yer wearin' out my heart fer worryin' about ye. Take pity on yer old Gran and stop gettin' hurt like this, would ye?"

"I'll try my best. Promise."

Before I sit, I notice Emmet seated on the loveseat. When our eyes meet, I see how upset he still is. "Would you guys mind giving Emmet and me a minute? I was an asshole and hurt him. I need to eat crow before I can eat my meal."

Gran gives me a shoulder hug and kisses my cheek. "Take yer time, luv. I have a fruit crumble bakin' in the oven. It might wash away the taste of crow if we put some ice cream on top."

I chuckle. "Awesome, thanks."

She winks and tilts her head. "Sloan, can ye help me start a new pot of tea, my boy?"

When Emmet and I have the room to ourselves, I shuffle over and ease onto the big couch. I'm not nearly as confident that I should be up and about now that I've left the horizontal comfort of my bed.

In fact, as the room starts to swell in a hazy spin, I'm pretty sure this trip to the family room was a mistake.

I need to get through this apology and eat my meal without collapsing. If I don't, it will convince Sloan to never again listen to me when I assure him I'm fine.

"You okay, Fi?"

I shake my head. "No, not really."

"Anything I can do?"

"Yeah, let me apologize, then hug me and say you forgive me for being an ass."

His smile is sad when he sits back. "Okay, shoot."

I take his hand in mine and squeeze. "First off, thanks for the save. Dillan and I were circling the drain, and Bruin and Dart wouldn't have been far behind. Maybe Bruin would've survived, or maybe he would've been trapped in the fae realm, I don't know. The point is, it wouldn't have ended well."

"For the record, I never wanted to save you two from dying. I didn't want you guys hurt at all."

"I know that. Still, you came through the door even though we left you behind. I'm so grateful you were too stubborn to give us the last word."

"Because you were wrong."

"Maybe. Or maybe, if you were there, you would've been diced right beside us and all three of us would've died."

"I guess we'll never know."

"I guess not." I don't even want to think about what would've happened if Emmet was there with us instead of here to come to save us. "Chumbawamba was classic. I *did* get up again. Now it will forever be my dying song."

"Your *almost* dying song."

I nod. "I'm sorry, Em. I get that we hurt you badly and I hate that. You know I would never intentionally cut you out of anything but despite you being amazing and talented and brave and a million other things, your gifts—at least for the time being —are support team."

He scowls and pegs me with a glare. "Is this you admitting you were an asshole and eating crow? Because if it is, you suck at it."

"I *am* an asshole."

"Agreed."

"But not for poking at your sore spot. I'm an asshole because I haven't worked with you to try to develop your offensive gifts. You got dunked in the pink river of fae goodness, and we've never done anything about it. As the ring leader of this circus, that was a stupid oversight on my part."

"Do you think there's something to develop?"

I meet his gaze and smile. "I absolutely do. When Sloan and Granda first started working with me, I didn't know what I had going on inside me. Fionn stamped me as his heir and whammied me with gifts, but it was working with them—training, meditating, and stretching myself—that brought those gifts forward. I should've done that for you."

He raked his fingers through his hair and sighs. "It sucks knowing you're the weakest link."

"Oh, I know that all too well."

He sits deeper on the couch and makes a face. "When have you ever felt like that?"

I laugh. "Only every day of our lives. I grew up with five handsome, strong, amazing brothers. Five guys who got good grades, charmed the ladies, and knew exactly what they wanted to do with themselves from the time we were kids."

"So, what?"

"Hello...I am the only girl, the socially awkward one, the one who thought she could grow up and make a living as a professional glassblower."

Emmet waves that away. "You've never been socially awkward. You simply have no filter, offend people, and put them off."

I laugh. "A fine distinction. My point is that I know what it's like to live among Clan Cumhaill and feel like everyone has it going on except you. It's like you're getting left behind despite knowing you have greatness bubbling inside you waiting to get out."

With an arm across my stomach, I ease to the front of the cushioned seat. "I love you like crazy, Em. You know that. I see your value. I know how brave and capable you are, but as the person Fionn put in charge of this, sometimes I have to make unpopular choices. I wasn't wrong to leave you behind, but I shouldn't have left without clearing the air. I almost died, ending us with hurt feelings and fighting. That can't happen."

Emmet blinks fast and looks off to the side. "I hate that people are always trying to kill you, Fi. What makes it worse is feeling useless to stop it." He draws a deep breath, his watery eyes welling fast. "Why didn't I get a sword or a staff and mad fighting skills? What's the universe saying? Why aren't I good enough to be a warrior like you guys?"

"You are, Em." I swipe at my cheek and swallow. "The way I see it, the goddess has something extra special planned, and it's a plan in the works. It's coming though. I know it is."

Emmet wipes his sleeve across his eyes and sniffles. "Well, I hope it hurries up because I hate feeling like this. I don't want to be jealous of you guys. I hate it."

I shift to sit next to him, my stomach muscles protesting as I settle. "I know you do. It'll turn around. You'll see."

"I meant what I said about not caring if I get fired from the department. I want to help you, Fi. Hell, if I were a better druid, I'd quit so I could."

I lean forward and meet his forehead with mine. "You're an amazing druid, Em. Don't doubt that. Doc knows it. We were all at that parade, but he chose to bond with you. You're going to rock this, but the goddess is saving the best until last, you'll see."

"Thanks. I want to be part of this. I need to help you or I'm going to go nuts."

"You can start by helping me right now. Any chance you can get me over to the table without Sloan seeing I can't get there myself?"

Emmet pulls back and flashes me a million-dollar smile. "I have you covered, sista. Don't you worry about a thing."

Twenty minutes later, I finish my fruit crumble and sit back in the chair. The inside of my stomach is happy. The outside is getting very achy. "So what happened after I collapsed? Is Keldane dead? Please tell me the Queen of Wyrms or one of the dragonborn chomped him up. That would make me smile for the rest of my life."

Emmet collects the bowls and sets them on the tea tray. "Sorry to burst your homicidal bubble. As soon as I arrived with the dragon brigade, his guards closed ranks and rode him off. He lives to torture another day."

"That's too bad." Dillan pushes his dessert around his bowl. "Him being dragon crunch and munch would've made my decade."

My phone rings and I wince, swiping to answer. "Hey, Da. Before you start...I'm fine. Dillan's fine. We learned a valuable lesson about our mortality, and we're still very tired and achy. Yes, we were impulsive and reckless...but can you love us tonight and lecture us in a few days? Please?"

Dillan blows me a kiss. He looks as tired as I feel.

There's a long pause at the other end of the line, then Da says very calmly, "I love ye all more than ye know. Heal up. Come home. We'll discuss this when we're face to face, and I can assure myself yer not gonna keel."

"Thanks, Da. We love you too."

"When *are* ye comin' home?"

Sloan leans toward the phone. "My father wants to keep an eye on them for a couple more days to ensure there are no magical side effects from their time in the fae realm."

"Does he think there will be?"

"No, but after assuming I was well and missing the festerbugs, I expect he'll be more stringent on his follow-up in the future."

Thinking about Sloan and the festerbugs nearly does me in. A wave of dizziness and nausea hits and I don't hide it well enough to fool anyone. Might as well admit defeat.

"Da, I love you and wish I could talk longer, but I've run out of steam. I need to lay down before I fall."

"But yer all right, *mo chroi?*"

"I will be. Promise."

"Yer well, Dillan?"

"A chip off the block, oul man."

"Emmet, I'm bustin' my buttons with pride fer how ye handled things, my boy."

Emmet smiles. "Thanks, Da."

"All right," Da says. "I'll call ye tomorrow to hear what Wallace says. Then, I'll see ye in a few. Take care of her, boys. She's too willful and stubborn to do it herself."

Sloan and my brothers all nod. "We will."

When the call ends, Sloan takes the phone and frowns. "Ye've overdone it when ye promised me ye wouldn't."

I shake my head, too tired to move. "Could you please *poof* me to bed and be right tomorrow?"

His expression softens. "Aye, *a ghra*. I can do that."

CHAPTER TWENTY

For all of the next day and the day after that, Dillan and I play the slow and steady recovery game. It's like when we were kids, and the chickenpox swept our house. Aiden and Emmet got them first, then Brendan and Calum, and finally Dillan and me. The two of us spent four glorious days at home with our mom after everyone else was well enough to return to school.

Even though we were itchy and felt gross, it's one of my favorite memories.

The two of us brought down in battle is less charming, but it's nice to hang out with him anyway.

It's also nice to recover in the grandparents' Shire. To be TLC'd by Gran is an extra-restorative treat.

I try my best to be a good patient, and Sloan even admits I did better than he thought I would.

He finishes packing up our things and zips our duffle when it's time to go. "One post-trauma examination at the clinic and we're heading home. Are ye ready?"

I'm sitting on the bed in the spare room, running my fingers through Manx's fur. "Sure, why wouldn't I be? My last encounter with your parents went well."

"Ye mean the one when ye were unconscious, and yer insides were hangin' out?"

"Yeah. No confrontations. No fighting. I think it was my favorite visit *evah*."

Sloan rolls his eyes. "Maybe from your viewpoint, but as the guy waking up to hear my father and his staff were piecin' yer guts back together again, it wasn't my favorite visit."

I snuggle Manx close and extend my hand for Sloan to hold. "We can agree to disagree. *Poof* us there, already."

He does, and we arrive in the outer chamber of the main examination room a blink of a second later.

"I'd like to go run to the grove and visit some friends if there's time, sham," Manx says.

Sloan smiles at his faithful companion. "Plenty of time. Da wants to examine both of us, and I promised if they were civil, we would stay for lunch and talk."

I hadn't heard that part of the plan, but I try not to react. If Sloan's ready to give his parents a chance to rebuild some bridges, I certainly won't argue. "I'm proud of you, Mackenzie. Take it from me. The high road is a tough one."

Sloan beams down at me and winks. "I don't know. Ye tend to take it more often than not, and ye make it look easy."

"Smoke and mirrors, sir. It's hard work."

"Well, I'll try. What's the worst that can happen?"

I make a face. "Why would you say that with me around? With the disaster magnet plastered on my back, that's begging for trouble."

He grins. "I think we've faced enough trouble this week. Yer quota is full. I'm confident about our odds."

I laugh. "I loves me a man who lives dangerously."

It's a little weird that my boyfriend's father has seen almost as much of me naked as his son. Not so much when we're in the clinic, but definitely when we're sharing a meal with his wife immediately afterward.

Wallace is an amazingly gifted healer, and I respect his skills a lot. Out of the clinic, he doesn't shine quite so brightly in my eyes. Hopefully, after almost losing his son and knowing how it affected him, he'll do better.

"What do you plan to do with yer time in Toronto?" Wallace asks Sloan over a meal of soup and sandwiches.

I'm thankful to be able to eat and not have to speak. The three can make small talk, and I'll make quick work of these toasted turkey and brie sandwiches Duncan crafted.

"Nothing is set yet," Sloan says. "I've spoken with the Grand Governor of the Toronto Guild, and we're discussing the possibility of me establishing an antiquities shrine and cataloging items of historical and magical significance."

"Similar to the work ye've done with Lugh and the Order all these years?"

Sloan sips his wine and swallows. "Similar, but the scope of the items would expand beyond druid and Celtic significance. With the Lakeshore Guild of Empowered Ones, there is all manner of sects, species, and magical creatures that I could learn about."

Wallace smiles and sets his cutlery across his plate. "It sounds like something you would enjoy."

He nods. "Fiona's boss at the Emporium is a Historian of the written word, so she and I have discussed how having an archive of this kind could work with the preservation of spells and craft in peril of being lost and forgotten."

Janet pegs me with a tight smile. "That's right. Wallace mentioned yer a clerk in a bookstore. How...quaint."

Whatevs. I adjust the linen napkin on my lap and smile. "Among other things, yes. I love working with Myra in the bookshop. She's an ash nymph and has taught me so much. She's also very understanding about me putting in time when my life events allow for it."

"I'm surprised ye work at all now that ye've landed my son and are financially free."

I'm ready for the jibe, and it slides right off me. "You're mistaken. My financial status hasn't changed. I have bills to pay and debts to clear and life expenses as always. I work at the soup kitchen and the bookstore to feed my soul. My position at the Guild is my true source of income."

Her gaze narrows on me. "Yer serious."

I look from her to Sloan and Wallace and back to her again. "Why wouldn't I be?"

"Ye expect us to believe our boy isn't payin' yer way?"

I shrug. "Believe what you want. Sloan might've bought the house, but between the five of us, we split the household bills and the groceries evenly."

"They insisted on it, actually," Sloan says.

"Well, we'll see how long that lasts."

Sloan squeezes my hand under the table. "Please, don't start, mother."

Janet waves her son's words away. "I *am* tryin' to understand...well, tryin' to believe is likely more accurate. I will concede that ye genuinely seem to care about my son. Goin' to the fae realm and breakin' the witch's mocker was nearly the death of ye and I'm grateful ye were successful."

I swish the wine in my glass around before I tip it back and pass the empty to Sloan to refill. "Him being alive is my thanks."

Janet taps a manicured nail against her sterling silver spoon. "Ye say yer not interested in his estate?"

"I'm not."

"Then we can end the bitterness between us and ye'll sign a legal agreement to that effect."

Sloan sets his spoon on his plate. "Drop it now, or we leave.

The only conversation Fi and I had about my estate was when I asked that if something happens to me, that she handle my affairs with the same consideration she's showed after her brother's passing. I did that because I have no faith you would do me the same honor. It's not Fiona's fault that I don't trust ye to value my wishes—that came from a lifetime of ye dismissin' who I am and not listenin' to what I say."

I take another long sip of wine. Talking about the money from Brendan's death makes me uncomfortable and sad. "Why does it have to come back to money? Sloan almost died. I'd think you'd be anxious to patch things up."

"We are." Wallace sets his cutlery down with great care. "*I* am. I hate that ye felt the need to move halfway around the world to find yerself, son. I see that the two of ye have somethin' special. If ye say yer granda's money had no part in it, I believe ye."

I shake my head. "Wait. His *granda's* money? It's not even *your* money you're fighting over?"

Sloan shakes his head. "When Da's father passed, he left the entire Mackenzie fortune to me."

"And bypassed…" I read the anger and disappointment in his parents' expressions and…oh, this makes so much more sense. I shouldn't find any of this amusing, but call me petty because I do. "Why did your grandfather choose to leapfrog a generation?"

"That's none of yer business," Janet snaps.

"Then why do you keep making it my business?"

Sloan scratches his head. "She has a point. Since ye won't let private matters remain private, let's air it out. The truth of it, Fi, is that when my parents were first married—"

"Don't ye dare," Janet spits.

"No," Wallace snaps, nodding at Sloan. "Tell her. Fiona deserves to know why she's bein' judged. Maybe then we can be done with all this."

Sloan looks at me and frowns. "Mam and Da were paired together as an arrangement, and it was a difficult beginning.

Early in their marriage, Mam had an extra-marital liaison. The two of them worked it out and rededicated themselves to the union, but Granda never forgave the indiscretion. Funny enough, he didn't trust her. He thought she was here solely fer the Mackenzie money."

"So, he willed everything straight to you."

"That's the gist of it, aye."

I meet his mother's gaze. She's still glaring at me with haughty judgment, but I see now, she's only deflecting. "After being judged and branded a money-grubbing freeloader, you thought you'd pay it forward and do the same thing to me? That's sad, Janet."

"I'm protectin' my son."

I shake my head. "No. You're protecting yourself. You're worried about this life and your station in the druid community. If Sloan is off with me and gets himself killed, you're worried you'll lose out."

"Which ye won't," Sloan interjects. "I've assured ye of that fact a hundred times. I've assured that Stonecrest Castle and yer accounts be left in yer possession. Why can't ye trust me to know my mind? Ye raised me and yet it's like ye haven't the slightest notion of my character."

"And that's shameful." Wallace throws up his hands. "I'm done with the whole argument. Ye say it's taken care of, I believe ye. The castle, the properties, the lands, the money, it's yers to do with as ye wish. I won't give it another moment's thought."

"Thanks, Da."

He nods. "I'll call the barrister this afternoon and withdraw the petition of objection."

"Just like that?" Janet snaps.

Wallace looks at her and smiles. "Yes, Janet, just like that. Our son grew up, and we missed it. Now, he's showin' us what it means to be an adult, and we missed that too. I won't miss anythin' more, not for money, for pride, or even for you, *a mhuirnin*. I want my son back in my life."

He stands and smiles at the two of us. "Shall we take our tea in the den? I want to hear all about yer new home before ye head off. I do hope to see it one day soon."

"You're home!" Calum and Kevin rush in from their room across the hall. They bump knuckles with Emmet and Dillan and pat Manx and Doc as the animal companions head off to their rooms to unwind. I release Bruin, and my bear lumbers past to catch up with his roomies.

Kev and Calum give Sloan an assessing glance.

"You're good?" Kevin asks. "All fumigated and fixed?"

Sloan opens his arms and does a runway turn. "Thanks to yer sister, I'll live to tell the tale."

"The Tale of the Designer Druid Who Barfed Blue Bugs," Calum says. "Catchy."

I groan. "I'll pass on the book. I suffered through the movie. Not a fan."

Sloan sets our bag on the dresser. "If I never see another festerbug, it'll be too soon."

"I bet." Calum grins. "I heard it got a little harried in the fae realm."

Dillan looks at me and winks. "Nothing we couldn't handle, eh, baby girl?"

"Um...*not*," Emmet chuffs. "When I got there with the dragon brigade to rescue their stubborn asses, they were both circling the drain."

I don't even try to front. "That is one hundy percent true. Emmet is the hero of the hour. Without him, Dillan and I and likely Dart would all be dead."

Calum hugs me. "I'm glad you're not."

"Check out her scar," Emmet says.

I pull up my shirt, and they both look faint.

"Fuck, Fi, why wasn't your armor up?"

"It was. Keldane disengaged it somehow."

Kevin scowls. "Did you know that could happen?"

"Nope. It was a teaching moment for sure."

Calum rolls his eyes. "No more lessons, thanks."

"Agreed. Thankfully, all's well that ends well. It's Emmet for the big win. He and Patty rallied the dragons and came to our rescue. I only caught a glimpse of the grand entrance, but it was epic in true Emmet fashion."

Emmet dips his head. "Thank you. As I like to say, if something's worth doing, it's always worth *over*doing."

I laugh. "True enough."

"Speaking of something worth doing," Kevin says. "We've been busy while we had the house to ourselves."

"TMI." I make a face and wave my hands. "I don't want to imagine what you two got up to."

Calum barks a laugh. "That's not what he meant, but yeah, having the house to ourselves was fun too. It was the first time in my entire life when there wasn't someone around or about to arrive. It was weird."

I know what he means.

Sloan and I had the house to ourselves for three days before everyone started moving in. It was freaky. I was accustomed to six people coming and going at all hours.

The silence was deafening.

"Okay, so if we're not talking about you two getting busy, what are we talking about?"

Calum waggles his eyebrows and grins. "Follow us to the man cave."

"I'll portal us," Sloan says. "Fi is still sore."

I offer him a loving smile. "I'm fine to walk."

"You're finer to portal." When he wraps an arm around my

hips and extends his other hand, the boys link up and we *poof* to the bottom of the basement stairs.

Before we left, the boys had been busily trying to take care of what I amusingly call "the incident."

I didn't bother trying to get the details because I have enough catastrophes on my calendar most days without borrowing more. Based on what I know, there was an event involving a large aquarium and four hundred gallons of water.

Since they were all buzzing around to take care of it without me getting involved, I let them have their way—a team-building exercise of sorts.

Why sweat the small stuff, right?

No one ended up near death, and they worked together to correct the situation. Besides, Sloan has the money to cover any damages and likes to be able to spend it.

"Oh, I like the new floor." Gone is the beige Berber carpet, replaced with a lovely hardwood plank floor.

Sloan grins. "I thought it went with the style and architecture of the house better than the carpet."

I snort. "Since you had to start from scratch anyway, might as well go for style, right?"

"Something like that."

Calum and Kev lead the way past the laundry area and the room Sloan is slowly transforming into his apothecary room and bring us into the main rec room.

I stop at the threshold, and my mouth falls open. "Wow. Seriously. This is unbelievable."

"Right?" Dillan grins. "I knew you'd love it."

I do. They guide me deeper into the room, and I try to take it all in. What used to be a rather plain room with a pool table in the center is now—

"It reminds me of the Rainforest Café." Sloan shakes his head, and I explain. "It's a chain of restaurants that bring the lushness and wildness of the rainforest into your dining experience. It's like this, but less authentic. Are these plants real?"

Emmet nods. "Yeah, Nikon helped a lot with transplanting sprigs and plants from different parts of the world. He thought we were crazy when we first pitched Dillan's idea to him, but geez, it came together while we were gone."

Sloan's taking it all in too, and I can tell even he's impressed. "Building the planter boxes along the walls was easy enough. The aquarium wall gave us some trouble—which I'm sure you figured out."

I laugh. "Well, three days of fans and Shop-Vac sounds and Dillan confiscating all my extra-large Ziploc bags. Yeah, I figured something bad happened. I envisioned a pool cue going through the glass."

Sloan shakes his head. "There was some confusion about the strength of the seal on the aquarium wall. It seemed all was in order until the pressure of the water proved different. It was a definite ah-ha moment."

I laugh. "More like an ah-fuck moment."

They all nod, chuckling.

Sloan nods. "Definitely that too."

Emmet points at the floor. "I like to think it was the work of the goddess because changing out a perfectly good carpet wasn't in the original plan and the hardwood is much better."

I study the gleaming planks and smile. "Agreed."

They give me the rest of the tour, the two rock walls of greenery, with little areas for Daisy and Doc to make themselves at home. There's a stone dome in the corner that mimics a cave for Bruin and above the cave, there's a climbing branch for Manx to lounge across.

The entire far wall is an aquarium with a glorious collection of exotic fish, and, of course, the last wall is a bar.

A gorgeous, professionally equipped bar with shiny brass beer taps, lit glass shelves, and all the favorite bottles lined up awaiting a good time.

My attention catches on one distinct bottle, and I point it out. "Is that what I think it is?"

Calum nods. "Nikon pulled it from his archive collection. He said you seemed to enjoy the last bottle so he donated it for the grand opening of the room."

"On one condition." Kevin holds up a finger. "He said you're not allowed to open it until he's invited for an evening, and the two of you open it together to christen the bar properly."

I snort. "Did he mention what 'christen the bar properly' entails?"

Sloan rolls his eyes. "Likely something about you being naked and polishing the counter."

The guilty looks Kevin and Calum flash us confirms it.

I laugh and hug Sloan's arm. "He's kidding, and you know it. The only man I get naked for is you…and your father when he's patching me up."

Emmet laughs. "Just the Mackenzie men. S'all good."

Sloan frowns at me. "Please don't put my father in the same category as you being naked. That's awful."

I laugh and stride off to explore the new tables. There's a ten-man poker table with felt and bumpers, which is cool, and a foosball table, and a—

"Wait a minute? No big screen?"

Sloan shakes his head. "No. We talked about it but decided this room will be for spending time together, drinking, playing, and hanging out. The telly upstairs is where we'll watch games and movies."

I scan the smiling faces of my guys and my chest swells. "I'm proud of you. This is a fantastic space, and you had to work together to pull it off. Yay team."

When the house settles down, Sloan and I head back upstairs to unpack and spend some much-needed quiet time together. "Home Sweet Home." I throw my hands up as I launch into the air and collapse into the familiar comfort of our antique bed. "I missed you, King Henry."

The deep baritone of Sloan's laughter sounds behind me, and he stands at the opening of the curtains. "I suppose if yer well enough to take a running leap into our bed, yer well enough to enjoy the pleasures of our bed. Shall I lift the halt on sexual exertion?"

"Yes, please…and thank you…and please."

He laughs again, goes back to shut and lock our bedroom door, and crawls in beside me.

"How long do ye think we have?" He draws his tongue down the column of my neck.

I groan and lift my wrist to check the time. "Da is off work in two hours. I'm sure he'll be here five minutes later."

"Two hours and four minutes it is."

CHAPTER TWENTY-ONE

Over the next few days, I regain full strength and am ready to get back to life. My scar is fading, and like I thought he would, Sloan made it his mission to work on a balm that will reduce the injured tissue of Keldane's scimitar.

He's doing well. It's far less pink and raw.

Now instead of it looking like the aftermath of a slasher film, it merely looks like someone drew a line across my body with a wide-tip pink marker.

The doorbell rings and I answer it with a smile. "Hey, Anyx. How's things?"

The brawny blond lion dips his chin and steps in out of the cold. "No complaints. Is everyone ready?"

Sloan, Manx, and I are ready to leave and Bruin's on board for the ride. "All set."

Anyx uses his Moon Called ability to flash us to the outer lobby of our Team Trouble Batcave. "He wants you two to test your access to the security system. We've had to iron out a few glitches while you were away."

"Sure." I pat the silver pendant against my breastbone and set my hand on the scanner.

A red line moves down the length of the screen and scans the palm of my hand. "Access granted," an AI voice says.

The lock on the door clicks open, and I let Manx in to look around. When Sloan finishes with his security scan, I open the door again, and we head inside ourselves.

"Fi! You're home." Andromeda rushes out of her office. She's wearing tight jeans and a loose-knit sweater. I marvel at how she can make a simple outfit look glamorous.

I should be used to it. Sloan is the same way.

The two of them exist on another level of beauty. Thankfully, they're as beautiful in character as they are in visage.

I meet her with a girlfriend hug and point through the glass wall of her office at all the paperwork. "How has it been holding down the fort?"

"Not bad. I think we're getting a rhythm going."

"Have you started with the SIU?"

She blinks and shakes her head. "Oh, you *are* out of the loop. No. After working together as a group for a little, your dad, Max, and I decided I'm better utilized here."

"I didn't know. Okay, so, who have we got in the SIU?"

"That would be me." I follow the feminine voice and turn to find Anyx's mate coming out of another office.

"Zuzanna, hi. You decided to hop onto the crazy train too, did you?"

The lion shifter smiles and winks at her mate. "I finally convinced a certain someone to trust me to protect myself and live my life. I'm very excited to have a job and be a double agent for Team Trouble."

I smile at Anyx. "Protective of your beloved, I take it?"

Zuzanna laughs and holds up her fingers to give me a measure. "A little *over*protective, one might say."

Anyx grunts. "Or perfectly justified in protecting my living soul after the things I've seen daily for years."

My living soul. Aww…our lion tough-guy is a romantic. "Well,

I'm glad you're part of the team. It'll be wonderful to see more of you."

"Having another woman on the team is good too." Andy adds.

I grin at Sloan. "We gotta keep our elbows up around over-protective men. Make sure they give us our space."

Sloan arches a manicured brow. "Perhaps yer man wouldn't be overprotective if ye weren't standing in the eye of every storm blowin' through town."

"Speaking of which..." Andy jogs back to her desk and returns with a Post-it with a name and address on it. "I received a call twenty minutes ago and thought we should check it out. The woman who called wasn't sure it was an empowered issue, but I assured her we'd rather err on the side of caution than let something slip into mainstream attention."

I accept the orange square of paper and read the address. "What was her concern?"

"She said she saw something strange outside her house."

"Strange like what?" Sloan asks.

Andy looks up at us and grins. "She saw a unicorn trot by on its way to the park this morning."

I bark a laugh. "Seriously?"

"I don't make the news. I only report it."

I shrug. "Okeedokee, we'll check it out. Manx, do you want to come? We'll have to pop home for your harness or you can opt out and stay home."

He shakes his fluffy cheeks and plods happily from over by the kitchenette. "No. I'm coming. We should maybe have a harness for me here for when we're in a rush."

I nod. "Good idea. We'll get you one." I grab my purse from where I set it on the conference table. "Okay, we're off to track down a unicorn."

"Or an old woman with failing vision," Sloan adds.

I chuckle. "Such a negative Nelly."

I wave to Zuzanna and Anyx on our way out. "Bye for now. Welcome to the team, Zuzanna."

The three of us step out into the foyer, and I wrap my arm around Manx when he stretches up on his back paws and stands against me. When I have a hold on him, I reach out for Sloan. "Home, James."

It only takes a moment to *poof* home, grab Manx's harness, and get our boy suited up for our first official trouble call. While Sloan's getting him harnessed up, I change out of my sneakers and into my winter boots. I was expecting an afternoon in the office. If I'm out working the streets, I need to be ready for February.

When we're ready, I check the address and zip it in my pocket. "Unfortunately, there's nowhere close by where you might have already been, and it's too cold to walk from somewhere you have. It'll be faster and warmer to drive."

Sloan nods and hands me my keys from the line of wall hooks where they hang. "When the weather warms up, you and I will explore all the nooks and crannies of your fair city so I'll be of full use to the team."

I take the lead out the door and wince as a blast of winter hits me in the face. "You're already of great use to the team, but yeah, that will be fun. Can you drive? I want to look up a few things as we go."

Sloan takes the keys and pulls up the collar of his peacoat to block the buffeting wind. He walks me to the passenger's side of my SUV and opens the door. Once I'm in and seated, he walks around to the other side and lets Manx in the back before climbing in behind the wheel.

While everyone is getting settled, I notice the curtains drop in the bedroom window at the house beside ours. I've been curious about the old woman we saw in the rocking chair for months now.

It's been too cold to catch her outside, and I haven't had the chance to invent a reason to go over and introduce myself.

Maybe I'm getting paranoid in my druid days, but something about her tweaked my curiosity.

"Where are we headed?"

I snap out of my mental musings and get back to the present. After pulling up a map on my phone, I hold it over for him to see. "Not far. The woman who called it in—Poppy Grainger—lives near High Park. I think her place is about the halfway point between the Medieval Times Dinner Theater and the Toronto Adventures place where you can rent a horse for an afternoon and go for a trail ride through King's Mill Park and the Humber Marshes."

"Yer thinkin' she saw a regular horse from one of those two places and misinterpreted it as a unicorn?"

"It's the simplest answer, but a unicorn would be cool."

He turns the key in the ignition, and my Hellcat's engine sputters. After a little clearing of its throat, the engine kicks in and the truck starts. "Does yer car need a tune-up?"

"No, that's normal for February. We abandoned her for a week while we were away. That's hard on the battery. It's good we're going for a drive. It'll get her charged up again."

He backs out of my parking spot in the back lane and pulls away from the house. "That's not an issue in Ireland."

"You don't get into the minus forties either."

"We could move somewhere warmer...like Ireland perhaps, or Majorca."

I smile. "Nikon has a place in Majorca. We should go try it out. Lay around on the beach, bask in the sunshine, drink fruity, tropical drinks."

"It sounds heavenly."

I continue with my phone searches and start tapping in my

search words for the unicorn hunt. "It does. Maybe for my birthday, we'll run away for a few days."

"It's a date."

"Barring any apocalyptic or preternatural disasters."

"Agreed. So, likely not going."

I laugh. "Such a pessimist."

"Which way am I turning?"

"South to Lakeshore, then west until you get to Exhibition Place." I go back to my first search results and expand the map to include both spots near this lady's home where she would see live horses. "Just what I thought, she likely saw one of the performance horses going by."

"A believer in Occam's Razor now, are ye? The simplest answer is often the right answer?'

"Or so I've been led to believe." I take in the activity of my neighborhood, happy to be home. "It's sad though."

"What is?" Sloan turns left with the lights.

"We're so good at our jobs that our first case is solved before we even arrive."

Sloan laughs. "Now who's cocky?"

I laugh and wave that away. "No. I'm still going to give the investigation the consideration it deserves…and honestly, I'd be far more excited if there is a unicorn rather than a woman suffering from a moment of senility."

He chuckles. "There is no such thing as unicorns."

"That you know of. A year ago, I would've said there is no such thing as leprechauns."

Sloan winces. "I wish ye wouldn't use that term. Ye might be friends with Patty, but if another Man o' Green happens to hear ye say it out loud, he won't be pleased."

"Sorry. You're right. I'll try not to say it anymore. I'll think it though."

He hits the indicator and takes us toward Exhibition Place.

"All right, I can't police what ye think but realize there are those who hear thoughts as well."

I pull the orange Post-It from my pocket and laugh. "Geez, a girl can't do anything around the fae folks."

"Ye can. Ye just have to be careful."

I read the address and point toward the intersection coming up. "Through the lights and left."

Sloan follows my instructions, and after a few more turns, we end up on a residential street.

"That's it there." I point at the brick semi-detached, which looks the same as every other house on the street.

The side of the semi we're visiting is well-kept, the walkways shoveled, the shrubs wrapped in burlap for the winter, and the porch steps salted to avoid anyone slipping.

The other half of the semi next door is the opposite.

"If this were my house, that would drive me crazy. Poppy obviously has pride of ownership. Her next-door neighbor—not so much."

Sloan points at the sidewalk and frowns. "Watch the salt on yer pads, Manx. I don't want it to burn your paws."

Manx heeds the warning and shifts to walk on the snow-covered ground beside the pathway up to the house.

Despite it being clear and dry, Sloan grips my elbow on the sidewalk and doesn't release his hold until we're safely on the porch.

I stomp my boots and knock on the aluminum screen door. A moment later, a lively old girl with dyed red braids and rosy cheeks answers the door. She looks like her name should be Pippy and not Poppy, but I keep that to myself. "Hello, I'm Fiona, and this is Sloan. Are you Poppy?"

Her gaze narrows. "I am."

"We're following up on your call about seeing a unicorn earlier. May we come in?"

She shakes her head. "No need. The animal wasn't in my house. It was clopping down the street like nothing was strange about it. It went into the park, right there, and has been there the past hour."

I follow her pointing finger and in the far distance, see the animal in question. "Perfect. Thank you for your time."

Poppy retreats inside to stay warm while we cross the street toward park. We're too far away and looking at the wrong end to see if it is, in fact, a unicorn.

It *is* a horse of some kind.

It's pawing at the snow with its front hoof and clearing spots to try to graze.

Our footsteps *crunch* through the crust of snow as our boots sink four or five inches to the hard ground below. Looking over, I smile at the fact that Manx's paws are wide enough to disperse his weight so he doesn't sink.

Animals are so cool.

When we get close enough to see the animal fully, we sidestep to get a good view. The first thing I notice is that the horse is mauve with pink and white swirls. The second is—"Holy crappers, would you look at that?"

Sticking two feet out from the front of her forehead is a horn that corkscrews in a smooth swirl like a never-ending soft-served ice cream cone.

A very tall, pointy, ice cream cone.

As we approach, we give her hindquarters a wide berth. After being mule-kicked by an angry centaur already this week, I'd rather not repeat the experience.

"Hello there, beautiful lady." I'm giddy inside and fight to keep from clapping my gloves and squealing.

A unicorn!

I freaking love my life.

Robust and built with a strong, muscled frame like her ordinary equine cousins, there are three notable differences. Her coat is mauve, pink, and white and swirls in pastel whorls. When she moves, the sunlight, even the winter not-very-sunny sunlight, makes her coat glimmer and glisten with sparkles. Annnd, of course, there's the two-foot horn sticking out of her forehead.

"She's amazing," I gush. "You are a-maaa-zing," I repeat in case she understands. When I can tear my gaze away from her, I blink up at Sloan. "She's real."

He shakes his head. "Unicorns aren't real."

I snort and ease a step closer so I can run a hand down her side. "Yet, I can see her and hear her and touch—"

I'm about to contact her when the icy attack hits. It knocks my shoulder back, and I spin away from the unicorn. I call my defenses and turn, ready to fight.

CHAPTER TWENTY-TWO

"Whoa. Wait." Sloan launches forward and grabs my wrist as I search for the source of the attack. "It was a snowball, Fi. Yer fine. We're not being assaulted."

I dial down my adrenaline and reach up to pluck the slushy residue from my hair and off my neck. Searching the nearby park, I find a little girl patting a second handful of snow together. "Get away from Contessa McSparkles."

After the past months of unsolicited attacks, I'm accustomed to my opponents being deadlier than an eight-year-old kid in a polka-dot snowsuit hurling snowballs.

I'm a bit thrown off.

I give her my back and release my armor and my weapon, and by the time I face her, I'm back to being my regular self.

"I'm not here to hurt Contessa McSparkles, hon. We were admiring how beautiful she is."

"Well, don't." She pulls her arm back in a wind-up and chucks her next projectile.

I bat the snowball to the side with ease. "How did you and your unicorn end up here in the park?"

"Duh...we walked."

I blink at Sloan, who looks as concerned as I am baffled. I can't tell if she's a human kid who stumbled into something magical or a member of the empowered community who did something unexpected with her powers.

I'm not sure how to bring up the subject.

"Where did the Contessa come from?" Sloan asks.

The kid looks at us like the two of us are daft. "Duh...I wished for her."

Okay, that's twice in two minutes that she's given us that response and I'm not a fan. This kid is a bucket of sunshine.

"What kind of wish was it?" Sloan uses the soft, charming voice he saves for calming me when I'm riled. I like to think of it as his 'tame the wildling' voice.

It's a perfect choice with this girl.

"Where were ye? Were ye holdin' anythin' at the time?"

"You talk funny."

Sloan nods. "I suppose I do. I'm not from here, ye see, so I have an accent."

"Are you an alien?"

"Uh, no. I grew up in another part of the world."

"Florida? We went to Florida and Disneyland last year. People there talked funny too."

Sloan looks at me as if his brain is cramping. "Not Florida, but the same idea."

"Back to Contessa McSparkles." I point at the giant, swirly purple equine, my wow-meter still redlining. "You wished for her, and she appeared?"

"She's *mine*. You can't have her." She points her finger at me, and I feel the push of magic against my mind.

So, an empowered kid, after all. That makes things a little easier. "Where do you live?"

Her gaze narrows. "Why?"

"Because I think we should talk to your mom or dad about how you wished for a unicorn."

"No," she protests, her tough-girl edge crumbling. "That will ruin everything."

By the quiver of her chin and the gloss building in her eyes, I figure we have about two minutes before she falls apart. "I'm not trying to ruin anything, sweetie, but Contessa McSparkles is too special and magical to keep. Your neighbors will see her. I'm sure your parents have told you how important it is to keep the magic world a secret, right?"

"I know that. I told Contessa we can't tell anyone she's a magical unicorn."

Sloan blinks at me, and I fight not to laugh. "I believe the two of you could keep the secret. The problem is if anyone sees her, they'll know she's special. Just look at her. She's much too remarkable for people not to notice."

"There you are." We all turn toward the arrival of a harried-looking man. His boot laces are untied, and his plaid-checked jacket is open and hanging loose as if he exited the house in a race to find his child. "What are you doing out here on your own, Markie? Mom is losing her mind."

The tears that had been glistening at bay start now in earnest. "Mommy won't let me keep Contessa. She said I had to wish her away. I won't do it."

The man seems to register our presence and stiffens. Before he panics about exposure, I pluck one of my new cards out of my pocket and extend my hand. "It's all right. I'm a Guild Governor. Markie was explaining to us how she wished for a unicorn."

I can't tell if the man's relieved I'm a Guild representative or not. He lifts his daughter onto his hip and shakes his head. "We didn't mean to cause trouble."

"As far as we know, there's been no true exposure. We'll have people look into it, but no one is in trouble here."

He lets out a long breath and seems to steady himself. "What now?"

"Perhaps ye could help us piece together what happened," Sloan says. "How did this wish come about?"

"I took the family to Rockin' Ramen last night for dinner. They have a wishing pond in the front lobby. I didn't think there was any harm in Markie throwing in a Loonie and making a wish…but here we are."

I smile at Contessa. "Yep. Here we are. Okay, well, I hate to say this, and I am sorry…but—"

Markie's father shakes his head and wraps his arm around his daughter. "You don't need to explain. She can't keep a unicorn in the city. Can I leave you to take care of it?"

"Ye can. Thanks fer yer help."

With a nod to Sloan, he turns and tromps away with a screaming eight-year-old in his arms.

As the crying dies down in the distance, my attention shifts to the next problem. "Okay, Contessa, what shall we do with you?"

"Are ye sure this is a good idea?"

"The best idea I can come up with in a pinch." I nod at Sloan and wrap my arm around Manx. When he takes my hand and sets his other hand on the pink and purple swirly unicorn, we *poof* uptown.

We materialize on the driveway of Garnet Grant's Toronto home a moment later.

"Do ye maybe want to check with the man first?"

"It'll be fine."

With a hand on Contessa McSparkles, I invite her to walk with us through the brick archway that leads to the Alpha's compound in Africa. It's Sunday, and I already texted Myra to make sure she and Imari are home.

"Did ye at least tell them why we're coming?"

"I said I had a big surprise for Imari."

Sloan's eyes widen. "Isn't there a rule of conduct that states yer not supposed to buy a pet fer another person's child without them knowing?"

"First off, I didn't buy her. Second, we don't even know if this magic will last. I'll explain where we are to Myra, and she'll take care of the rest. She'll know how to put it so Imari understands."

Sloan looks doubtful, but he trusts my instincts, so he goes with it. "Into the lion's den, then."

Walking through the magical barrier that portals us to the African compound makes my ears pop. Other than that, and slight tingly pressure on my skin, I'd never know we traveled anywhere.

Contrasting the blustery winds of winter with savannah heat is shocking. The moment we step through the compound archway, I start to unzip and undress.

"Fiona!" Imari runs from the oasis pool in her bathing suit. "What did you bring?"

I jog forward and pick up Imari if only to stop her from rushing at the unicorn with flailing arms. The little orphan bear in my arms isn't much bigger than my four-year-old nephew, but from what we can figure out, we think she's closer to an undernourished six.

When Myra meets up with us, I set Imari on her feet and take her hand. Myra's vertically slit eyes widen when she takes a look at what I've brought. Strangely beautiful to begin with, they now dance with amusement. "Yes, Auntie Fi. What *did* you bring?"

"Ladies, I give you Contessa McSparkles. A little girl in the city wished on a magic fountain and got a unicorn. The Contessa can't stay in the city, and I don't know how long the magic will last, but I thought you might enjoy her in the meantime."

Myra eases closer and strokes the horse's bulbous side. "You brought us a swirly pink and purple unicorn. Isn't this the most perfect little girl's wish ever?"

"Right?" I grin, excited to be with girls of my own heart. "Look how beautiful her horn is."

As we're chatting, several of the Moon Called members of Garnet's pride wander over to join us. I've learned from Myra the people here range in species from lion to wolf to coyote to any number of other species, but Garnet makes no distinction between them.

They are Moon Called. Therefore, they are a pride.

"Can I ride her?" Amari asks.

Myra frowns. "Let's wait until she gets settled and maybe Daddy can get you a saddle and some reins to hold onto. I don't want you falling off."

"Can I sit on her? Just for a second?"

Myra meets the gaze of a tall brute of a male and nods. "Dornan can lift you, and we'll see how she responds. If she doesn't like it, we won't upset her by treating her like a pet."

Imari nods. "Deal. Just for a second."

Sloan and I step back while Dornan hoists Imari up onto Contessa McSparkles. As a dutiful aunt, I pull out my phone and start taking pictures. I send one off to Garnet with the caption,

Brought your daughter a unicorn. Best auntie evah!

The reply comes almost immediately.

Seriously, WTF?

I giggle and wait. If he's not super busy intimidating people or bloodying bad guys, he'll be here in—

"Only you, Fiona. Seriously."

I turn and grin at the scowling male. He's wearing his calf-length slicker, and with his ebony hair long and wind-blown, he looks like a deadly mercenary out of a Mad Max movie...but I see beyond that.

He shucks off his jacket and lets it drop to the artificial turf that makes up their compound grass. Seeing Imari on top of the unicorn, he slows his roll and dials back the hostility. "Dornan, take her down."

The man does as he's commanded and seems unaffected by the violence lacing his alpha's tone.

When Imari is set back onto her feet, she runs to her foster daddy and leaps into his arms. "Look, Daddy. Do you see how beautiful my unicorn is?"

"I see, my darling." Garnet pegs me with a glare. "Why don't you and Mama go get some apples and carrots and see if the unicorn is hungry?"

Imari squeals and a moment later the two are hurrying into the massive ranch bungalow built into the stone steppe.

Garnet turns to me and crosses his arms. "All right, Lady Druid. I'm listening."

I start at the beginning and fill him in about following up on the woman's call and finding Markie in the park with the unicorn. "I figured eliminating the risk of exposure was the priority, so I brought her here. Now, we'll go to the Rockin' Ramen restaurant and see what we can find out about their wishing well."

Garnet rolls his eyes, but he's only moderately annoyed and maybe not even at me. "Fine, but if this ends up breaking her heart because her unicorn turns into a hell beast and I have to slay it, it's on you."

"Having a bad day, Garnet? Because, wow, you flipped from fancy-free to darkly-disturbed faster than usual."

He draws a deep breath and exhales heavily. "Apologies. I hate the idea of Imari heartbroken when this ends badly."

"Maybe it won't."

He shakes his head. "No. Likely when you terminate the source of the wish, the unicorn will cease to exist."

"Then we'll explain that to her. She understands magic. We'll make sure she understands Contessa McSparkles is here for a good time, not a long time."

His amethyst gaze falls on me. "Are you waxing philosophical using lyrics from songs again?"

"Yeah. Trooper. Great song."

He points toward the arch. "How about you go figure out what allowed a unicorn to materialize in our city, and I will explain to my daughter that her amazing new pet will evaporate by tomorrow."

I make a face. "Why don't you let Myra flag that one? You're in a mood, cranky pants."

He stiffens his arm and points more fervently.

I take the hint. As I'm zipping up and putting myself back together to leave, Myra and Imari return with a basket of possible unicorn snacks. "See you later, girlies. Love you."

"Love you, too," Imari waves. "Bye, Sloan. Bye, kitty."

Myra meets my gaze and tilts her head toward Garnet. "Everything okay?"

"Sure. You girls enjoy Contessa McSparkles…and remember to enjoy her every minute while she's here because we don't know how long the magic will last."

"I remember," Imari says. "Maybe Jackson and Meg can come to play this afternoon and see her before she's gone."

Myra nods. "That's an excellent idea. We'll call them right now."

It fills my heart with all the warm fuzzies to know Imari's besties are my niece and nephew. The little bear shifter might not have had much of a family until now, but we'll make up for it. "Have a great day. Laters."

Rockin' Ramen is a funky Asian restaurant near the core of Toronto's Downtown tourist area. It caters largely to visitors who have come to check out the CN Tower or attend a sporting event at either the Rogers Centre Dome, BMO field, or the Air Canada Centre. It's pretty big, as restaurants downtown go, and by the people milling around outside waiting to get in—it's popular.

"Wow. This might take a moment."

Sloan frowns. "Let me take Manx home, and we can get a table and eat while we assess the situation."

"Sounds good. I'll get into line. See you at home, puss."

Sloan and Manx stride off down the block and into a side street while I get into line. I've advanced to stand between the double glass doors by the time he's back. He gets a couple of dirty looks as he slides past people, but they settle once they see he's with me.

He pulls off his gloves and blows into his cupped hands. "The food smells good."

My stomach growls to punctuate the point, and I shrug. "I didn't know I was hungry until I smelled it."

"Ye need to take better care of yerself. With the kind of injuries ye sustain regularly, ye need to give yer body all the help it can get."

"That's why I have my very own touch healer."

He rolls his eyes and winks at a couple of college girls smiling at him from further up in line. They seem quite taken with him and giggle as they whisper something that makes a third girl turn to look.

Without giving it even a moment's consideration, he shifts the conversation back to me. "So, the girl's father said the wishing pond was inside the front lobby. That must be what he's talking about there."

I follow his extended finger to the rock and plant waterfall lining the wall on our left. There's a long bench in front of it by the entrance, and farther in, it becomes the backdrop for the hostess stand.

Once we advance into the restaurant and can move around a little, I step over and look beyond the rocks. There are koi swimming in the water and dozens of coins glistening at the bottom of the pool.

Turning back to the line, I chuckle at two of the three girls making conversation with Sloan. He sees me notice and holds his hand out to welcome me back to the line.

The girls giggle and move back up to their spot.

"Making friends?"

Sloan shrugs. "Honestly, I don't know what that was about. They asked me if I'm the actor who plays the Duke of Hastings. Apparently, I'm the spitting image of him."

I shrug. "No idea. I'm not current on TV shows right now. Too much real life to deal with."

"Agreed. So, what did you see?"

"Nothing clandestine, koi and a couple of dozen coins in a moat. Nothing that suggests—wait, you don't suppose there are that many magical wishes invading the city, do you? That's a lot of wishes for us to track down."

Sloan leaves me in line to go look and returns with a frown marring his pretty face. "I wouldn't think there's much to worry about. Most people wish for money or love or health for themselves or a loved one."

"Good point. So even if something like that came true, the average person wouldn't necessarily attribute the good fortune to the power of the fae world."

He dips his chin, taking in the surroundings. "Exactly. The only two things we need to worry about are the wishes outside the scope of normal life."

"Like swirly purple unicorns."

"Right. Then, our second concern is stopping it from happening again."

I understand the logic of shutting this down, but honestly, it's sad. There's a real wishing well. Why do I have to be the party pooper to take it away?

"Because yer an adult and it's yer duty."

I meet Sloan's gaze and giggle. "Sorry, I didn't realize I spoke out loud."

He chuckles and ushers me forward with a hand on the small of my back. "Blessed be. Table for two, please."

The woman at the hostess stand gives him a weird look, pulls two menus, and hands us off to a runner.

"So, not a fae establishment. I take it that's what you were testing for?"

"It was."

We're seated close to the restaurant's front and have a clear line of sight to both the wishing pond and the hostess and kitchen area.

"So, what now?" I ask.

"Now we eat."

CHAPTER TWENTY-THREE

Sloan and I go through the Rockin' Ramen menu and can't decide between three entrees, so we order them all, intending to take the leftovers home for later. The food comes quickly and is hot and delicious. There's nothing left to take home.

"Ohmygawd, I'm so full." I lean back from the table and shake my head at the empty dishes. "I can't believe we ate all that. I was hungrier than I thought."

Sloan wipes his mouth and smiles. "It must be all the fresh Toronto air we got today."

I laugh. "Fresh. That's a generous way to put it."

He catches the eye of our server and points at his glass for a refill. "I can't speak ill of your city, *a ghra*. It's my city now too."

"I love that."

When our server returns to the table with Sloan's drink refill, he gestures at her name tag and leans in. "One question before you leave, Akira. How long has there been a wishing pond at the front of the restaurant?"

She glances over her shoulder. "The koi pond...as far as I

know, it's been here since they opened. I've only been here a year, so I can't say for sure."

"But since you worked here, it's always been there?"

"Yeah."

"And people regularly toss coins in it? That's not new?"

"No. People have always tossed a coin in as they leave."

"What about maintenance?" I ask. "Has anyone serviced or maybe cleaned the pond recently?"

She lifts her shoulder and sighs. "I don't know. Maybe you should talk to the owner's wife, Sandra. She'll know."

Sloan straightens in his seat. "Is Sandra here?"

With a glance around the busy restaurant, she indicates a brunette by the servers' pick-up window wearing a white blouse and a black vest and slacks. "That's her."

Sloan nods his thanks and pulls out his wallet. "I think we're ready to settle up." He looks at me and smiles. "Unless you're anticipating dessert."

I hold my hands up in surrender. "I would explode."

He winks and shifts his attention back to Akira. "Just the bill then, thank you. If you wouldn't mind letting Sandra know we'd like to speak to her, I'd appreciate it."

I giggle as he flashes the poor girl one of his sexy smiles and she pretty much melts into a puddle beside our table. "I'll tell her, and I'll be right back with your bill."

When she walks away, and it's only the two of us once more, Sloan notices my amusement and shrugs. "What? Why are you laughing at me?"

I wave away his concern and lean across the table. "I didn't realize you possess the gift of persuasion. You never mentioned it as one of your Spiritual disciplines."

"Because it's not."

I flick a lazy finger toward where Akira is printing out our bill. "I beg to differ. When you fluttered those dreamy dark eyes and flashed your sexy smile, you affected her ability to think clearly. I'll have to keep an eye on you and make sure you're not coercing young ladies to do your will."

He rolls his eyes at me. "Yer ridiculous."

"Maybe, but I'm not wrong."

My train of thought is derailed as the owner's wife Sandra steps up to our table. "Hello. I hear you have a question about the koi pond?"

Sloan smiles, and I'm glad she's directing the question at him because I have no idea how he's going to handle this. What's he supposed to say? Did you know your wishing well gave a fae girl a unicorn?

"Yes, I do," Sloan says, smiling. "One of your customers mentioned his family was in here not long ago and wished on a coin dropped into your koi fountain. I merely wondered what kind of magic you use to fulfill the wishes?"

The woman blinks and chuckles. "Excuse me? Oh, you're serious." She sobers and shakes her head. "No magic. It's a few fish swimming in a fountain by the door."

"How often do you clean out the coins?"

"My husband does it when we're closed for the holidays between Christmas and New Year's Day."

"Does he do that himself or have someone come in and tend to the fish?"

The woman glances around the room and frowns. "What's this about? You can't seriously believe luck can manifest from tossing a Loonie in with some fish."

Sloan smiles. "Not really, no, but our friend was certain his daughter's wish came true. We said we'd keep an open mind and follow up."

Nodding, the woman eases back. "Sorry I couldn't help you more. Have yourselves a nice weekend."

After she leaves, Sloan accepts our bill from our server and tosses a hundred onto the plastic payment tray.

While Akira bustles off to make change, I tilt my head toward where Sandra retreated to speak to a member of her staff. "She didn't seem like she knew anything about it."

Sloan shakes his head. "No, she didn't but *he* might."

The weird look on his face has me wondering what I'm missing. I glance at the man by the hostess stand he's indicating and see nothing that makes me suspicious of him. "Why do you think that?"

He reaches across the table and takes my hand. "Because my ring is showing me something interesting."

I lace my finger with his and rub my thumb over the bone ring that chose him to have true sight. When I open myself up to its magic, the restaurant flutters, and the glamor of the mundane dissolves away.

The man at the hostess stand looked totes ordinary when we came in, but now that I'm looking at him through fae eyes, there's nothing normal about him. He's close to seven feet tall with blue ink covering his bald head, face, and neck. His eyes are glowing gold, and as we watch him, his head turns, and he meets our gaze as if he knows we're on to him.

"What is he?" I feel a strange flutter in my mind.

Sloan doesn't answer. He's mumbling something, and a surge of his energy tingles up my arm from our joined hands. A moment later, the flutter in my mind is shoved away with a violent push. It's like someone slammed my mind closed and battened down the hatches.

"What did you do?"

"I warded our minds."

"What is he?"

"A djinn."

I've heard of djinn—both the drinking kind and not—and know our connection to the magic wish pond just got more interesting. "Aren't they like the genies of the fae world?"

"They are."

"You think he spiked the pond."

Sloan nods. "Very likely."

"Why?"

"A djinn gains power by granting wishes, but they have to deal with humans and can get tangled up and even enslaved doing so."

"Like Barbara Eden in *I Dream of Jeannie* or Will Smith in *Aladdin?*"

"Those are Hollywood entertainment. We're talking about real life."

"Right, I know. So, in the real world, what do djinn do? Are they hostile? What are we up against?"

"Hostile is a relative term, I'm afraid. They're not much for a physical confrontation if they can avoid it, but they have reality-warping powers and can manipulate matter and energy. They can also possess psionic powers like telepathy, clairvoyance, and a kind of psychic erosion."

I make a face. "So, they don't want to get into a fistfight, but they have no problem melting your brain?"

"If ye want to put it that way, aye. That covers it."

"*Noice.*"

Akira is back with Sloan's change, and she sets it down for him. "Is there anything else I can help you with?"

Sloan brightens. "Actually, there is. That man at the hostess stand. Who is he?"

"Darren...no, Dan. I'm pretty sure his name is Dan."

"Yer not sure? Is he new here?"

She nods. "He started right before the holidays. I haven't worked with him much. He mostly keeps to himself."

"Thanks fer yer time." Sloan stands and rounds the table to help me with my coat. "Ye've been a big help. Go ahead and keep the change."

"That's over fifty dollars."

He graces her with an easy smile. "It's fine. Treat yerself to somethin' nice."

I chuckle as he shucks on his coat and checks that we haven't left anything behind. "You realize she thinks you're flirting with her, right?"

His dark brows furrow as he glances around. "Who?"

"Akira. You gave her a huge tip and sent her off with a wink and a smile."

He shakes his head and places his hand at the small of my back as he does. "Yer ridiculous. Try to focus."

By the time we make our way to the hostess stand by the exit, our djinn dream maker is nowhere to be found.

"The gentleman who was here a moment ago," Sloan says. "Is his name Dan? He looked familiar, and I wanted to say hello. Do ye know where he got off to?"

The hostess glances around and frowns. "No. Maybe he went on his break."

Sloan nods. "We'll wait a moment over by the koi and see if he comes back if ye don't mind."

She shifts her hand through the air. "As long as you stand out of the way."

We shift out of the traffic of hungry customers, and I smile at the natural setting indoors. It's soothing...the trickle of water running down the wall of stone, the colorful fish working their way along the two-and-a-half-foot moat to the pool area near the door, and the green, rubbery plants growing in behind.

"This fountain area is quite lovely."

"It is." Sloan reaches toward the water, his lips moving in silent conversation.

His powers tingle against my skin, and when he straightens, I cast him a curious smile. "Whatcha doin'?"

"What ye said about it bein' lovely is true, but people shouldn't throw money into the water. The metal and germs aren't good fer the fish. I simply spelled the water to keep it pollutant-free for them."

"Aw…safeguarding the fishes. Nice guy."

"Safeguarding nature is part of—"

I leave Sloan talking and push past the line of people to get out on the street in time to see Dan the djinn driving away in an old Dodge Daytona. Grabbing my phone out of my pocket, I dial up Emmet. "Hey, have you left the station yet?"

"No. I was about to go change to leave."

"Don't bother. I have a runner and could use some police backup."

"You got a name and addie?"

"It's Dan, he's a djinn, and he's driving a Dodge Daytona."

Emmet snorts. "Say that three times fast. Okay, have you got anything I can actually use to track him down?"

"The custom plate on the muscle car was three, whiskey, one, sierra, hotel, echo, sierra."

He chuckles on the other end of the line, and the tapping of keys on his keyboard ends. "The custom plate, three wishes, belongs to one Dantarion Jann…"

As he reads out the address, I repeat it aloud to Sloan, who has now caught up to me. "That's not far from us. We'll meet you there."

"On my way."

When Emmet hangs up, I end the call and dial Garnet.

"Good evening, Lady Druid."

I grin. "You don't sound like you want to maul me and chew me up anymore. Does that mean Imari's day with her unicorn went okay?"

"Likely one of her best days in life. Your sister-in-law came over, and the kids played unicorn games all afternoon. Contessa is remarkably forgiving during ring-toss. They played that for close to an hour."

"Myra got pictures, I hope."

The deep baritone of his amusement rings in my ears. "It's lucky the times have moved to digital instead of print photos. Myra would bankrupt me in a day if I had to pay for developing like I used to."

"Well, good. I can hardly wait to see them. Listen, the reason I called was to give you an update." I go on to tell Garnet about the wishing well and the djinn at the restaurant. "Emmet's meeting us at his apartment now, although we're not sure he'll even head back there."

"Text the address to the team chat, and I'll have Anyx join you. Djinn can be nasty to deal with."

"Thanks. Sending it now."

Once that's done, I pull up the address on Google Street Maps and smile. "If you *poof* us into the Emporium, we can start there, and we only have to walk two or three blocks."

Sloan looks at me and smiles. "We drove yer SUV. We can drive there."

I laugh. "Good point. I never thought of that. Let's go."

Crossing the downtown core isn't too bad this early on a Sunday evening. Once we get off Lakeshore and onto the Gardiner Expressway, we make good time. All in...it takes us under ten minutes to get there.

Sloan pulls my truck against the curb next to where Emmet and Anyx are sitting in the front seat of Emmet's and Calum's Lexus. When our engine cuts off, we all bail out and meet up on the sidewalk.

"How do you want to handle this?" Emmet asks.

Anyx looks at me to make the call, so I go with my gut. "We might know *who* but we don't know *why*, yet. Let's assume this was an error in judgment and go in with a soft touch. If things go badly, we have enough power between the four of us to take out one djinn."

They nod and agree with my plan.

"Okay, let's go meet Dan the djinn."

The address Emmet got off the system says Dan owns the second floor of the triplex across the street. It's a nondescript building with a metal fire escape on the side.

"Should someone watch the side exit?" Emmet asks.

"I've got it," Anyx says. "Let me know if you need me."

"Will do." The three of us open the front door and head up the public stairs. "How does fighting a djinn go? If his glamor is five-foot-eight and the real man is seven-foot-two when you punch him in what you think is his face, is it actually his chest?"

Sloan blinks at me. "Are these truly the things that fill yer mind at a moment like this?"

I pause, my knuckles raised and ready to knock on the door. "Yeah. Why? Don't *you* wonder about things like that?"

"No."

Before I crack the door panel with my knuckles, I remember Sloan's spell from earlier. "Batten down Emmet's hatches. I don't want Dan to make his brain mush."

Emmet makes a face and takes a step closer. "Yes, please. I don't want mush for brains."

Sloan repeats whatever he did for me at the restaurant, and when he gives me the go-ahead, I knock.

We wait a moment, and when nothing happens, I signal for Emmet to take point. "Do the 'This is the police' thing."

Emmet flashes me a grin and moves to the front of our group. "Dan Jann—" he snorts, "Okay, that sounds awful when you shorten his name." He straightens and starts again. "Dantarion Jann, this is the police. Open up."

The *clack* and slide of the deadbolt bring out my smile, but when the door opens, I realize my celebration is premature. It's the room full of djinn who are smiling now.

Emmet looks at me and rolls his eyes. "I blame you for this. You and your stupid curse of a Fianna mark."

CHAPTER TWENTY-FOUR

S loan takes in the gathering of bald, inked, djinn giants and curses under his breath. "What were ye just sayin' about the four of us havin' enough power to take out one djinn?"

I smile and give a little finger wave to the men inside. "Hello, boys. What have we here—a club meeting?"

The man from the restaurant, Dan steps forward and grins. "Hello, Lady Druid. Thank you for coming."

I scan the faces of the other eight men. "You were expecting us?"

They assess us with blank expressions, but I suppose if they're mental manipulators, they don't let much slip. "We learned of the new team you've put together and wanted to test how effective you would be. We weren't certain who or how many to expect, but we're pleased with your response time and your resourcefulness."

Anyx steps into the apartment, and Sloan closes the door. I meet Emmet's gaze, and he sticks his phone back into his pocket. Good thinking, Em. No sense having the muscle out in the cold when it's obvious no one here is fleeing.

"Let's make sure I have this straight. You allowed young

Markie to wish for a unicorn to test how long it would take for us to piece it together and track it to you?"

Dan the djinn nods. "Exactly right, and it took you less than five hours from the time we phoned it in."

"So, Poppy, the woman living across from the park is part of this too?"

He shakes his tattooed head. "No, but her mind was malleable and her proximity to the park fortunate. We used her as a starting point for contact. We couldn't have a unicorn running around Toronto and risking exposure, after all."

"Good. I'm glad we agree on that. So, were there other wishes I should be tracking down?"

"None that can be traced to the empowered world. The others involved hopes, health, help with work, that sort of thing. Nothing to concern yourself with."

I check with Anyx and Sloan, and they seem cool with that answer. "Fine. As long as it doesn't come back to bite us in the butt, we'll leave it at that."

Another of the men stands from where he was seated in the living room. I recognize him from the Guild meetings. We've never spoken, and I've never seen him without his glamor, but I'm sure it's him. "The djinn have survived from the days of what you would call ancient Persia, Lady Druid. We know well our duty to remain in the shadows. That is why we were interested in your team."

I search the men's faces, waiting to see if anyone is going to expand on that.

"Ye want to join the effort," Sloan says beside me. "Yer thinkin' that with yer skills in manipulation, havin' a djinn on the team would make cleanin' up exposure easier."

By the relaxed smiles around the room, Sloan gets full points for his assessment.

"All right," I say. "We don't have an application process, but if you give me the name and background information of the person you're nominating, I'll take it back to the team. We'll do an extensive background check and discuss it with Governor Grant."

Dantarion collects a file folder from the top of the table and hands it to me. "I look forward to working with you, Lady Cumhaill."

I tuck the folder under my arm. "No promises, but we'll consider your proposal."

Emmet opens the door, and we're backing out of the apartment when another thought occurs to me. "Oh, what about the unicorn? I found her a home but told the little girl it was temporary. Will she disappear now that we've completed your test?"

He lifts his palms. "The draw on our magic is in the execution of a wish. The animal exists now. If you wish for me to end that, I can, but it causes no issue for us if it has found a home and won't expose our world."

"Cool. Then let's leave Contessa McSparkles where she is and see how it goes. Three kids will be thrilled to spend more time with her."

Dan dips his chin. "As you wish."

Sloan pulls my truck into my spot, followed closely by Emmet pulling into his. The three of us go through the gate and cross lawns to our house, chatting about the success of our first official case.

After we take off our boots, I hand Emmet my coat and take the folder into the open concept main floor to open it on the dining table. "It's cool we caught the attention of the empowered folks with Team Trouble. I was wondering what the people think about a response team."

"It seems they like it and want to get involved." Sloan fills the kettle and turns it on.

Emmet scoops up Doc as he heads toward the stairs. "We have

to make sure Maxwell stays under the radar. Even if new members join the tactical team, we still want to make sure his cover isn't blown."

"Agreed. I don't think he fully understands the danger he's in if one of the more violent races finds out he knows about them and decides they don't like it."

Emmet lifts Doc, and the marten winds his way up onto my brother's shoulders, his bushy brown tail curling around his neck. "Manx and I were thinking," Doc says. "We'd like an exit so we can go to the grove even if everyone is out. Is there any chance we can get access to come and go?"

"Like a doggie door, you mean?" Manx and Doc scowl at me. "Sorry. Like a druid companion door, you mean?"

Manx grins. "Exactly. We would have to ward it to keep out the elements and the undesirables, but yes."

Sloan meets my gaze and shrugs. "It's fine with me, but I agree, we'll have to ward it to restrict access to only those we want to come and go."

"I'm sure Dora can help. She rocks on warding."

Dora rocks on a great many magical practices.

Emmet pats Doc Marten's head, and they turn toward the stairs. "Let me change out of my uniform and grab my laptop. I'll come down and help with the initial background check for Dan the djinn."

I wave that away. "Let's do that tomorrow. Tonight, I was thinking of invading next door and checking in on the old man. I miss seeing him every day."

Emmet laughs. "We're only next door, but yeah, sure. I'll change and meet you over there."

When the floorboards creak above our heads, I lean into the stairwell and call upstairs. "Calum and Kev, we're headed next door for a visit. Do you want to join?"

Calum jogs down the stairs with his skunk companion

stretched out in the cradle of his arm. "Daisy and I are game. Kev got called into work at the last minute."

"The gallery or the theatre?" Sloan strolls over from the counter with two mugs of tea in his hands.

I accept mine with my thanks and sip it.

"The gallery," Calum says. "Apparently, some snooty guy who bought a house on the Bridal Path is looking for artwork. He wanted a private showing. He's rich and paranoid or something."

I chuckle. "The Bridal Path. How much did he pay?"

Calum grins. "We looked it up. The house was listed for eighteen million."

I flick my hand. "Oh, is that all?"

"Yeah, he said—" Calum holds up one finger. "Speak of the devil." He answers the call as Emmet comes down the stairs looking fresh in jeans and the sweater I helped him pick out for Yule with Sarah.

"What? Wait. Slow down, Kev. Who's there? What's happening?"

Calum is on the phone but rushing to get his shoes on, so we do too. When he straightens, he looks faint. "Keep your head down. We're on our way. I love you."

He hangs up and looks like he might throw up. "Sloan, tell me you know where the gallery is."

"Yer sister gave me the tour. What's happening?"

"A dozen fae freaks with lots of teeth busted in and are beating on the rich guy."

I hold out my hand. "Sloan will take us, then get Da and the others."

Sloan doesn't look happy about it, but there's no time to argue. He grips our hands and *poofs* us straight into the gallery. We'll have to clean up whatever exposure that costs us afterward.

When I see the torrent of hell we've materialized into, I release Bruin and call my armor.

"Hurry back, hotness," I say to Sloan, who is gone in a split second.

Assessing the situation, I curse. I have no idea who this guy is or what inspired a nest of whatever the hell these are to come after him, but it's obvi they aren't here to make terms.

Calum launches off to find Kev, and I fish my pendant out of my shirt. Pressing the sigil, I focus. "Backup."

We've never tested the pendant's cavalry option, so I hope it works. I think it will because a pulse of magic snaps between my fingertips, and the pendant starts to glow.

I call Birga and engage at the same time Sloan's back. He brought Aiden, Dillan, and Da. Nikon flashes in a moment later. Garnet and Anyx are there too.

"The gang's all here." I dive into the fray.

"Focus on something ferocious," I shout at Emmet. "Call your animal form. See if adrenaline helps."

"These are leviathan," Garnet shouts. "Decapitation is the only thing that will slow them down."

Good to know. I turn back to Emmet. "Something with long, sharp claws."

Emmet doesn't seem to be having much luck transforming but grabs a wicked hunting knife off someone and dives in the best he can. I shift to stay close to him when I'm knocked sideways.

Bruin sees me stumble, but it's only that—a stumble. Before the guy can take advantage, I regain my footing and turn, weapon raised.

Behead them, eh?

Not my favorite play, but you gotta do what works.

The guy who shoved me looks pleased with himself. He flashes me a grin, tips his head back, and opens his mouth to show me about six rows of long, serrated teeth.

I'm not sure if I'm supposed to be intimidated, but at best, it's gross. The two of us engage, and I'm holding my own when I see a second guy tag into the fight with Emmet.

Two on one is not cool.

"Bruin, incoming." I spin and kick my guy backward and straight into the reach of Killer Clawbearer. That leaves me free to help Emmet.

While my brother faces off with one, I grunt and swing Birga at his second opponent. The man's head comes off in a spray of black ichor and hits the gallery's polished floor with a meaty clunk.

"Emmet, tee him up for me."

Emmet nods and works the second guy back toward me. "Batter, batter, batter...swinnng batter."

Emmet throws himself back at the same moment I grip Birga's staff and swing. Beheading people isn't easy. It takes a lot of upper-body strength, and after two, I'm not sure how much more decapitation I've got in me.

Thankfully, when I assess the room, not much more is necessary. "Where'd everyone go?" I pant, counting the dead. "We're short four guys."

Garnet's lion shakes his ichor-covered paws and transforms back into the man. "Nikon portaled them into our containment room. It's a protocol we've been working out. This will be our test. If we have the materials and the warding correct, no one should be able to travel in or out of that cell except Nikon, Sloan, Anyx, or I."

"Cool. So, while we battle, the transporters can dump people into a holding cell. I like it."

Anyx rises from all fours to stand before us. He spits and wipes at his ichor-covered mouth. "What the fuck is this about?"

"No idea. We got a distress call from Calum's partner, Kevin." Mentioning Kev brings my concern back to the fore. "Calum? Kevin? Are you guys good?"

"We're good," Calum shouts from the back room. "I figure it's best to keep everyone back here until the authorities take care of a few things, right?"

Smart boy. "Yes. Keep everyone safe while we assure the danger is clear. It won't be long. S'all good."

I check the vast space. I'd never thought about it, but the wide aisles and open spaces of a gallery make it an opportune place for a battle. Cleanup of the floor will go quickly.

Cleanup of the walls and ruined artwork...not so much.

"What was this about?" Garnet asks.

I glance around and come up blank. "No idea. Calum mentioned they had a VIP buyer coming in tonight."

Garnet points at the beaten form of a pulpy dead guy bleeding all over the floor.

"From what we know, he bought a home on the Bridal Path and asked for a private showing of the artwork. Kevin said he was paranoid about something."

Garnet frowns at the bodies and the loose heads lying around, oozing on the polished marble floor. "It seems he had reason to feel that way."

"So, what now?" I ask. "I know nothing about leviathan or why they'd slaughter a rich guy at a gallery."

Garnet doesn't seem any more enlightened. "Anyx and I will make the bodies disappear. Someone, see what kind of security footage was recorded. Forward it to the team and wipe it from the system. I'll call in my cleaner to handle the bulk of the ichor. In the meantime, Niall and Fi, you two start the debrief with the gallery staff and see what they know."

Dad strikes off toward the back. He looks murderous, but for once, I don't think it has anything to do with Garnet or being set on a task by him. My instincts say this is all about one of his boys being caught in the cross-hairs of violence.

Kevin is ours. He always has been.

"You're with me, Bruin."

My bear lifts his black nose to the air and grunts. "This was fun."

I chuckle. "Glad you enjoyed it. Now, away you go before you give some unsuspecting human a heart attack on an already bad night."

"I'm a mess, Red."

"I see that. We'll take care of that when we get home. For now, I'd prefer you with me even if you look like a tar kettle tipped over on you."

Bruin ghosts out and spirits his way into my chest. I pat the flutter beneath my fleece top and head toward the back room to find Da and the others.

CHAPTER TWENTY-FIVE

"Yer sure Mr. Montclair never mentioned the nature of his concerns?" Da asks.

He's sitting around the staff table with Kevin, his boss Paul, and the event hostess they use when VIPs come in, Carina. The three of them look shaken and disheveled but relatively unharmed. Calum looks like he's barely holding it together.

I head over to the little kitchen counter, turn to stand beside him, and bump his shoulder. "Is he okay?"

"Yeah. He did good. When the incoming force swarmed the client, he recognized there was nothing to be done and focused on saving Paul and Carina. He got them locked back here and phoned us."

"We've trained him well."

Calum is practically vibrating with emotion.

I slide my arm under his and link our fingers. "Deep breaths, bro. Focus on him being all right. He's right there in front of you, and he's fine."

I've been working on connecting and casting soothing energy like Sloan sends me when I need steadying. I focus on Calum and give it a try. With my intention set, I send him peace and love.

The moment it takes hold of him, he casts me a sideways glance and smiles. "You're too much, Fi, you know that?"

"Is that good or bad?"

He leans sideways and rests his head on mine. "It's good...very good. Thanks."

Easing him is all the thanks I need. "Da is finishing up. Why don't I have Sloan take the two of you home while we work on what happened? You can have the house to yourselves for a few hours and smooth some of the rough edges that something like this causes."

He shakes his head. "I want to be part of it. I want to know who the fuck these guys were and why they attacked."

I squeeze his hand. "I'll keep you in the loop. You can be a cop tomorrow. Tonight, be Kev's rock. Trust me on this. When the adrenaline wears off, both of you will need a moment to assure yourselves that it's over and he's all right."

"When did you become the authority on relationships?"

"Normal ones? I'm not. Ones where two people are skirting danger and holding on for dear life? I earned my wings."

Calum nods. "Yeah, you have."

Sloan and Emmet return from their duties and flash me a thumbs-up.

Da nods, finishes at the table, and thanks them for their time and cooperation. "Can we help ye home? Emmet and Dillan can escort ye if ye like?"

Paul shakes his head. "No. I picked Carina up on my way in and have my car. I'll drop her home and come back to deal with the damage."

Kevin shakes his head. "No. Calum and I will handle things tonight. Come back in the morning once you've had a chance to put the attack behind you."

Paul considers that before he nods. "I suppose there's not much I can do until I have a copy of the police report to supply the insurance company."

Da nods. "I'll write it up and stop by around eleven with your paperwork. Will that work?"

Kevin's boss looks gutted but agrees. "I don't think I can face seeing the damage tonight anyway."

Kev pats the man's shoulder. "Leave it to us. Take Carina home, and I'll meet you here in the morning. We can look at things then."

Paul stands and retrieves his coat off the hook on the wall. "Thank you, gentlemen. I knew Calum's family are cops, but I never realized how beneficial it would be in a crisis. I am so grateful you came to our rescue."

I take no offense at being left out of the "gentlemen's" club. To a mundane, human world, I don't look like I'd be much of an asset in a situation like tonight. Paul and Carina probably think I tagged along.

When Paul and Carina are gone, I take Kevin's keys and ask Sloan to take him and Calum home. The rest of us return to the storefront to check on the gallery cleanup.

Dillan whistles between his teeth. "Wow. It looks better already. Nice work."

Garnet leaves Anyx to direct the preternatural cleaning crew and joins us. "Everything sorted with the witnesses?"

"Seems so," Da says. "The buyer was a new client. They didn't have much on file for him, but we have a name, address, and a credit card number."

"And the security cameras?"

Dillan steps up for that one. "The security cameras are hooked up to the owner's laptop. I forwarded what we got from the attack and erased it, but it looks like it's also uploaded into a cloud file. Cracking something like that is above my pay grade."

Garnet pulls out his phone and scrolls through his contacts

before making his selection. "I have a job for you...Yes, right now. I'm passing you over to the person who knows more, but the gist of it is a hack and wipe of a cloud file." He hands the phone to Dillan. "Tell him what you know, and he'll take care of the rest."

Dillan steps away to do that and Sloan returns. "They're home and settled. I suggested some time in the hot spring to wind down."

"That sounds about right," Da says. "How about we clear out of here and let the cleaners do their jobs?"

"Where do ye want to go?" Sloan asks.

"To the Batcave," I say, more enthusiastically than the situation calls for. "Sorry. I got excited there for a sec."

Da chuckles. "A fine idea. We'll go to the team office. Someone will need to stay here and lock up."

Emmet holds out his hand. "Give me the keys, and I'll stay with Dillan. When the cleanup crew finishes, we'll lock up and text Sloan for a pickup."

With that settled, I hand my brother the keys and the slip of paper with the security code.

Emmet looks at me and laughs. "Okay, Fi. Let it out."

I grin. "To the Batcave!"

Between Sloan and Garnet, we arrive safely in the outer foyer of our team's home base and scan in to unlock the doors. I text Nikon where we are, and he responds that as soon as Garnet's men arrive to guard the cell, he'll join us. Then I send Sloan back to the gallery to collect Dillan and Emmet and bring them here when the cleaners finish.

Once inside, the first thing I do is give everyone the tour pointing out where the bathrooms, kitchen, and safehouse suite are. "Having a bed here will be handy for those long nights when one of us needs to crash for an hour."

Garnet arches a brow. "The safehouse suite is intended for compromised members of the community to stay while we sort out dangerous situations."

"And for naps," I add.

Garnet rolls his eyes and turns to point at a closed cabinet in the corner. "There are three laptops in docking stations in there. Help yourselves to one whenever you're here and need one."

Aiden heads straight over and sets up on the conference table. "What's the name of our vic, Da?"

"Arthur Lloyd Montclair," he reads off his notepad, following with his address and his credit card info. "Grant, did ye happen to smell what species of empowered Mr. Montclair was?"

"No." Garnet is activating the projector wall and calling up the footage from the attack. "The stench of leviathan drowned out my sense of smell. My lab will have preliminary findings within the hour."

I watch over Aiden's shoulder as he accesses the Toronto PD data system and punches in the victim's deets.

"Are we connected to the law enforcement systems?" I look at Garnet and my father.

"We are," Da says. "One of the perks of having the Deputy Commissioner of the RCMP on our side. He pulled a few strings and voilà, we're hooked up."

"Speaking of which," Andromeda comes in from the hall with John Maxwell following close behind. She's carrying a large pastry box, and Maxwell has two trays of coffees stacked in carriers. "I felt the all-call and picked up John on the way in. What happened?"

I grab an apple fritter and fill Andy and Maxwell in.

"Everyone's well?" She blows over the rim of her coffee.

"Shaken but no damage done."

Da shoots me a look. "Except to the man lyin' dead in the Guild morgue. If ye ask him, I think he'd disagree."

I wince. "Yeah, sorry, except to him and the leviathans who attacked him."

"Leviathans," Maxwell runs his fingers through his short, silver hair. "We haven't talked about leviathans yet."

"Don't feel bad." I wave that away. "I didn't know they existed until I was staring at six rows of teeth and Garnet was calling for decapitation."

"Truly ugly motherfuckers." Dillan walks through the glass doors with Emmet and Sloan. "They bleed this gross black goo that is slick as grease."

Andy makes a face. "That's disgusting."

"You aren't wrong, beautiful." Dillan lifts the lid of the pastry box and picks a cruller. "We could all use a shower. Hey, do we have showers here?"

"We do." Garnet points the way.

Emmet laughs and picks a Hawaiian with sprinkles. "A shower probably won't help anyway. Oil and water and all that. Fighting leviathans is like wrestling an oily pig at a country fair."

I snort. "Like that, was it? How do you know?"

Emmet grins. "Wouldn't you like to know?"

Andromeda's gaze is bouncing from one of us to the other. "You're a lot to take in all at once."

I nod. "True story."

Some people believe you live this life alone—you face your trials, you rise or fall on your own merits, and when you leave this life, your actions speak for themselves.

I pity them.

I look around—at Sloan, Dillan, Emmet, and Da, at Maxwell and Garnet, Aiden and Andy—and what I see is the strength and motivation to help me through the trials. Loving people makes the chaos in life bearable, enjoyable even.

It's the balance that keeps you getting up in the morning.

Balance. Good and evil, dark and light, chocolate and peanut butter.

Nikon flashes into the foyer and bounces in to join the party a moment later. "So, what did I miss?"

"Nothing of importance." Garnet steps back from the projector and reaches up with the clicker to start the surveillance video. "Things are just getting interesting."

I take in Team Trouble and couldn't agree more.

Things *are* just getting interesting.

Thank you for reading – *A Druid Hexed.* While the story is fresh in your mind, and as a favor to Michael and me, click HERE and tell other readers what you thought.

A star rating and/or even one sentence can mean so much to readers deciding whether or not to try out a book or new author.

And if you loved it, continue with the Chronicles of an Urban Druid and claim your copy of book seven:

An Immortal's Pain

AN IMMORTAL'S PAIN

The story continues with *An Immortal's Pain*, coming April 18, 2021 to Amazon and Kindle Unlimited.

Pre-order now to have it delivered to your Kindle on as soon as it publishes!

AUTHOR NOTES - AUBURN TEMPEST

FEBRUARY 26, 2021

Six books in and I feel like Fiona and the gang are only beginning to get their druid groove on. Michael and I talked about where this series might end and we agreed, it's too soon.

Honestly, his actual words were, "You are fucked. This family of characters is so damned good. Fans, including myself, are not going to want it to end at six."

I took that as high praise coming from Michael, and knowing how loyal and special his fanbase is I definitely don't want to disappoint.

The good news is, I signed on for at least three more, so you're stuck with me for a while longer. After that... who knows, maybe Fiona will have said everything she has to say, or maybe we'll go for an even dozen.

Also, I get asked quite often about audio. There is progress on that front too, so stay tuned for dates and announcements when we know more about when you can start listening to the series. I'm quite excited to hear the stories aloud.

I'm halfway through An Immortal's Pain and am loving the mythology and adventures we're having. Can you guess by the title where we're going for that one? I'm sure you've got a good idea. I can't wait to read what you think.

Tons to look forward to,

Blessed be,
Auburn Tempest

P.S. If you enjoy my writing and read sexy steamy romance, my pen name for the books I write Paranormal and Fantasy Romance is JL Madore. You can find me on Amazon.

CONFESSIONS OF AN URBAN FANTASY AUTHOR

FEBRUARY 25, 2021

Thank you for not only reading to the end of this story, but these author notes as well!

I have a confession, and that is I prefer magic users over any other types of characters in an Urban Fantasy story.

It's a bias, I know. I'm working hard to give the fighters in the group the love they deserve.

Perhaps it's the fact that Magic Users can't wear most armor. There is some 'rule' that they can't cast spells with all of that weight on them.

I would have preferred to be given a chance. I mean, suppose I wore enough armor to stop that annoying arrow from piercing my chest. Do you know how annoying it is to play a game and I'm minding my own M-U business in the back of the group, waving my hands around like I'm swatting flies when out of nowhere, an arrow pierces your chest?

No?

Well, it's annoying and painful.

Magic users have to use so much of their treasure just buying ingredients. Have you SEEN how expensive eyes of newts (the red ones, not the green ones) have risen lately?

And don't get me started on how those who play thieves moan and complain about having to get their knives sharpened.

With a little work, the little whining brats can sharpen their own tools…Out on the road!

I suggest they try carrying along an extra ten or fifteen healing potions for chest wounds caused by arrows.

I guess that's still a sore spot with me.

HA! A pun. Get it? Sore spot… as a magic-user, I'm getting nailed in the chest all of the damned time with arrows.

It got so bad that even the barbarian (who, by the way, is way more intelligent than one would think with all of their grunting and monosyllabic answers) picked up a shirt with a target painted on the front as a joke.

A barbarian punked me. A magic-user!

We get no respect.

What we get is arrows…lots and lots of arrows.

Just wait. When I reach the tenth level, and I can cast a lightning storm I'll have those paladins quaking in all that metal armor. Then I'll have them jerking around as a million volts go through their limbs.

I think I'll wait until they have had to wade through a river.

<< Snippet from the diary of the late Wizard Montalbon. The rumor was he took two arrows to the chest and couldn't reach his pack of healing potions in time.>>

As transcribed by Michael Anderle

ABOUT AUBURN TEMPEST

Auburn Tempest is a multi-genre novelist giving life to Urban Fantasy, Paranormal, and Sci-Fi adventures. Under the pen name, JL Madore, she writes in the same genres but in full romance, sexy-steamy novels. Whether Romance or not, she loves to twist Alpha heroes and kick-ass heroines into chaotic, hilarious, fast-paced, magical situations and make them really work for their happy endings.

Auburn Tempest lives in the Greater Toronto Area, Canada with her dear, wonderful hubby of 30 years and a menagerie of family, friends, and animals.

BOOKS BY AUBURN TEMPEST

Auburn Tempest - Urban Fantasy Action/Adventure

Chronicles of an Urban Druid

Book 1 – A Gilded Cage

Book 2 – A Sacred Grove

Book 3 – A Family Oath

Book 4 – A Witch's Revenge

Book 5 – A Broken Vow

Book 6 – A Druid Hexed

Book 7 – An Immortal's Pain

Misty's Magick and Mayhem Series – Written by Carolina Mac/Contributed to by Auburn Tempest

Book 1 – School for Reluctant Witches

Book 2 – School for Saucy Sorceresses

Book 3 – School for Unwitting Wiccans

Book 4 – Nine St. Gillian Street

Book 5 – The Ghost of Pirate's Alley

Book 6 – Jinxing Jackson Square

Book 7 – Flame

Book 8 – Frost

Book 9 – Nocturne

Book 10 – Luna

Book 11 – Swamp Magic

Exemplar Hall – Co-written with Ruby Night

CONNECT WITH THE AUTHORS

Connect with Auburn

Amazon, Facebook, Newsletter

Web page – www.jlmadore.com

Email – AuburnTempestWrites@gmail.com

Connect with Michael Anderle and sign up for his email list here:

Website: http://lmbpn.com

Email List: http://lmbpn.com/email/

Social Media:

https://www.facebook.com/LMBPNPublishing

https://twitter.com/MichaelAnderle

https://www.instagram.com/lmbpn_publishing/

https://www.bookbub.com/authors/michael-anderle

Made in the USA
Middletown, DE
05 April 2022